"This amusing holiday tale about love lost and found again
is heartwarming. Quirky characters, snappy dialogue
and sexy chemistry all combine to keep you laughing,
as well as shedding a few tears...."
—*RT Book Reviews* on *Merry Ex-mas*

"*Merry Ex-mas* is the absolute perfect holiday book!
It has everything great women's contemporary fiction
should have—a great storyline filled with romance,
humor and a bit of mystery tucked in here and there,
fabulous personable characters filled with charm..."
—*Sharon's Garden of Book Reviews*

"An engaging humorous tale of
three sets of ex-couples coming together over the holidays.
The ensemble cast makes for a fun frothy frolic
as the ghosts of Christmas past reunite..."
—*Harriet Klausner* on *Merry Ex-mas*

"Roberts' witty and effervescently funny holiday novel
will warm hearts. Realistic characters populate the pages
of this captivating story."
—*RT Book Reviews* (Top Pick) on *On Strike for Christmas*

"Roberts' charming holiday-themed contemporary story
set in the Seattle area offers hope, comfort,
and a second chance for those who believe,
and a nudge to change the minds of those who don't."
—*Booklist* on *The Snow Globe*

"Within minutes of cracking open the book, my mood was
lifted.... The warm, glowing feeling it gave me lasted for days."
—*First for Women* on *The Snow Globe*

"This lighthearted and charming read will appeal to fans of
Kristin Hannah's magical, light romances and readers
who enjoyed Roberts's previous holiday offerings."
—*Library Journal* on *The Snow Globe* (starred review)

"Witty characterizations, slapstick mishaps,
and plenty of holiday cheer."
—*Publishers Weekly* on *The Nine Lives of Christmas*

SHEILA ROBERTS

The Lodge on
Holly Road

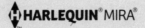

Recycling programs
for this product may
not exist in your area.

ISBN-13: 978-0-7783-1661-9

The Lodge on Holly Road

Copyright © 2014 by Sheila Rabe

For questions and comments about the quality of this book, please contact us at
CustomerService@Harlequin.com.

Printed in U.S.A.

For Sandy Hamilton, aka Santa Colorado

Dear Reader,

Can you remember the thrill of coming downstairs as a child on Christmas morning and rushing to see what Santa left for you under the tree? I can! Good old Santa Claus, a kid's best friend. And you see him everywhere: at shopping malls, in parades, at family holiday gatherings. There he is, ho-ho-ho-ing, handing out treats and generally making everyone feel good.

Except everyone doesn't always feel good during the holidays. Strained relationships, hard times, grief and loss can steal our holiday joy. With that reality in mind, I got to wondering what would happen if Santa were to lose his Christmas spirit. What if a man who once loved to play Santa Claus was coping with grief and didn't want to be jolly anymore? And what about the people he'd find himself interacting with? What if they were having problems, too? If several people who were facing holiday challenges all found themselves gathered together in one spot for Christmas, how would they cope?

Well, just to see, I gathered a bunch of people together at the Icicle Creek Lodge in Icicle Falls and asked them to help each other figure out how to have a merry Christmas. I hope I succeeded and I hope you'll enjoy this holiday tale of love and laughter.

You can always find me on Facebook. And please visit my website, www.sheilasplace.com, to find out more about Icicle Falls, the Hallmark Channel original movie based on my Christmas novel, *The Nine Lives of Christmas,* my contests and more. And let me know what *you* do to make Christmas special.

Merry Christmas to you, your family and friends!

Sheila

The Lodge on
Holly Road

Chapter One

Jolly Old Saint Nicholas

The toddler wasn't simply crying. Oh, no. These were the kind of earsplitting screams that would make the strongest department-store Santa want to run for his sleigh. Her face was a perfect match for James Claussen's red Santa suit, and both her eyes and her nose had the spigot turned on full blast.

What was he doing here, sitting on this uncomfortable throne, ruling over a kingdom of fake snow, candy canes and mechanical reindeer? What had possessed him to come back to work? He didn't want to be jolly, even imitation jolly.

"Come on, Joy," coaxed the little girl's mother from her spot on the sidelines of Santa Land. "Smile for Mommy."

"Waaah," Joy responded.

I understand how you feel, James thought. "Joy, that's a pretty name for a pretty girl. Can you give your mommy a big smile?" he coaxed.

"Waaah," Joy shrieked, and began kicking her feet. The black patent leather shoes turned those little feet into lethal weapons. Come tomorrow he'd have a bruise on the inside of his left thigh.

"Ho, ho, ho," James tried, but the shrieks only got louder.

Okay, this was as good as the picture with Santa was going to get. He stood and handed off the child, who was still kicking and crying, barely dodging an assault to the family jewels in the process. The jewels weren't so perfect now that he was sixty-six but they were still valuable to him and he wanted to keep them.

Shauna Sullivan, his loyal elf, sent him a sympathetic look and ushered up the next child, a baby girl carried by her mother. Rosy-cheeked and alert, probably just awake from a nap, the baby was dolled up in a red velvet dress with white booties on her feet and a headband decorated with a red flower. She was old enough to smile and coo but not quite old enough to walk or, thank God, kick Santa where it hurt.

This baby girl reminded him of his daughter, Brooke, when she was a baby, all smiles and dimples. Big brown eyes that looked at him in delighted wonder. Oh, those were the days, when his kids were small and Faith was still…

Don't go there.

"And what would this little dumpling like for Christmas?" he asked, settling the baby on his lap.

For a few seconds it looked as if she was actually concentrating on an answer. But then a sound anyone who'd had children could easily recognize, followed by a foul odor, told him she'd been concentrating on something else. Oh, man.

"Smile, Santa," Krystal, the photographer, teased, and the smelly baby on his lap gurgled happily.

James had never been good with poopy diapers but he gave it his best effort and hoped he looked like a proper Santa.

Finally, they were down to the last kid in line. Thank God. After this, Santa was going home to enjoy a cold beer.

That was about the only thing he'd enjoy. Oh, he'd turn on the TV to some cop show, but he wouldn't really watch it. Then he'd go to bed and wish the days wouldn't keep coming, forcing him to move on.

He especially dreaded the next day, December 24. How he wished he could skip right to New Year's Day. Or better yet, go backward to New Year's Day two years ago, when he and Faith were planning their European cruise.

Stay in the moment, he told himself. *Stay in character.* He put on his jolliest Santa face and held out a welcoming arm to the next child.

This one was going to be a terror; he could tell by the scowl on the kid's freckled face as he approached. He was a big, hefty burger of a boy, wearing jeans and an oversize T-shirt, and could have been anywhere between the ages of ten and thirteen. Logic ruled out the older end of the spectrum. Usually by about eight or nine, kids stopped believing.

"And who have we got here?" James asked in his jolly I-love-kids voice.

Normally he did love kids and he loved playing Santa, had been doing it since his children were little. He'd always had the husky build for it, although when he was younger Faith had padded him out with a pillow. No pillow necessary now. And no need for a fake beard, either. Mother Nature had turned his beard white over the past few years.

These days he wasn't into the role, wasn't into Christmas, period. Santa had lost his holiday spirit and he was starting to lose his patience, too. Very un-Santa-like. He should never have agreed to fill in today, should have told Holiday Memories to find another Santa.

His new customer didn't answer him.

"What's your name, son?" he asked, trying again.

"Richie," said the boy, and landed on James's leg like a ton of coal.

"And how old are you, Richie?"

"Too old for this. This is stupid." The kid crossed his arms and glared at his mother.

"So you're twelve?" James guessed.

"I'm ten and I know there's no such thing as Santa. You're a big fake."

Boy, he had that right.

"And that's fake, too," Richie added.

James was usually prepared for rotten-kid beard assaults, but this year his game was off and Richie got a handful of beard before James could stop him. He yanked so hard he nearly separated James's jawbone from the rest of his skull. For a moment there he saw stars, and two Richies. As if one wasn't bad enough.

"Whoa there, son, that's real," James said, rubbing his chin, his eyes watering. "Let's take it easy on old Santa."

Now Richie's mother was glaring, too, as though it was James's fault she'd spawned a monster.

"Look, Richie," he said, lowering his voice. "We're both men here. We know this is all pretend."

And Christmas is a crock and life sucks. So deal with it, you little fart.

James reeled in his bad Santa before he could get loose and do any damage. Good Santa continued, "But your mom wants this picture. One last picture she can send to your relatives and brag about what a great kid you are." *Not.* "Can you man-up and pose so she can have a nice picture of you for Christmas?"

Richie scowled at him suspiciously, as if he was up to some strange trick.

James sweetened the holiday pot. "I bet if you do, you'll get what you want for Christmas." Now the kid was looking less adversarial. James pressed his advantage. "Come on, kid. One smile and we can both get out of here. Whaddya say?"

Richie grunted and managed half a smile and Krystal captured it. "But you're still a fake," Richie said.

And you're still a little fart. "Ho, ho, ho," James

replied, and rocketed the boy off his leg, sending him flying.

"Hey, he shoved me," Richie said to his mother, and pointed an accusing finger at James.

"Trick leg," James said apologetically. "Old war injury. Merry Christmas," he called and, with a wave, abdicated his holiday throne.

"Okay," he said to Shauna, "I'm out of here." Thank God today was over. He was never doing this again. He didn't care if every Santa on the planet was home with the flu.

"You can't go yet," she protested, and began looking desperately around the mall.

After a ten-hour day? Oh, yeah, he could. "No kids, and it's ten minutes till the end of our shift. We'll be okay to leave. Right, Krystal?"

Krystal frowned. "Well…"

It was nearly five o'clock. All the moms and kiddies were now on their way home to make dinner. The next Santa crew would arrive soon to deal with the evening crowd. All they had to do was put up the Santa-will-be-back sign. What was the problem? Maybe Shauna and Krystal felt guilty about stealing a couple of extra minutes from work.

Not James. He'd worked hard all his life and he had no qualms about stealing a few minutes for himself now. For over forty years he'd been a welder at Boeing. Then he'd come home and work some more, putting that addition on the house, mowing the lawn, cleaning the garage, repairing broken faucets.

Of course, he'd also realized the importance of

playing—backyard baseball with the kids, Frisbee at the park, board games on a rainy Sunday afternoon. And real life had taught him that you had to take advantage of everything good, even little things like getting off ten minutes early. Because you never knew what cosmic pie in the face was waiting for you around the corner.

"Come on, ladies," he said, putting an arm around each of them and trying to move them in the direction of the Starbucks. "The eggnog lattes are on me." They still balked. He'd never known the women to turn down a latte. He glanced from one to the other. "Okay, what's going on?"

"It's a surprise," Shauna said.

James frowned. He hated surprises, had hated them ever since Faith got sick.

"It's a good one," Krystal said as if reading his mind.

And then he saw his daughter hurrying down the mall toward him and the heaviness settling over him was blown away. There she was, his brown-eyed girl, all bundled up in boots and black leggings and a winter coat, her hair falling to her shoulders in a stylish light brown sheet. Once upon a time, it had been curly and so cute. Then suddenly she'd decided she needed to straighten her hair. He never could understand why the curls had to go. But then he'd never understood women's fashion.

He'd also never understood why she thought her face was too round or why she thought she was fat. Her face was sweet. And she was just curvy. As far as he was concerned she was the prettiest young woman in Seattle. That wasn't fatherly prejudice. It was fact, plain and simple.

"Daddy," she called, and waved and began to run toward him.

Krystal had been right. This was a good surprise.

"Hello there, angel," he greeted her, and gave her a big hug. "Did you come so your old man could take you to dinner?"

"I came to take my old man somewhere special for Christmas," she said. "Thanks for not letting him get away," she told his holiday helpers.

"No problem," said Shauna. "Have a great time."

"For Christmas?" James repeated as Brooke linked her arm through his and started them walking toward the shopping mall's main entrance.

They were going somewhere for Christmas on the twenty-third? Did that mean she wouldn't be spending Christmas with him and Dylan? It was their first Christmas without Faith (well, technically their second since she'd died on December 24 the year before). He'd assumed he and his son and daughter would all be together to help one another through the holidays.

But she was an adult. She could do what she wanted. Maybe she'd made plans with friends. If she had, he couldn't blame her for wanting to escape unpleasant memories. Maybe she'd found someone in the past couple of weeks and wanted to be with him. She shouldn't have to babysit her dad.

"Don't worry, Daddy," she said. "I've got it all under control."

He didn't doubt that. Like her mother, Brooke was a planner and an organizer. She'd organized their Thanksgiving dinner, gathering his sister and his cousin and her husband, assigning everyone dishes to bring.

But what was she talking about? "Got what under control?"

"You'll see," she said with a Santa-like twinkle in her eyes.

Oh, boy, another surprise. "What are you up to, angel?"

"I'm not telling, but trust me, you'll like it."

He wouldn't like *anything* this season but he decided to play along. "Okay, lead on."

He hoped she hadn't spent too much money. Kindergarten teachers didn't make a lot and he hated to think of her spending a fortune on some fancy meal. He'd be happy enough with a hamburger. Anyway, he'd rather eat in the car than go into a restaurant dressed in his Santa suit.

They were out of the mall now and at her trusty SUV. She complained about her gas mileage but he was secretly glad she had this vehicle. It had all-wheel drive and handled well in the snow, so he didn't have to worry about her when she was driving in bad weather. Seattle rarely got much of the white stuff, but they'd had a couple of inches earlier in the month and the weatherman was predicting more by New Year's.

James had always loved it when they had a white Christmas. It meant snowball fights with the kids and hot chocolate afterward. Faith would lace his and hers with peppermint schnapps.

"No frowning allowed," Brooke said as they got in.

"Who's frowning? Santa doesn't frown."

"He never used to," Brooke said softly.

"Well, Santa's getting too grumpy for this job. It's about time for the old boy to pack it in."

His daughter shot a startled look in his direction. "Daddy, are you crazy?"

"No, I'm just…" *Sick of this ho-ho-ho crap.* It would never do to say such a cynical thing to his daughter. "Ready for a break," he improvised.

"You can't take a break," she protested as she drove out of the parking lot. "You're Santa."

James studied the crowd of cars rushing around them, people busy running errands, going places, preparing for holiday gatherings with loved ones. Most of the men in Seattle would be out the following day, frantically finding gifts for their women. He wished he was going to be one of them.

He reminded himself that he still had his kids. He had a lot for which to be thankful, and if Brooke had plans for Christmas, well, he and Dylan could make turkey TV dinners and eat the last of the cookies she'd baked for them, then watch a movie, like *Bad Santa.* Heh, heh, heh.

Now they were on the southbound freeway. Where

were they going? Knowing his daughter, it would be someplace special.

He smiled as he thought about the contrast between her and his son. Dylan would come up with something at the last minute, most likely a six-pack of beer and a bag of nachos, their favorite football food. Naturally, Dylan would help him consume it all.

James was wondering what downtown Seattle spot his daughter had picked for dinner and was hoping it was in the Pike Place Market, where anything went in the way of dress, when they exited I-5 onto I-90, heading east out of Seattle. "Dinner in Bellevue?"

"Maybe," she said, determined to be mysterious.

They passed Bellevue. And then Issaquah, getting increasingly farther from the city. Where the heck was she taking him?

When they reached North Bend at the foot of the Cascades, he said, "So, we're eating here?"

"Actually, dinner's in the backseat," she said, nodding over her shoulder to a red cooler. "I've got roast beef sandwiches and apples and a beer for you if you want it."

If they weren't going out to dinner, then where were they going? Now he began to feel uneasy. How long was he going to be stuck in this suit? "Okay," he said, making his tone of voice serious so she'd realize he was done fooling around. "What's going on?"

"We're going to Icicle Falls," she said brightly.

"What?"

"This is a kidnapping."

That was not funny. "Brooke," he said sternly. "I'm not going to Icicle Falls."

"Daddy," she said just as sternly. "We're *all* going to Icicle Falls. For Christmas. I booked us rooms at the Icicle Creek Lodge."

"You can't spring this on me, baby girl," he said. "I don't even have a change of clothes."

"Not to worry. Dylan's bringing clothes when he comes up later."

He should've known she'd think of that. She'd probably given her younger brother a detailed list. He tried another argument. "I can't leave my car at the mall."

"Dylan's picking it up after work and driving it to Icicle Falls. See? Everything's under control."

No, it wasn't. It wasn't remotely under control. James was getting hauled off to some stupid Bavarian village that would be chock-full of Christmas lights and happy tourists when all he'd wanted was to spend Christmas at home with his kids. Being depressed because his wife wasn't there with them. And making the kids feel bad. Ho, ho, ho.

"We thought we should do something different this year," Brooke added gently.

Maybe she was right. They could've tried to celebrate the way they'd always done with a big dinner on Christmas Eve, followed by a candlelight service at church and then pancakes and presents in the morning and friends over in the afternoon to sing

Christmas carols and eat cookies. But it would all have been hollow and empty.

Still, he'd planned on trying. He'd bought a bunch of Christmas movies for them to watch and stocked up on cocoa, put up the tree and stuck their gift cards in among the branches. "I figured we'd have Christmas at home," he said. Now he sounded like an ingrate and he didn't want to do that. Anyway, it was too late now. They were halfway to Icicle Falls. The Polar Express had left the station.

"I think this will be good," Brooke said. "It's our gift to you."

"Your gift?" Staying in some lodge would be expensive. "Oh, no. I'll take care of it."

"Daddy," she said firmly. "You've always taken care of us. And you've always been Santa," she added, smiling at him. "Now it's our turn. So don't ruin the game."

He sighed and looked out the window at the stands of evergreens they were rushing past. He guessed he could play along.

As long as nobody asked him to be Santa this year. Because Santa had lost his Christmas spirit and he didn't care if he ever found it again.

Chapter Two

All I Want for Christmas Is...

"What are you doing?" screeched Mrs. Steele, startling Missy Monroe.

This was not good because Missy was in midcut. The scissors took a slide and an extra half inch of hair disappeared.

"Ack!" Mrs. Steele cried.

"Sorry," Missy muttered.

"Stop!" Mrs. Steele commanded. "That's too short!"

It sure was now. "I'm sorry," Missy said earnestly. "I thought you said you wanted to go shorter so the cut would last."

"Shorter, not bald," snapped her unhappy customer, scowling at their reflections in the mirror.

Short of gluing the woman's hair back on, there was nothing Missy could do now. "I think, once we've styled it, you'll like it."

"Style? You have no style. How did I get stuck with you, anyway?"

Missy had just been thinking the same thing about Mrs. Steele. But she'd been the next available stylist, and there'd been no way she could wiggle out of taking the woman. She strongly suspected all the other stylists had been dawdling over their haircuts in an effort to avoid getting the old witch. Dummy her. She should've dawdled, too.

Nobody liked Mrs. Steele. She was sixty-something and skinny and wore a frown right along with her expensive clothes. Maybe if she ate more chocolate she'd be happier. Or if she went to some couture hair salon. But Mrs. Steele was notoriously cheap, which was why she was at Style Savings Salon. She never tipped and she was never happy, no matter what you did.

"Well, it's too late now," Mrs. Steele said with an irritable flick of the hand. "You've already gotten the color wrong. I guess I shouldn't be surprised that you can't cut hair, either."

Mrs. Steele had picked that color, but now it was Missy's fault. Sooo unfair. She loved doing hair and helping women look their best, but sometimes she hated this job.

"Don't worry," she said. "It'll look nice." Well, the cut would, anyway. If Mrs. Steele had listened to her advice, the color would have been perfect, too. After a certain age, raven's-wing black didn't do a woman any favors.

Fortunately for Mrs. Steele, Missy knew what she was doing. She'd find a way to blend in this little slip of the scissors. She snipped some more and then put in some of the salon's hair root lifter. This really *was* going to look nice…if only Mrs. Steele would stop frowning.

But all the product in the world, all the careful styling, couldn't redeem the fact that Missy had failed to be psychic and know what Mrs. Steele had really wanted, which was probably to look like Jennifer Lawrence or some other movie star. (Good luck with that.)

Mrs. Steele glared at herself in the mirror, her thin lips pressed together in an angry line. Then she glared at Missy. "My God, but you're incompetent."

She was not! She did hair, not plastic surgery. If Mrs. Steele wanted a miracle, she should have gone to church. Missy bit her lip to keep in the angry words.

Now everyone in the salon was staring, all the other last-minute holiday customers no doubt thanking God that they hadn't gotten stuck with the incompetent stylist, all the other stylists thankful that they hadn't gotten stuck with Mrs. Steele. Missy could feel the heat of embarrassment over this undeserved criticism from her collarbone to the roots of her powder-blue dye job.

"I'm sorry you're not happy," she said.

"I'm certainly not. The color's wrong and the cut is awful. I'm not paying for this."

Oh, great. Mrs. Steele was going to walk, and that meant it would come out of Missy's paycheck.

"And I'm not coming back here," she added as Missy removed the plastic cape.

"Good riddance," muttered the stylist next to Missy as Mrs. Steele stormed out the door.

"I thought her haircut was pretty," said the woman sitting in the chair.

It was, darn it all. Well, never mind. In another hour she'd be done and out of here and on her way to having the best Christmas ever. She got her broom and swept up the raven's-wing black locks left behind by the old crow, all the while hoping that a big tipper would come in before they closed.

The door opened and in came—oh, no, not this guy. Again, all the other stylists started cutting in slow motion. Nobody wanted Larry the lech.

"Welcome to Style Savings," sang out Shiloh, their manager. She went to where their cash register and appointment schedule sat to get old Larry checked in.

Larry was somewhere in his forties and, more than anything, he resembled the Pillsbury Doughboy. He was the king of the boob grazes, and there wasn't a stylist in the salon he hadn't hit on, including Missy. And she'd bet that today he was going to be all hers. Goody.

Sure enough, Shiloh was giving her The Look. She set aside her broom and came over to conduct Larry to her chair. She could practically feel his pervy stare burning her butt as they crossed the salon. Ugh.

She settled Larry in his chair and fastened a

cape around his neck. "What would you like today, Larry?"

"You," he said with a wink.

Gag. If she was married she could flash him her ring.

But marriage had never happened for her. Men had happened, two to be exact, one for each kid. Man Number One had been what some might have considered a youthful mistake, but she'd loved him like crazy. And when she got pregnant, they'd planned on getting married…until he tried to break up a bar fight and got killed for his trouble. Right before he'd been about to enlist in the army, too. Even though she'd had a child with him, his parents hadn't bothered to make a connection with their grand-child. Hardly surprising considering that they'd pretty much written off their son.

That was sick and wrong if you asked Missy. People could change. She would never write off *her* kids. They were the best part of her life, even if things hadn't worked out with their dads.

And boy, things really hadn't worked out with Man Number Two, who was also out of the picture but for a completely different reason. She'd jumped into that relationship, driven by loneliness, anxious to find a father for Carlos. Man Number Two had been separated from his wife. They'd been ready to get a divorce…until wifey informed him she was pregnant. He told Missy just as she was about to break the news of her own pregnancy to him. (She'd read somewhere that condoms were 98 percent effective. Leave it to her to land in the 2-percent category!) His family was happy that he'd finally "come to his senses" and was reuniting with his wife. They'd never said anything to her face but she knew they'd never approved of her. She wasn't about to stay around and be accused of screwing up the man's life. So, figuring a pregnant wife trumped a pregnant ex-girlfriend, Missy had decided to let him go and stick with single parenthood. She was already raising a child on her own. What was one more? By Man Number Three, she was using more reliable birth control, but she wasn't making smart choices. He hadn't been good father material. He hadn't even been good boyfriend material, the cheating rat.

After a couple more short-lived love attempts, she wised up and realized it was better to be alone than to settle. In fact, better to live up to her own potential as a woman than to worry about meeting a man who'd make everything fall into place.

Still, every once in a while she'd see a happy couple strolling the mall and sigh. Why were there so many Mr. Wrongs out there and so few Mr. Rights?

That wasn't all she wondered. Sometimes she wondered how she was going to give Carlos and Lalla the kind of life they deserved.

But when those grim thoughts came along she pushed them firmly away. Yes, she'd made some mistakes and not everything had gone according to plan, but she had two great kids and she'd manage somehow. She was only twenty-six. She had time.

Someday she was going to work at a fancy salon and be successful. And someday maybe her prince would come, ready to exchange his Corvette for a minivan, and carrying a wedding ring in his shirt pocket. Meanwhile she had…Larry.

"Larry, you know I'm not into guys," she lied.

"I think lesbians are sexy," he said.

"Let's soak your head, er, wash your hair," she said.

Larry always wanted his hair washed. That gave him a close-up view of the boobage.

She got him all washed up, trying to keep her boobs out of range. (Larry often had to scratch his nose during the process and his hands usually got lost on the way there.) Then it was time for a cut. His hair was thinning so he kept it long and shaggy in an attempt to compensate. He always reminded the stylists that he only wanted a little trim. After the incident with Mrs. Steele, Missy was going to take off barely anything.

She began, oh, so carefully, snipping.

"Could you take a bit more off here," he said, pretending to reach for his ear. Before she could dodge his pudgy paw he'd scored his first boob graze. "Oh, sorry," he said.

Yeah, that was why he was leering.

Was it the final straw, or rather follicle? Had she inhaled too many fumes while giving Bessy Hart her perm a couple of hours ago? Was she going insane? Who knew? But something got into Missy. Maybe it was the spirit of the Grinch.

She gave Larry a wicked smile and cooed, "No problem." Then she picked up a section of hair and made a radical cut. Oh, that felt good. *Let's do it again.* Another section of hair disappeared.

"Whoa," said Larry. "Just a trim. Remember?"

"Trust me. I know what I'm doing," she said with a Grinchy grin, and more of Larry's hair vacated his head. Then she got out the clippers.

"Whoa, stop," Larry cried.

Too late. She was already running the clippers up the back of his head.

"Hey," he protested, trying to move his head. That got him a nick in the ear. "Yow! What's with you?"

"Just giving you a trim," she told him sweetly. "Like you said."

"That's no trim! It's a scalping."

"Oh, Larry, I'm sorry," she said. "I guess we'd better stop." With half his head buzzed and the other half shaggy. Hee, hee.

"You can't stop now! I look like a freak."

Yeah, it would be a shame to look like the freak he was. "Well, Larry, if you promise to keep your hands to yourself we'll finish this."

"What do you mean?"

She didn't say anything, merely stood there, staring at him in the mirror until he actually made eye contact.

Then he scowled. "Okay, okay."

She rewarded him with a smile. "You're going to look totally buff."

"Buff, huh?" He thought a moment. "Yeah, buff is good."

When she was done, Larry's hair was ready for the marines. Too bad the rest of his body wasn't.

She handed him a mirror and turned the chair so he could see the back of his head.

He nodded approvingly. "Hey, it's not bad. I kinda like it." He smiled up at her. "Nice job."

Oh, great. She'd earned the undying devotion of Larry the lech. "Um, thanks," she said.

She took off the cape and Larry forgot his promise and decided to stretch. She was too fast for him this time and danced backward, away from his lecherous paws. He frowned.

But when he paid, he gave her a ten-dollar tip.

She watched him go out the door and sighed. "Why do I feel like a pole dancer?"

Shiloh was next to her now. "You should be so lucky. Pole dancers make a lot more than we do."

Two more cuts, two more decent tips and then she left to collect the kids from the babysitter and hit the road for their Christmas adventure. So far their Christmases hadn't exactly been something you'd put on a greeting card. Often there'd been a boyfriend involved and a fight, or a tipsy neighbor stopping in to share the yuletide cheer, drink in hand, always a scraggly bargain tree with cheap presents that broke by the end of the day or weren't what the kids really wanted.

She wasn't going to come through in the Santa department this year, any more than she had last year, since Carlos still wanted a dog. It was hard to produce a dog when her landlady didn't allow pets. "All that barking, my nerves couldn't take it," Mrs. Entwhistle said whenever Missy broached the subject.

Mrs. Entwhistle lived in the other half of the duplex Missy rented and was hard of hearing. She probably wouldn't hear a Saint Bernard barking in her ear. She sure never heard when the teenagers down the block were partying till all hours of the morning or racing their cars. Or when the couple across the street had too much to drink and started yelling loud enough to drag Missy out of a sound sleep.

"Dogs are so messy," Mrs. Entwhistle would add, strengthening her argument.

So were children. Missy never pointed that out. The last thing she wanted was Mrs. E. deciding she didn't want children living next door, either. So, no dog for Carlos. They couldn't really afford a dog, anyway. But how did you explain that to a seven-year-old?

And then there was Lalla. Oh, how she wanted a grandma. This was even more impossible to produce than a dog. It had just been Missy and her mom when she was growing up. So there was no grandma by marriage. And Missy's mom was no longer on the scene. After wrapping her car around a tree while under the influence, Mom had gone to climb inside that great whiskey bottle in the sky.

Still, in spite of the no-dog-no-grandma thing,

Missy was going to give her kids a wonderful Christmas this year. They were going to Icicle Falls to stay at the Icicle Creek Lodge, a big, beautiful place with a fireplace in the lobby and rooms that had fireplaces, too. At Christmas, the B and B not only provided its usual breakfast but dinner on Christmas Eve and Christmas Day. One of her clients had told her about the place, and she'd been saving for it all year. This was going to be a Christmas her kids would never forget.

She could hardly wait to get up there and show them the real, live vintage sleigh in the lobby, decorated with greenery and ribbons and filled with presents and teddy bears. There'd be no dog and no grandma in there, but staying in such a cool place should make up for the fact that Carlos was getting a stuffed dog and Lalla was getting a princess doll.

The kids were literally bouncing with excitement when she picked them up. Or maybe it was a sugar buzz, since her girlfriend Miranda's three kids were also bouncing. And yelling. And jumping on Miranda's tired couch. Miranda was very fond of Oreos and thought them an excellent afternoon snack, usually ignoring the carrot and celery sticks Missy gave her to dole out. ("Hey, the kids like Oreos better.") Carlos's pants were muddy and ripped, a sure sign he'd been playing in the run-down playground half a block away, hopefully not unsupervised, and Lalla's dress had a chocolate stain on the bodice while her ever-present tiara sat crookedly on top of her cornrows. Obviously, they had enjoyed themselves.

"Are you guys ready for fun?" she asked, hugging them both.

"As if they don't have fun here," snorted Miranda.

Of course they had fun at the babysitter's. She gave them junk food and they could watch cartoons all afternoon. Miranda had a good heart, but was she a good influence? If only Missy could afford to put the kids in some fancy day care with planned activities and…carrot sticks.

Well, down the road. She wouldn't always be at Style Savings. Oh, no. She was already looking at employment sites online. She'd done makeovers for a couple of her friends and was putting their before-and-after pictures in a notebook so she could show just how expert she was when she finally went to interview at that high-end salon. Unlike her mother, who never got beyond waiting tables at the nearby breakfast place, she was going to make something of herself. She was going to make her children proud.

And, meanwhile, this Christmas, they'd be making a memory worthy of the Hallmark Channel (which she'd be able to afford someday). She thanked Miranda, then said, "Okay, guys, let's go," and with a squeal they bolted for her beater Honda.

"Have a great time," Miranda said, giving her a hug. "And don't do anything I wouldn't do." Which pretty much left the field wide-open.

The kids were already buckled in when she got

to the car. She put on her own seat belt and then turned on the radio, choosing a local station that was playing Christmas carols. All right. *Now* they were ready. They pulled away from the curb, singing "Jingle Bells."

They'd only just entered the freeway when Lalla yelled from the backseat. "Stop it, Carlos!" This was followed by, "Mommy, he's poking me."

"Carlos, cut it out," Missy said in her firm mommy voice.

"I'm bored," Carlos complained.

"Well, look for Priuses," she suggested. Dumb suggestion because this game called for the first person who saw a Prius to say "Beep-beep" and slug the other Prius hunter in the arm. "Never mind," she amended. "Just…" She fumbled around in the paper bag on the seat next to her and found what she was looking for. She tossed the plastic bag of munchies into the back. "Have a carrot."

"Yuck," said Carlos.

"Yuck," parroted Lalla.

"Well, you guys sure aren't getting any more sugar," she informed them.

"Are we there yet?" Lalla demanded.

Hmm. Maybe she should've picked someplace closer for their perfect Christmas.

Chapter Three

It's Beginning to Look a Lot Like Christmas

Olivia Wallace's Icicle Creek Lodge was decked out for the holidays. Her oldest son, Eric, and his burly friend Bubba Swank had hauled in her antique sleigh from the lodge's storage garage and it was now set up in the lobby, brimming with brightly wrapped faux presents. The staircase banister was dressed in greenery, and mistletoe had been hung in various key spots around the lodge and in the private family quarters. The big tree on the front porch was decorated with lights. Red poinsettias filled in any gaps.

Olivia Wallace smiled as she surveyed her domain. George would have been so proud.

That thought always comforted her. And made her a little wistful. How she wished her husband was here to help her run this place. Not because Eric wasn't doing a wonderful job. He loved the lodge as much as Olivia did, and would probably take it over someday. No, it was more because she knew how happy she and George would have been. They'd shared the vision for this place and he'd never lived to see what a huge success it had become. They'd grown, added on, developed a reputation. Oh, yes, George would have loved this.

Well, most of it. Olivia hid a frown as one of her more difficult guests came down the stairs with his wife, his rolling suitcase thump-thumping behind him. He missed the last step and went tottering off sideways.

Oh, no! Please don't fall. This descendant of Ebenezer Scrooge would sue her by New Year's Day if that happened.

He righted himself, thank God, and she could hear him muttering all the way across the lobby to where she was manning the reception desk. "Those stairs are uneven."

At times like this Olivia really didn't like being an innkeeper. She braced herself for the barrage of complaints.

Sure enough, Mr. Braxton marched to the reception desk, his wife walking behind him like a reluctant shadow, and slammed down his keycard. "We didn't sleep a wink last night."

"I'm sorry to hear that," Olivia said.

"The people down the hall were up partying all night."

There had been two younger couples who'd been en route to Seattle to spend Christmas with family and had decided to stay the night. Olivia had suggested they try Zelda's for dinner and they'd gone merrily off, full of good cheer. They'd probably overindulged in huckleberry martinis or the other house specialty, a Chocolate Kiss. She imagined they'd been a bit noisy on the way back to their rooms. Still, that wasn't her fault.

"Making a racket in the hall at all hours," Mr. Braxton continued.

"I'm terribly sorry," Olivia said. "I do wish you'd come down and said something to me. I'd have been happy to talk to them."

"Ha! Come down in my bathrobe and pajamas? I think not. And breakfast this morning."

Olivia stiffened. "What about breakfast?"

"All those carbs."

No one made crepes like Olivia. She served them stuffed with wild huckleberries and berry-flavored whipped cream. And she always served some sort of protein along with them. "If I remember correctly, breakfast also included sausages," she said, some of the sweetness seeping out of her voice. "And fruit."

"I thought it was very good," said Mrs. Braxton, her voice barely above a whisper.

Her husband ignored her. Now he produced his printed bill. "I want a refund." Behind him, his wife studied her feet.

Ooh, of all the cheap, contemptible… Olivia would have liked nothing better than to tell this man exactly what she thought of him.

But men like this rarely saw their shriveled souls for what they were. So, instead of saying, "You win the bad-boy lump of coal award for the day," she said, "I'm sorry your stay wasn't to your satisfaction. We try hard to give all our guests a pleasant experience."

"Well, you failed with me!"

"I can refund fifty percent of your room price." Sometimes, when guests had a complaint (and that was rare), Olivia gave them a gift certificate for a free night. Not Mr. Edward Braxton. She had no intention of encouraging him to return.

"I want a full refund," he insisted.

This man was a bully. And there was only one way to treat bullies. "Mr. Braxton," she said firmly, "you stayed in a lovely room with a beautiful view. We even left Sweet Dreams chocolates on your pillow."

"My wife ate mine," he muttered.

"*And* we gave you a lovely breakfast this morning, featuring my very own gourmet crepes. Which you ate. You made no complaint at breakfast, nor did you inform me of any special dietary needs when you registered. And there was a place on your registration form to do so. Now, you are a businessman, correct?"

He looked at her suspiciously. "Yes."

"Then I ask you, would you give yourself a full refund?"

His brows formed an angry V. "Now, see here."

"It's Christmas, and in the spirit of the season, I'm offering you a fifty-percent discount. Would you

like it?" she finished in a tone of voice that plainly
said, "Take it or leave it."

"Fine. I'll take it."

"An excellent decision," she said.

"But I don't like it," he growled after they'd finished the appropriate paperwork.

"I'm sure you don't," she agreed.

"Come on, Thelma," he snapped at his wife, and
made for the front door.

"Bah, humbug," Olivia muttered as she walked
through the door marked Private into her family's
living quarters.

Right now the only family living there was Eric
and her and Muffin the cat. They could easily make
room for a wife. And children. Or remodel.

Three bedrooms were at the back. The rest of the
family quarters was like any other small home, entered through a front door with a window of etched
glass. Once inside, visitors found a great-room-style
layout with a small but state-of-the-art kitchen, a
dining area and a cozy living room, complete with
an electric fireplace, where she could hang Christmas stockings.

Three stockings hung there now. One was marked
Olivia, and her boys usually slipped in a couple of
stocking-stuffer-size boxes of Sweet Dreams chocolates. The next stocking in line had Eric's name on
it. That she would fill with nuts and candy bars and
his favorite hot sauces and jellies from Local Yokels,
which specialized in Northwest products. The last
stocking belonged to her younger son, Brandon, who

was currently in Wyoming but who managed to get home for Christmas every year. Brandon was her wandering boy, trying to find himself. But his internal compass always brought him home for important holidays. His stocking would get filled with Snickers bars and Corn Nuts, his all-time favorite snack.

Normally the sight of her decorations cheered her. The ceramic nativity set on the mantel had been a gift from her mother-in-law years ago, and she cherished it. Her little tree was loaded with ornaments she'd collected over the years. And she'd hung mistletoe in the archway between the kitchen and dining room. She frowned at it. Why did she put that up every year?

Her frown deepened. All right. This was a very bad attitude she had brewing. She'd been perfectly happy until her encounter with her grumpy guest.

"Mr. Braxton, I am not going to let you ruin my day." She picked up her knitting (a scarf she was finishing for her friend Muriel Sterling-Wittman for Christmas) and got to work. Knitting always made her feel good. She imagined herself poking Mr. Braxton in the bottom with one of her knitting needles, and that made her feel even better.

She'd barely gotten started when the doorbell rang. Oh, she knew who that was, and the mere thought of what she'd find when she opened the door was enough to drive the memory of Ebenezer Braxton from her mind. Yup, there stood Kevin from Lupine Floral, looking like a fashion model in his trendy jeans and gray wool coat. And he was wearing the red scarf she'd knit for him the Christmas before.

"I have something for my favorite innkeeper," he sang, holding out a huge holiday floral arrangement.

"You'd better not let Ann Marie or Gerhardt Geissel hear you say that," Olivia cautioned with a smile. Although, knowing Kevin, he said the same thing when he delivered floral arrangements to them.

He grinned and winked. "I can see you're all ready for Christmas here at the lodge."

"Of course we are. It's my favorite time of year."

"This place could be a movie set," he said with a dramatic sigh. "Olivia, you are the queen of Christmas."

"Well, if I'm the queen, then you and Heinrich are my princes. I look forward to your lovely arrangements every year. Please tell him that."

After a few more pleasantries, Kevin was on his way to flatter more of the residents of Icicle Falls, and Olivia took the arrangement over to the kitchen counter and removed it from its box. As she'd expected, it was a feast for the eyes with red and white roses, delicate ferns and baby's breath. Candy canes bloomed inside the big red ribbon bow wrapped around the vase. Gorgeous.

She didn't have to read the card to know it was from Eric but did, anyway, just so she could delight in the message. "Merry Christmas to the world's best mom. Love, Eric."

She pulled a tissue from her sweater pocket and dabbed at eyes that had suddenly grown misty. She had such a wonderful son. She was so lucky that he'd opted to stay in Icicle Falls and help her run the lodge. As if that wasn't enough, every year he sent her a Christmas bouquet. He'd been doing it for fourteen years, ever since George died. At first the arrangements were small and simple, fitting a young man's budget, but as he'd gotten older they'd gotten more elaborate. And more expensive.

The door from the reception area opened and he walked in.

"Look what came," she greeted him.

"Well, whaddya know. I guess Santa came through again."

"Santa Son," she said with a smile. "They're lovely. I wish you wouldn't be so extravagant, though."

"You're worth it," he said, stopping to kiss her on the cheek before going to the refrigerator to forage for lunch.

"There's leftover potpie," she said. As if he didn't know; as if that wasn't what he was looking for. It was one of his favorite meals and she made it for him on a regular basis.

"Got it," he said, pulling out the casserole dish. "So, has everyone checked out?"

"All but our last guests. I haven't seen them yet."

"The couple with the baby? They just left."

"Well, then, that's it until our Christmas guests start arriving. I'll get their room and the Braxtons' cleaned after lunch."

He shook his head. "Why you gave Morgan time

off the day before Christmas Eve I'll never understand."

"Because we don't usually have that many rooms to clean. She can have a break and we can save some money."

"We don't need to save money anymore. And it would be nice if you didn't kill yourself right before the Christmas rush."

"Cleaning two rooms isn't going to kill me. I'm not that old yet."

Her son wisely didn't argue the point.

She fingered a red rose. "I'm glad we've got so many people staying with us for the holidays." Having other people to think about made it so much easier.

"Yeah, we've got plenty this year."

"It's going to be wonderful," Olivia predicted.

"As long as we don't get any more Braxtons," Eric said. "I hope you didn't give him a refund."

"Did he ask you for one?"

Eric nodded. "Ran into me in the upstairs hall. Please tell me you didn't give in to that jerk."

Olivia shrugged. "Fifty percent off."

Eric shook his head. "You're too soft, Mom."

"Well, it's Christmas."

"That doesn't mean you have to humor jerks like Braxton."

"I couldn't bring myself to be as small as him, not at Christmas. Anyway, he'll get what's coming to him. We all do at some point." And sometimes people got what they didn't deserve, like losing a spouse. Olivia shooed that thought away. "Heat me up a little of that potpie, will you? Then I'm going to get those rooms cleaned and finish my shopping before the day gets away from me," she said, forcing cheer into her voice. "Can I pick you up anything?"

"Nah, I'm fine. And I'll clean the rooms. I've done all my outside work for the day and I need something to do."

He was always working, but she decided to let him have his way.

"All right, then, you're in charge," she said when lunch was done and she was ready to leave for the store. Actually, he was pretty much in charge even when she *was* at the lodge, which left Olivia free to enjoy cooking for their guests. What would she do without him?

It was a question she asked herself a lot lately. She wanted her son to find a nice woman and settle down, but so far no one in Icicle Falls had fit the bill. What if Ms. Right lived somewhere far away and didn't want to move to Icicle Falls? Olivia wasn't sure she could run the lodge alone, wasn't sure she wanted to. But she hated the idea of closing it. It had meant so much to George. And to her.

What will be, will be, she told herself. Meanwhile, she had a lot to be thankful for. Eric was here, helping her. And Brandon, her baby, would be coming home for Christmas. Both her boys at the lodge. It was going to be a perfect holiday. Well…almost perfect. As perfect as it could be without George.

Once at the Safeway, she got busy picking up the

items on her grocery list. Her friends Pat Wilder and
Ed York had come in to get some lunch at the deli
and she stopped to visit with them for a few minutes. Honestly, those two acted more like infatuated
teenagers every day, she thought as she made her
way to the produce department.

She realized she was suddenly feeling slightly
Scroogey herself. She could have blamed it on the
grumpy Mr. Braxton but she knew the real reason.
Still, it was better to have loved and lost than never
to have loved at all.

Probably better to quit hanging mistletoe around
the lodge, too.

No, no. People needed to celebrate. Someone
would make good use of that mistletoe, even if it
wasn't her. She made a quick detour to the baking
aisle, grabbing some chocolate chips and more flour.
When she got home she was going to bake cookies.

Eric had dinner with his mom, then left her finishing up a knitting project and enjoying some old
Christmas movie on TV to go meet up with his pals
for a pre-Christmas beer fest at Zelda's, a favorite
hangout for locals and tourists alike.

He found the place brim full of holiday cheer
and people. A tree dressed up in pink ribbons and
lights greeted visitors when they came in and the
bar was decorated with silver tinsel and bells. The
cocktail waitresses all wore Santa hats. So did half
the customers.

Eric went over to the table where Bubba Swank

and Rob Bohn were waiting for him. They hadn't waited to order, however, and had both already made a dent in their beers. Bubba raised his in salute. "Merry Christmas. Got your shopping done?"

"Of course," Eric replied. "Unlike you slobs, I don't leave it till the last minute."

"You also don't have anybody but your mom to shop for," Rob said.

His mom and his brother, but it didn't take long to buy iTunes and Bavarian Brews gift cards. "Yeah? And who've you got to shop for besides Ivy?" Eric retorted. Rob and Ivy had a couple of kids, but Eric knew who bought the presents for them, as well as all the other people on their Christmas list.

"My parents," Rob insisted. "And my brothers."

"And *you* buy their presents? Not your wife?"

Rob was silent, and Bubba gave a snort.

"So, you going to Seattle to see Gina?" Eric asked Bubba.

"First Christmas with the girlfriend," Rob put in. "I'm betting that's a yes."

Bubba frowned at his beer. "Actually, that's a no."

"Uh-oh," said Eric.

"Uh, you still have the girlfriend, right?" asked Rob.

Bubba shook his head. "She broke up with me day before yesterday. By text."

"Seriously?" Of course, breakups happened all the time, but Eric was surprised to hear about this one. Bubba was a nice guy, good-looking with a six-pack and the kind of strong jawline that seemed to draw women like a magnet. He owned a big place on Mountain View Drive and had a successful business. Plus he was a great guy. If Bubba couldn't hang on to a woman, what hope was there for someone like Eric, who wasn't exactly calendar-boy material and who worked running his mom's lodge?

"That's harsh, man," Rob said. "How come?"

"She said she didn't see it going anywhere."

"Which meant she didn't want to move," Rob deduced.

Bubba nodded. "I think that's about it."

"I guess she doesn't know what a gold mine Big Brats is. Did you tell her you're a millionaire?"

Bubba shook his head again and took a long swig of beer. "Only a half millionaire. She can probably do better in Seattle."

"I doubt it," Rob said. "But that's the problem when you get involved with tourists. They come up for some laughs and then they return to their real life. You were good enough to flirt with, hang out with this summer, but when it came right down to it…"

"I guess I should've known," Bubba said with a shrug.

"Yeah, you should have," Rob said. "Drink local and date local."

"First you gotta find someone local," Bubba said. "We can't all meet a cute little cheerleader in high school and live happily ever after."

Now Rob wasn't looking quite so happy.

"Uh, you guys are okay, aren't you?" Bubba asked.

Rob smiled but it seemed forced. "Sure. We're okay."

"Yeah?" Eric wasn't buying it.

"Okay, we've got some shit going on. Well, I've got some shit going on."

Rita Reyes was at their table now, ready to take Eric's order. "Merry Christmas, Eric," she said. "How are things at the lodge? Are you guys full up?"

"Not quite," he said. "There's still time to make a reservation for Christmas dinner."

"Someday I'm gonna treat myself and do that. Your mom's Christmas dinners are legendary. So, what can I get you?"

"Hale's Mongoose."

"I'll have another," Rob told her, and she nodded and hurried off. "There's a fine-looking sugarplum," he said, admiring the view as she threaded her way among the tables.

"Hello," Bubba said, tapping him on the head. "Married man?"

Rob frowned.

"So, what's going on with you two?" Eric asked, returning them to the subject at hand.

Rob contemplated his beer. "Sometimes I wonder if, aw, I don't know. I think we got married too young."

"Don't tell me you're thinking of leaving Ivy," Eric said.

"I don't know," he said again. "Sometimes I feel like I missed out somehow."

Eric couldn't believe his ears. Rob and Ivy were the perfect couple. In fact, he'd envied his old high school buddy. Rob seemed to have the perfect life. He'd married into a great family, and Christmas Haus, the shop he and Ivy owned, was a gold mine. It was originally called Kringle Mart, and they'd recently changed the name and doubled their business. In addition to sitting on a gold mine, he was married to a pretty woman who was about as nice as they came. A perfect life, a perfect marriage. If Rob couldn't make it, who could?

Lately, Eric had been feeling the pull toward marriage. It seemed as though all his friends were happily paired off, either married or in a serious relationship. Well, it had until tonight.

"You're nuts if you leave," he told Rob.

"Yeah, probably," Rob agreed. "But I wish I'd stayed single like you, man. Your life is your own. You can do what you want. All of that, plus good home cooking."

Who was he kidding? Eric's life was tied up in running the lodge and watching over his mom. Yeah, the home cooking was great and there was nothing else he'd rather do than run the lodge, but living with your mom didn't exactly make for a great sex life.

"Yeah, right," he said. "My life's so great, that's why I'm hanging out with you two—who, by the way, are a real pair of downers."

"Love can be a downer," Rob said morosely.

Rita was back with their beers. Just in time because Rob had swilled all of his. He lifted up his glass. "Okay, guys, here's to the new year. Let's hope it gets better."

"I'll drink to that," Eric said. And *better* for him would include a woman. He was getting tired of his bachelor existence, tired of things not working out. His younger brother didn't seem to mind going through women like candy but Eric did. He was ready to settle down.

Except if someone in a practically perfect marriage like Rob could be discontented, if a nice guy like Bubba couldn't hang on to a woman, what chance did he have? And where was he going to find Ms. Right? Date local, great idea. But he'd tried the local girls and nothing had come of it. He'd even expanded his search to nearby Wenatchee and that hadn't panned out, either. Was he too picky?

No, he decided. It wasn't picky to want what his folks had. They'd been so happy. Maybe that was some older-generation thing. Maybe it didn't work that way for people his age anymore. Who knew?

All he knew was that hanging out with his friends should have put him in a good mood and instead they were a holiday bummer.

Never mind, he told himself. *Santa's still alive and well, and it's Christmas in Icicle Falls. Your life's not so bad.*

But hey, Santa, if you're listening, it could be better.

Chapter Four

I'll Be Home for Christmas

"What do you mean you won't be coming for Christmas Eve?" John Truman's mother demanded.

John had not been looking forward to this conversation, which was why he'd put it off to the last possible minute. "I'm doing something with Holland."

"With her family?" his mother asked suspiciously. When it came to Christmas and her kids, Mom didn't like to share.

"No. Just the two of us. But we'll be back Christmas Day."

His mother harrumphed. "That's all well and good, but it'll just be us on Christmas Day. What am I supposed to tell the aunts and uncles, and your cousins? And Ben's bringing his fiancée, too."

As if John hadn't already met his big brother's girlfriend a million times. Anyway, if all went according to plan, he'd be showing up on Christmas Day with a fiancée of his own.

When he shared this with his mother, she wasn't all that excited. "So, you're going to do it."

"Yep. We're driving up to Icicle Falls tonight to stay in this really cool B and B and I'll propose on Christmas Eve. Then we'll come by the house on Christmas Day and show you the ring."

There was a long moment of silence on his mother's end. "Well, John, we love you and you know we'll welcome her into the family."

And that was as much as he was going to get out of his mother. She and Holland hadn't quite warmed to each other yet. Mom thought Holland was self-centered. Translation: Holland didn't always want to go along with Mom's social plans for the family. Holland thought Mom was controlling. Translation: Holland didn't always want to go along with Mom's social plans for the family. They were both strong women but John knew they'd really come to love each other. Eventually. Once Mom got over the idea that Holland wasn't good enough for him.

All moms thought that about their kids, right? Except she loved his brother's fiancée, probably because Margo fell right in with everything Mom wanted to do, from impromptu family picnics to Father's Day barbecues. But Holland had a family of her own, and an important job at a Seattle ad agency. She had a social life, too. She had girlfriends, and a book club, and that all took time. And she and John had friends. They couldn't necessarily drop what they were doing and come running whenever Mom called. That was what Holland said when she balked at Mom's latest plans for family (and girl-friend) solidarity. Fortunately, she'd never said it to Mom's face, or there would've been hell to pay.

"I just hope you know what you're doing," his mother added.

Oh, yeah. Feeling the motherly support here. "Thanks, Mom."

"You haven't even been together a year."

"Eleven months." Close enough. And they'd known each other before then. They worked in the same downtown building and had hung out at lunch sometimes.

"And you two did have that rough patch," she continued.

"Everybody has rough patches, Mom." He remembered his parents doing their share of fighting when he was in grade school. "Anyway, that was months ago." He and Holland had worked things out since then. Okay, so they still had a fight once in a while. Every couple had disagreements, right? "We're fine now." And they were going to have a great time up in Icicle Falls, where he'd booked them a room at the kind of classy place Holland would love, with a fancy lobby and fireplaces in the rooms. Oh, yeah. It was going to be totally romantic. He had everything planned out. A late dinner at one of the local restaurants, shopping the next day, followed by a romantic sleigh ride and maybe some skating in the outdoor rink in the town square. Then, after Christmas Eve dinner, he'd whip out the ring he'd bought, get down on one knee and ask her to marry him. After that they'd have champagne in their room, get a fire going in the fireplace and heat up the sheets. Oh, yeah. Holland was going to be blown away.

"I just don't want to see you hurt," his mother said.

Had his mother been a wet blanket in another life? "What makes you think I'll get hurt?" He wasn't an idiot, for crying out loud.

Another silence on the other end of the line. "Honey, sometimes you're not…"

"Not what?"

"Not very realistic."

Okay, sometimes he *was* an idiot. But how could he have known Sarah Schoop was out to use him? Okay, so she'd gotten him to buy her a few expensive presents. He hadn't minded. He liked being generous. Maybe he liked being obtuse, too. He and Sarah would probably still be together if his mother and sister hadn't done an intervention after his sister overheard Sarah asking him to pay for her boob job. They'd explained that Sarah loved him only for his 401k. Yeah, Sarah was a mistake. But he was older and wiser now. Once a guy passed thirty, he developed a little more discernment. And one thing he knew—Holland didn't need to use him. Well, except as a sex toy.

"You need a woman with a good heart," said Mom.

"Holland has a good heart."

"I'm sure she does…somewhere."

"Mom," John said sternly, "you're talking about the woman I love."

"Don't remind me," she said.

"Okay, I have to go," he said, pissed.

"All right, but what am I supposed to tell the family tomorrow?"

"Tell them that the next time they see me I'll be engaged."

That didn't make his mother happy but it sure made him smile.

He was barely off the phone with Mom when his smartphone rang. This time it was the love of his life. "Hey," he said. "I'm just leaving to pick you up."

"Yeah, about that."

Oh, no. His mind latched on to the image of a building getting whacked by a giant wrecking ball. He could practically hear the crack and crumble of his carefully laid plans. "What?"

"I have to work late."

Two days before Christmas? Was she working for Ebenezer Scrooge?

"You go on up and I'll meet you there."

Oh, yeah, take two cars to a romantic getaway. "No way. We'll wait and go tomorrow morning." He'd paid a good chunk of change for the room but so what?

"No, you may as well have fun. Just go on up."

How was that supposed to be fun without her? Here he was, planning to sweep her off her feet, and instead she was pulling the rug out from under him. "I'm not going up without you. That's lame."

"No, it's not. Anyway, you paid for the room. You might as well use it."

"It wouldn't be the same without you. I'll wait and we can go up later, after you get done at work. I'll drive. You can relax."

"There's nothing relaxing about the way you drive," she informed him.

John frowned. Honesty was important in a relationship, but sometimes Holland was *too* honest, especially when it came to his flaws. "Thanks a lot," he muttered.

"Come on, John. Don't be like that."

"Like what?"

"All disappointed and grumpy."

Kind of hard not to be disappointed. He'd had this all planned, and she'd known about it for a month. Since when was she so gutless that she couldn't tell her boss she couldn't work late?

"It's been a sucky day. I just want to get a good night's sleep in my own bed," she continued, further bruising his ego.

Yeah, God forbid she'd want to cuddle up to him. They were serious, an item. Weren't they supposed to want to be together?

"So I'll see you up there tomorrow. Where are we going again?"

"The Icicle Creek Lodge," he said, but not grumpily. He was not grumpy.

"Okay, see you there," she said, and ended the call.

No matter what Holland said, he wasn't going to

go off and start their romantic getaway alone. "This reeks," he grumbled as he tossed his phone onto the seat next to him and drove home.

Home was a one-bedroom apartment in Seattle's Belltown. He guessed he'd find some Bruce Willis movie on Netflix and kick back with a beer.

And let that room at the Icicle Creek Lodge sit empty?

Yeah. That was the gallant thing to do because what kind of turd-brain went off and started a romantic weekend without his girlfriend?

A pissed one.

The car was all loaded with the champagne in the trunk, along with his suitcase. And, as Holland had pointed out, the room at the Icicle Creek Lodge was paid for. So, he could go home to his apartment and sit around feeling grumpy or he could go on up to Icicle Falls and check in to a really cool place, get everything ready for when she came up tomorrow. Hmm.

No, it didn't feel right.

Still, he'd already paid the money. He called Holland again.

"What?" she snapped.

"Are you positive you don't want to go up tonight? I'll give you a back rub when we get there," he promised. Holland loved his back rubs.

"No, I don't. I'm not sure when I'll get done and I'm tired from having to come in early. And I told you, I had a sucky day. I'll see you up there tomorrow. Okay?"

Well, there was no reason to get snappy. Oh, except for PMS. And if that was what was going on he'd be better off letting her get a good night's sleep.

"Fine," he said, a little snappish himself. "I'll see you tomorrow."

"See you tomorrow," she said in a quasipatient tone of voice, as if she was dealing with someone who was a severe trial.

He knew when to give up. If she wanted to take two cars and waste gas, fine. "Okay." He wanted to urge her not to take all day getting up there, but then he remembered that possible PMS thing so he didn't. Instead, he said, "See you when you get there." He added, "I love you, babe," but she'd hung up. Well, he was the more romantic of the two of them. Weird, but there you had it.

He was also the thriftier of the two, probably because he didn't make as much as she did. There was nothing wrong with being thrifty, and hey, if she was determined to bring her own car, then he'd go up tonight.

He turned toward I-90, brought up Pandora and got the Christmas music going. Once he hit Icicle Falls he'd maybe enjoy a late dinner at Zelda's restaurant, where he'd planned to take Holland, just to check it out. And wish she was there.

She'll be there tomorrow, he reminded himself. And then everything would go according to plan.

He made good time until he neared Snoqualmie Pass. Then the sleeting rain that had started around Bellevue turned to snow and traffic slowed down.

There was a veritable logjam of cars in the spot designated for putting on chains, and with the way the snow was coming down, he could see why chains were required. Maybe Holland wouldn't want to deal with that. Damn. He knew he should have waited and come up with her.

He quickly called her and got an impatient hello. "Hey, chains are required."

"Okay, thanks."

"Uh, you okay with doing that?" This was their first time going to the mountains together. What if she couldn't put on chains?

"I do know how to put on chains, John," she said.

"Okay, fine. You home yet?"

"Yeah, and I'm about to take a bath."

Oh, there was an image to make a man smile. "Get good and relaxed," he said. "See you tomorrow."

"Okay, bye." And then she was gone.

He pulled up behind a Honda that had seen better days, where a woman in a black parka and jeans and tennis shoes was struggling to get chains around one of her rear tires. Unlike Holland, who was leggy and svelte, this woman filled out her pants with a well-rounded bottom. She wore glasses and had curls of blue hair escaping from a red knit hat. Two little kids, a Latino boy and a cute little girl with big brown eyes and cornrows, were hanging out the back windows, trying to catch snowflakes in their mittened hands. Meanwhile, the woman was still struggling with the chain. It wasn't hard to see why; she wasn't wearing gloves. Her hands had to be frozen. She stopped to blow on them and glared at the chain.

Here was a job for Super John. He got out of his car and came over. "Can I help you with that?"

She looked up at him gratefully and rubbed her hands together. "That would be great. I just can't seem to get these stupid chains on."

"It's hard when your hands are cold."

"I forgot to pack my gloves. Here we are, going to the mountains, and I forget to pack gloves. Can you believe it?"

"Looks like you were packing for more than yourself," John said. The girl had joined the boy at his window and was now regarding John. She was cute as a button with her big brown eyes and that goofy tiara on her head. Her parka was a little frayed but clean. The boy's coat looked too small for him but it, too, was clean and his mittens looked new.

"My mom needs help," said the boy. "I could've done it."

"I'm sure you could," John agreed. He wondered what had happened to these kids' dads. This woman sure wasn't alone because she was a dog. She had a round face and blue eyes and Angelina Jolie lips. Cute, he thought. Not that he was interested, of course. It was just an observation.

He introduced himself to the mom and learned her name was Missy Monroe. Cute name, too. "Where are you guys headed?"

"To Icicle Falls," she said. "We're going to spend Christmas up there."

"No way. Really? Me, too," he said.

"All I want is to get there in one piece. I've never put on chains before," she confessed.

She had them laid out properly, with the connector facedown. Unfortunately, she was putting them on the wrong tires. "Well, you made a good start," he said, "but I'll bet this is a front-wheel-drive car, which means you need those on the front tires."

She took that in. "Oh. Oops."

"Easy to fix," he said. "Let's move the tires off the chains and try again."

She nodded and hopped behind the wheel. Moments later the chains were matched with the correct tires.

"Gosh, I'm glad you came along," she said as he hooked them up. "Even if I got them on, they would've been useless."

"No problem," he said. Yeah, good thing he'd decided to come up today. Otherwise, this poor woman would've worked away at those chains until her hands turned as blue as her hair. "So, where are you staying in Icicle Falls?"

"We've got reservations at this place called the Icicle Creek Lodge."

"No way," John said again. "That's where I'm staying." That made her face light up like a Christmas tree. Uh-oh. Maybe she thought he was single. "Uh, with my girlfriend," he added.

Her face reddened. "Oh." She looked over to his car, where there was plainly no girlfriend.

Now he felt embarrassed. "She had to work late. She's joining me tomorrow."

The woman nodded slowly, taking that in. "Oh."

"And are you, uh, meeting someone?"

"No." For a moment she seemed a little sad, but that was replaced by a forced brightness. "Just the kids and me. We're going to have a perfect, old-fashioned Christmas."

He nodded approval. "Great." He finished with the last chain and stepped away from his handiwork. "Okay, you're good to go."

"Thanks," she said, and smiled at him as if he was some sort of genius.

He waved away her thanks. All in a day's work for a holiday superhero. "If you have any problem, I'll be right behind you."

"Well, I guess I'll see you there," she said.

"Yeah, see you."

"And thanks again for helping me with the chains."

"No worries."

She gave him a bashful smile and then hopped into her car. He could hear her instructing the kids to buckle up. The car started and the sounds of "The Little Drummer Boy" drifted out to him. The son leaned his head out the window and waved, and John waved back.

"Come on, Carlos, we're not moving until you're buckled in and the window is up," said his mom.

Up went the window and the car chunk-chunked its way back onto the highway. John gave them one last wave and then got busy with his own chains. Someday that would be him, he thought as he pulled back onto the highway, taking his kids up to the mountains for Christmas. Maybe they'd even cut their own Christmas tree.

They'd have to do that without Holland. She wasn't much into hiking, even in nice weather.

But she liked to shop and she liked good wine, and that was another reason he'd picked Icicle Falls. He'd done a search for holiday getaway spots in Washington and the town had come up at the top of his search list. It wasn't hard to see why. In addition to its charming town center it had lots of those cute shops chicks loved, along with local wineries and good restaurants. Oh, yeah. It was a Holland kind of place. And the Icicle Creek Lodge was the frosting on the red velvet cake. They were going to have a great time.

Chapter Five

Do You See What I See?

There were oohs and aahs from the kids the moment they hit town. Driving past all those buildings with the fancy paintings on them and the cute little signs dangling above the doors, the potted Christmas trees strung with twinkle lights sitting on every corner, it was as if they'd gone to Germany for the holidays. One shop even had a life-size Nutcracker standing guard outside. Wow.

Once they'd gone through the town itself, Missy's directions sent her down Icicle Creek Drive, a wooded road surrounded by snowy woods. "See the llama farm?" she said, pointing. "That means we're almost there."

Sure enough, there was Holly Road, the side road veering off the main drag. She turned onto it and followed a scenic, curved road. She could already see herself walking down it, taking the kids into town to see the sights.

Then she saw their home for the holidays. Carlos and Lalla stared in awe at the Icicle Creek Lodge as if it was the Taj Mahal. It was pretty impressive—a big stone-and-timber building that looked like something from another time with a sweeping front lawn carpeted with pristine snow. The roof was strung with icicle lights and a tree bejeweled with colored lights sat on the front porch, which ran along the front of the building. Oh, yes, just like in the picture.

"Wow!" cried Carlos, racing toward the lodge.

"Not so fast," Missy said. "I need you to help me carry in our stuff."

"I can help," offered John Truman, who had just gotten out of his vehicle. He'd caught up with them quickly after chaining up his own car and, true to his word, had been behind them all the way like some sort of guardian angel.

He sure was a cute guardian angel, with hair the color of red some women would pay a fortune for and freckles strung across his nose. He wasn't as good-looking as other men she'd fallen for but she was willing to bet he also wasn't a sleaze bucket.

There would be no falling for this guy, she reminded herself. He was already taken. "That's okay," she said, handing a grocery bag of snacks to Lalla, who, like her brother, couldn't seem to stand still.

"Mama," Lalla gasped, "I just saw Santa Claus."

"There's no such thing, stupid," Carlos told her scornfully.

"Is, too!" Lalla shot back.

"Don't call your sister stupid," Missy scolded. She wanted to add that there was, too, such a thing as Santa, but couldn't quite bring herself to do it, considering that Santa had been rather a disappointment to her children, especially Carlos. "Where did you see Santa, princess?" she asked her daughter.

Lalla pointed to the lodge. "I saw him go inside."

"Santa doesn't stay in houses," Carlos said impatiently. "He lives at the North Pole."

So much for not believing in Santa, Missy thought with a smile, and gave her son the backpack with his clothes.

"Maybe he's visiting friends," John said. Missy had a trash bag with the kids' presents in it and he insisted on carrying that, as well as the beat-up carry-on suitcase she'd picked up at a garage sale.

"Maybe we'll see him," Lalla said, and hurried up the front walk.

"Race you!" Carlos dashed ahead of her.

"I think they're stoked," John observed.

"They're not the only ones," Missy said. Oh, yes, this was going to be such a great Christmas. And she didn't need a man to make it great. Still, as she made her way up the walk with her new friend beside her, she couldn't help wishing he wasn't already taken.

James wished he was in jeans and a shirt instead of this red Santa suit. If he were, he'd be more inclined to linger and talk to Olivia Wallace, the friendly owner of this B and B who was checking them in, supervised by a big orange cat sitting on top of the check-in desk. There was something pleasant about this woman, something that said, "Take a deep breath, relax, everything will be all right."

She was plump and round-faced. Her hair was as gray as his, a pretty silver-white, softly curled and very feminine-looking. Put her in a red skirt and a lacy blouse and some granny glasses, and she could pass for Mrs. Claus. She'd moved her wedding ring to her right hand, which told him she was widowed. It would be comforting to talk with someone who'd been where he was.

Olivia smiled. "I swear, you're the most realistic Santa I've ever seen."

Realistic or not, who went out in public dressed like Santa? He felt like an idiot. "I don't normally parade around in this outfit," he said.

"I kidnapped him from work," Brooke explained. She petted the cat and it purred and leaned into her hand for more. "He's a professional Santa."

"Oh, that must be fun!" said Olivia.

It had been. Once upon a time. James shrugged.

"He's been Santa for as long as I can remember," Brooke continued, warming to the subject. "At family gatherings, for church events, orphanages, fundraisers. He always goes to Children's Hospital and visits the kids."

Okay, this was becoming embarrassing. And now voices outside announced that more guests were arriving.

"I think I hear children," he said. "Let's get out of here before they see me and wonder what Santa's doing wandering around the lodge two days before Christmas."

"They'd probably love to meet you," Brooke said.

Well, he didn't want to meet them. "Honey, I really want to change out of this outfit."

"Of course," Olivia said, handing over the keycards for their adjoining rooms. "We serve breakfast from eight to ten. If you have any special dietary needs that weren't addressed when you registered, please let us know. Christmas Eve we'll be offering a special dinner at six and on Christmas Day we'll serve dinner at five."

"Fabulous," Brooke said.

"The elevator's right around the corner if you prefer to use it. I hope you'll enjoy your stay." Olivia smiled at both of them again, but her smile seemed to linger on James.

"I hope we'll see you around," he said, and then felt instantly guilty. That had been…too friendly. His wife had been gone only a year. He had no right to be smiling at a woman, taking in her generous curves. Her breasts.

His thoughts traveled back to Faith's mastectomy. A double. She'd mourned the loss of her breasts, but he'd just been glad to have her alive, still with him. Who cared about the breasts? Of course, she'd talked about reconstructive surgery and that had made him nervous. Even though it was a common procedure, what if something happened?

Something *had* happened. She'd barely gotten her new breasts when the damned cancer came back, this time in her spine. He'd nursed her the best he could, tried to learn to cook. But his specialty had remained heating soup. Thank God they'd had friends who brought over hot dishes. Thank God for his daughter. He wished he was thanking God that his wife was still alive.

Now the voices were getting nearer. Santa was in no mood to see anybody. He grabbed Brooke's suitcase and marched for the elevator.

She hurried after him, catching up with him just as the doors opened. As they stepped off the elevator and walked under the archway toward the hall where their rooms were, she said, "Oh, look. Mistletoe."

That made him even grumpier. But it wouldn't do to be grumpy when he was with his daughter and she'd gone to so much trouble to make their Christmas good. "Well, then, I'd better kiss my angel," he said, and gave her a hug and a kiss on the cheek.

She hugged him back. "We're going to have fun."

"Yes, we are," he lied.

"Look!" came a childish voice from the lobby. "There he is."

Crap. "Okay, let's go," he said, and picked up his pace.

"I saw him!" Lalla cried, pointing to the third landing. "He was right there and he was kissing a lady."

If he was on the third-story landing, he was gone now. The kids would love it if there was somebody here playing Santa Claus. Missy hadn't taken them to the mall to see Santa yet and she'd love to get their pictures taken with him.

Of course, they'd written letters to Santa. She'd helped Lalla write hers and it had read, "Dear Santa, I love you. Please bring me a grandma. My grandma is in heaven with the angels and can't bake me cookies or read me stories. Merry Christmas. We will try to make you some cookies if Mommy can buy some cookie mix." They hadn't gotten around to the cookies, but Missy had assured Lalla that Santa would bring her something, anyway.

Carlos hadn't been quite so loving in his letter. He'd written it himself and it was short and to the point. "Dear Santa, if you kant bring me a dog furgit it. Merry Kristmas, Carlos." Well, okay, so Santa wouldn't come through. They'd still have fun.

How could they not? She looked around the huge, beautifully decorated lobby. The carpet was dated but in pristine condition with a muted floral pattern. Sturdy ornate furniture gathered around a big fireplace on the back wall, impressive with its style and the carving on the mantelpiece. The fireplace was laid with wood, ready to be lit, and Missy could envision herself standing in front of it. A grouping of three large potted poinsettias sat on the coffee table and two wingback chairs flanked it. A baby grand piano occupied space in one corner and Missy knew from what she'd read on the website that later that evening someone would be seated at that piano, giving the guests a concert. But best of all was the antique sleigh sitting front and center in the lobby. It was decorated with red ribbon and greens and filled with presents and teddy bears. Some delicious aroma hung in the air, bringing the promise of cookies.

"Well, aren't you two the most beautiful children ever," the woman at the reception desk greeted them. "What are your names?"

"I'm Lalla. I'm named after a Orca princess." Lalla pointed to her tiara.

"Moroccan princess," Missy corrected her, and Lalla nodded vigorously.

"Of course. Anyone can see you're a princess," said the woman.

That was the plan, always had been, from the moment Missy learned she was having a girl. She'd picked the name, not just because of her daughter's mixed ethnicity and skin color, but because she wanted Lalla to know she was special and to grow up confident that she could become anything she wanted. There would be no low self-esteem in *her* family. No, sir.

"This is Carlos," Lalla continued. "He doesn't believe in Santa."

The woman put a hand to her heart. "Oh, dear. I'd better not tell Santa that. It will hurt his feelings. You know, Icicle Falls is his favorite place to visit," she said, lowering her voice conspiratorially.

"I saw him," Lalla said eagerly. "Who are you?"

"I'm Olivia Wallace, and this is my home. I hope you'll enjoy staying with us. We have you and your family in 205," she said, addressing both Missy and

John, who'd been standing next to Missy, enjoying the show. She handed a little envelope with the key-cards to John.

He turned red from his neck to the tips of his ears. "Um, we're not really together. We just, uh, met on the way up."

Olivia flushed. "Oh, excuse me."

"John put the chains on my car," Missy told her.

"Well, that was nice. It's good to see that chivalry is still alive and well," Olivia said approvingly.

"It sure is," Missy agreed. "Okay, guys, let's go see our room," she said to the kids. They were off with a whoop, racing for the stairs. "And don't run," she called, trailing after them with their bags.

She was still within earshot, so she heard Olivia say to John, "Now, there's a sweet young woman."

"Yeah, she's pretty nice," John said.

He thought she was pretty nice. She thought he was pretty nice, too. Pity he wasn't in the market for a woman.

Except that even if he was, a classy guy like that who drove a nice car and not an old beater wouldn't want to hang out with a girl like her, someone who lived in a dumpy neighborhood, shopped at Goodwill and garage sales and fed her kids mac and cheese from a box. At least she didn't smoke anymore. She'd kicked that habit and was already saving money as a result. Still, she'd never make enough to put her in his class. Men like John dated girls who worked in offices and shopped at Nordstrom and Macy's, girls who never got their hair done at inexpensive salons.

She frowned. It shouldn't matter what a person wore or what sort of car she drove. It was what she was like on the inside that counted. And on the inside Missy was an office-working, Nordstrom-shopping, high-end-salon kind of woman. Someday, someday soon, she'd have the life to prove it. And meanwhile, she was staying at a classy place and giving her kids a classy Christmas. *So there,* she concluded, lifting her chin. That chin-lifting stuff wasn't such a good idea, made it hard to see the stairs. She tripped, and her suitcase slid down a couple of steps. Oops. She grabbed it and kept on going, her cheeks burning. *Nordstrom on the inside,* she told herself.

John watched out of the corner of his eye as Missy Monroe and her kids went up the stairs. He wondered if Missy was seeing someone, if there was some man hoping to step into her ready-made family. There had to be someone. She was too cute and too sweet to be totally on her own.

Although if she *was* seeing someone, he probably would've come up here with her. After all, who did Christmas alone?

None of your business, he reminded himself as Olivia gave him his keycard.

"You're in 207," she informed him.

Right next door to the Monroe family. For a millisecond he wondered if he wanted to be that close to Missy and company. He felt a little like an alcoholic who'd just been offered a bottle of twenty-year-old Scotch.

But then he chided himself for being stupid. Yeah, Missy was cute, but so what? He was in love with Holland, and he wasn't some low-life scum who hit on other women when he was about to become engaged, so it was no big deal. That resolved, he went to his room.

Oh, man, Holland was going to love this. The room had it all—antique furniture but a state-of-the-art TV and DVD player, a small fridge for his champagne, a view of the mountains out the window, a snowy-white comforter on the king-size bed and an electric fireplace. Oh, yeah. This was going to be romance to the max. He could picture Holland and him in that big bed going at it and then cuddling together, watching the flames. If only Holland had come up tonight.

Well, she'd be here tomorrow, and that would come soon enough. Meanwhile, what was he going to do with himself? He went to the window and looked out. The snowy scene beckoned him. What the hey, might as well go check out the town, find something to eat.

He heard whoops coming from 205 as he walked past and for a moment wondered what Missy and her kids were going to do now.

Never mind. He wasn't up here to hang out with

Missy Monroe and her kids. He was here for a romantic getaway with his girlfriend.

Who hadn't arrived yet. With a sigh, he walked down the hall.

Chapter Six

Santa Baby

Brooke had experienced some doubt regarding the wisdom of her holiday kidnapping when her father first failed to get into the spirit of the thing, but only for a few minutes. Over the past year, Daddy had seemed to collapse in on himself, changing from the sociable man he'd always been to a hermit who preferred to sit at home and stare at the TV. That was not Daddy, and something had to be done.

"He'll be okay," Dylan kept saying whenever she'd brought up the subject of what to do about their father. "You've gotta give him time. Jeez, *I* still miss Mom."

As if she didn't? As if there hadn't been a day in the past year when she hadn't wished her mother was alive, when she hadn't gotten blindsided by a memory and burst into tears? But she had a job and a Sunday school class to teach. And friends getting married and having babies. And that meant bridal

showers and baby showers to shop for and wed-
dings to attend (where friends tried to match her up
with brothers and cousins, none of whom ever mea-
sured up to her idea of the ideal man). Life wasn't
a card game where you got to throw in your hand
and say, "I fold."

And that was exactly what her father was doing.
Granted, he'd had a rough time of it, first with taking care of Mom and then with having to live without her. But Brooke was starting to get worried. In
the past few months he'd hardly cleaned the house,
totally neglected the yard and had constantly made
excuses when any of his friends invited him out for
dinner. She'd thought he'd return to his seasonal job
as a department-store Santa, but he'd even pulled
the plug on that, and had only filled in for the past
two days when his former boss begged him to help
out. He couldn't go on like this. It wasn't healthy.
So a change of scene was what the doctor had or-
dered (Dr. Brooke, that is).

He'd perked up once they got to the lodge and
smiled approvingly when they entered and he saw
how beautifully the place was decked out for the holidays. And he'd smiled again when they were checking in. Of course, he wasn't happy being stuck in his
Santa suit but Dylan would be arriving any minute,
and once Daddy had a change of clothes they could
go wander around town and admire the Christmas
lights. Then, later, they could enjoy the piano concert
in the lobby and the home-baked Christmas cookies
that had been promised on the website.

The cookies probably wouldn't be as good as Mom's, and Brooke found herself wishing she'd taken the time to whip up another batch of gumdrop cookies to bring along. Maybe it was just as well she hadn't, though. That would remind them all of Mom.

She'd flipped on the switch for the fireplace, and her father was currently relaxing on his bed with his black boots and his Santa jacket off while Brooke sat at the desk, checking out the notebook filled with glossy pages about the various shops and restaurants in town.

"I've heard about this Christmas shop," she said, turning the binder so her father could see. "We might want to go there tomorrow."

He nodded. "Looks nice." He let out a sigh. "Your mother would have loved this place."

Brooke could feel the sting of incipient tears. It had probably been unrealistic to think they could simply outrun their grief.

Still, Mom would have wanted them to participate in the joys of the season, and this town seemed tailor-made for that.

"Yes, she would," Brooke said. "And I bet right now she's up in heaven, smiling down on us."

For a moment she feared he was going to cry, but he nodded gamely and forced a smile.

Yep, they were having fun now. They needed Dylan and his goofy sense of humor to liven things up. They'd been waiting almost an hour. What was taking him so long to get up here?

She'd called twice but only got his voice mail; she hoped that meant he was somewhere in the mountains and didn't have reception. If that was the case, at least he was getting close.

As if on cue, there was a knock at the door. Finally. Brooke hurried to open it, but instead of her brother she found Olivia Wallace, bearing a tray with grapes, Brie cheese and crackers.

"Oh, good, you're here. I thought perhaps you might be when no one answered next door. This is your complimentary fruit and cheese," Olivia said. "I hope you enjoy it."

"We will," Brooke assured her. She was aware of her father scrambling to put his jacket back on so he wouldn't look like a slob.

But Olivia wasn't coming in to visit. She wished them "Bon appétit" and then left.

"That was thoughtful," Daddy said as Brooke set the tray on his bedside table.

As if the woman had done it just for them. "It's included in the price, Daddy."

His brow furrowed. "I hate to think what you kids are spending on this."

"You're worth it," she said, and kissed his cheek.

Twenty minutes later most of the cheese and grapes were gone, and Brooke was anxious to get her father out of his room and experiencing the sights and sounds of the town, but there was still no sign of Dylan. She took her cell phone from her purse and called him again.

"Yo," he answered.

"Where are you?"

"I'm in the lobby checking in."

"Finally," she said.

"Hey, I had to work late."

Dylan was a systems analyst at Microsoft and working late happened sometimes. Everyone couldn't be lucky enough to be a teacher.

Although her brother never saw her as lucky. "I'd go nuts if I was stuck in a room full of snot-nosed kids making paper chains," he often said.

Brooke always thought this was ironic considering the fact that, at twenty-four, her brother was the world's oldest child. He could play video games for hours, never remembered important dates like birthdays and anniversaries and had yet to master the art of wrapping a Christmas present. His idea of a gift bag was a paper sack. Sheesh.

And she did more than make paper chains. She helped young minds discover and learn new things. She loved her job and she could hardly wait to have children of her own. She didn't want to raise them by herself, though, so that meant she needed to find a man. Why was it so hard to find a good man these days, anyway?

Another few minutes, and Dylan entered the room. He looked like a younger version of their father with a boyish face and a husky build. And, like Daddy, he sported a beard. Only unlike Daddy, his was brown and he kept it trimmed close to his face. In addition to being cute, he was also charming and never lacked for girlfriends. But he was far from ready to settle down.

"Ho, ho, ho. Merry Christmas," he said.

"That's my line," Daddy joked. He got off the bed and came to hug his son.

"Great choice, sis," Dylan said to Brooke. "This place rocks."

"Have you seen your room?" she asked.

"Just dumped my stuff in there." He handed Brooke a plastic grocery bag. "Here's the eggnog you wanted."

"Thank you," she said, and moved to store it in the little refrigerator.

"Never mind the eggnog," her father said. "Give me my clothes."

Dylan's easy smile fell away, replaced by a look of panic. "Clothes? Crap."

He'd forgotten to go by Daddy's and get some clothes! She was going to kill him. "Please tell me you didn't forget." Why was she bothering to even say that? He had.

"Oh, man. I totally spaced. My bad."

"Your bad is right," she snapped in frustration. She'd planned everything, made their reservations, picked up their father. All Dylan had to do was pick up Daddy's car and bring some clothes for him. How hard was that? "I can't *believe* you forgot the clothes," she wailed. Her well-laid plans, all ruined.

"Hey, there's stores up here," Dylan said with a frown.

She knew he hated it when she went into older-sister mode and got on his case. But darn, she hated it when he acted like the baby of the family and got all irresponsible. "There won't be any stores open by now," she said, frowning, too. "And Daddy doesn't want to be stuck in his room all night."

"I'm fine," her father said. "I can find something on TV. You kids go have fun."

The only thing she'd have fun doing was throttling her irresponsible brother and that would hardly make for a warm and fuzzy family Christmas. She let out a huff of exasperation. "I'm going to go ask where we can buy some clothes," she announced, and yanked open the door.

As she left she heard her brother say, "So, what channels do we get?"

Great. They'd both watch some stupid movie with things blowing up and that would be that. Their first night in Icicle Falls with its snowy streets and pretty Christmas lights and the boys would be watching Bruce Willis save the world. She scowled as she marched downstairs.

The plump and friendly Olivia was not at the reception desk. Instead, a tall man with dark hair receding from his hairline and glasses was busy helping two older women check in. They were both dressed in heavy winter coats, leggings and snow boots. The short one wore a felted red hat over curls still as blond as if she were twenty and not seventy-something. "And in about an hour we'll have a piano concert down here in the lobby," he was telling them.

"That sounds wonderful," declared the other

woman. She was as tall and skinny as her companion was short and chunky, and her salt-and-pepper hair hung in a long, lanky curtain to her shoulders. "Didn't I tell you this was a good idea, Vera? It beats staying home wondering if those spoiled brats of yours are going to come by."

The plump Vera had been smiling up until that moment. Now she took her keycard from the man and calmly told her companion, "At least I *have* brats."

"If that's the best marriage can do, I'm glad I never got married," retorted her friend. "Come on, let's go up to the room. I want to call and make sure Tiger is all right."

"Talk about spoiled," Vera muttered as the two women walked past Brooke. "That cat's better treated than most children."

"That's because he's better behaved than most children."

And so the bickering continued as the two women towed their suitcases toward the elevator.

Well, fa-la-la, Brooke thought as she approached the reception desk. The man behind it looked more attractive the closer she got, and she realized he was younger than she'd originally thought. Maybe early thirties. He was well built and had a strong jaw and brown eyes behind those glasses. No wedding ring on his left hand. Not that she was actively looking. Okay, she was. Sort of.

"Hi," he greeted her. "May I help you?"

"I hope so," she said. "My father and brother and I all have adjoining rooms on the third floor."

"Is there a problem with your rooms?" he asked, his voice incredulous.

"No, no. They're great. But we do have a problem."

Now he seemed mildly suspicious.

At that moment Olivia reappeared from a door behind the reception desk. "Oh, hello," she said to Brooke. "How is Santa settling in?"

Her son looked at her, brows knit.

"I kidnapped my father from his Santa gig," Brooke explained, and the man nodded and smiled. He had a pretty darned sexy smile. *Let's get back to why you came down here,* she told her wandering thoughts. To Olivia she said, "I'm afraid Santa's not doing very well. My brother forgot to bring up my father's clothes and he's got nothing except his Santa costume."

That made the man behind the counter snicker.

Brooke decided his smile wasn't so sexy, after all. She supposed her father's predicament sounded funny, but it wasn't. He wasn't going to go strolling around the streets of Icicle Falls in his Santa suit, and that meant there'd be no getting him out and lifting his spirits. She frowned, and Mr. No Longer Sexy coughed and cleared his throat, then donned a more serious expression.

"Of course, he'd fit right in if he did go out in it," Olivia said. "I'm sure you got a glimpse of how the town is decorated when you arrived."

"Yes, it's lovely," Brooke said. "But the problem is, well, he's not in much of a Santa mood this year."

"Oh, dear."

"I was hoping you could tell me if there's someplace in town where we might find him some clothes."

Olivia shook her head and bit her lip. "We've got Manly Man, but I'm afraid they closed for the holidays yesterday. It's a family-run business and they're on their way to Florida to be with family."

"We've got some places where you can get an Icicle Falls sweatshirt," the man put in. "And a jacket."

Maybe he could wear them over his red pants.

"But they're closed now," said Olivia. "And he could get coveralls at the hardware store but by now they're closed, too. Wenatchee isn't far, though, and tomorrow you'll be able to find a store there that sells men's clothing."

Brooke sighed. It looked as though they'd have to wait until tomorrow to get something for Daddy to wear. Tonight he'd be stuck in his room. Which would probably be fine with him. But it wouldn't be fine with her. He could watch TV at home. This was Icicle Falls, for crying out loud. They were supposed to be having fun, making new memories.

"You know," Olivia said thoughtfully. "I might have something to tide you over until you can get to a store. Let me look around and I'll come up in a few minutes."

"Oh, if you could, that would be great," Brooke said. "Thank you."

"No promises, but we'll see what we can do."

Brooke went back to the room to give the boys her good news and found them stretched out on her father's bed watching some gory action movie. Oh, yes, this was how she'd envisioned their holiday getaway. Not.

"Where are you planning on finding clothes for this guy?" Eric asked his mother after their guest had gone back up the stairs. "If he's hefty enough to play Santa, he won't fit any of mine."

"I still have a few things of your father's."

Eric looked at Olivia in surprise. "We took everything to Goodwill."

"Not everything."

She'd kept a pair of George's slacks, a sweater, two of his shirts. Silly, she supposed, but seeing them hanging in her closet had made her loss seem less final. She'd actually taken his old red plaid flannel shirt to bed with her every night the first month he was gone, holding it close, inhaling the lingering scent of his cologne. She'd kept back a half-empty bottle of the cologne, too, and occasionally dabbed some on the shirt. Eventually the cologne had run out and she'd hung the shirt back in the closet, resigned herself to her loss and picked up the pieces of her life. She'd reopened the Icicle Creek Lodge for business and moved forward as best she could. And with the help of her girlfriends, the LAMs (Life After Men), who were also dealing with life single-handed, she'd coped with widowhood. She could spare the pants and the red flannel shirt for a day.

"Oh," Eric said, obviously nonplussed.

"You keep an eye on the front desk and I'll bring a couple of things up to the Claussens. We still have the Spikes and the Williams family to check in."

He nodded, and she slipped through the door to the family living quarters before he could ask her any questions about why she was still hanging on to her deceased husband's clothes.

Mom had kept some of Dad's clothes? After more than ten years? This was news to Eric.

In a way, it didn't surprise him. They all kept reminders of Dad. Brandon had his old signet ring and it never left his finger. Eric treasured Dad's old watch and his fishing pole, and every time he went fishing he thought of Dad and the conversations they'd had on the banks of the Wenatchee River, talks about girls and things a man shouldn't do, not unless he wanted to go blind. Talks about how it didn't matter whether you won or lost the basketball game, that what mattered was doing your best. His dad had taught him that the most important things a man could have were good character and good friends.

Eric had his pals, but he'd lost his closest friend the day the old man died. What must it be like for his mom?

She and Dad had been inseparable. And this lodge had been their big dream come true. Life had been blue-sky beautiful until the day Dad's friends from the hiking club came and told Mom what had happened... She'd been in the kitchen, baking cookies to put out for some of the guests. She'd fainted and the baking sheet she'd been holding had dropped to the floor, raining chocolate chip cookies everywhere. They'd stayed on the floor for two days until Eric went into the kitchen and cleaned them up.

The community had rallied around her. Dot Morrison had donated gift certificates to all the lodge guests for a free breakfast at Pancake Haus. The Sterling sisters had come in and helped with room cleanup. And the Geissels, who owned Gerhardt's Gasthaus, had taken in guests who'd booked rooms for the following month. Her friends Pat and Muriel had raised enough money from community donations to cover the lost income. Eric had paid the bills and kept the books straight while his mother walked around like a zombie.

Their first Christmas without his dad had sucked. Mom had managed to make some of the usual treats, but early Christmas morning, when they would've gathered to snarf down Dad's pumpkin pancakes and exchange gifts, there'd been a big hole. Yes, Mom had made the pancakes, and yes, there'd been presents. But there'd been no joking, no big, booming laugh. No father.

Life went on, but not always smoothly. The Christmas his mom had gotten a boyfriend was not good, and Eric and Brandon had succeeded in driving him away in a hurry. Needless to say, later he'd felt bad.

He and his mother had talked about that whole incident a few years ago. "It's just as well," she'd said with a shrug of her shoulders. "He wasn't your dad."

No one was. But now that he was older, Eric often regretted his youthful overprotectiveness. Mom was lonely. He saw it in her eyes every Valentine's Day, when she watched lovers going off to their rooms. And he saw it at Christmas, when she watched couples kissing under the mistletoe and sighed. He wished she'd stop hanging the damn stuff. But, of course, she wouldn't. She wasn't the type to deprive others of happiness just because she was unhappy. Mom was the kind of woman who loved to do for people. Hell, she loved *being* with people.

In fact, she worked hard to make sure she wasn't alone, going to the movies with Dot Morrison or hanging out at Muriel Sterling-Wittman's place, tagging along as a third wheel with Pat Wilder and Ed York. It was a poor substitute for having a man.

If he hadn't been such a shit when he was young and encouraged Brandon to follow suit, she might have married that guy who was hanging around after Dad died. Or some guy. Maybe even old Henry Figg, who liked to come in for the Sunday-morning brunches. It seemed that now she was trapped in the role of widow.

Poor Mom. Brandon was already off living his life. What was Mom going to do if Eric found someone and moved out? Not away, of course. He'd never do that. Icicle Falls was his home and always would be. And he'd never leave her in the lurch to run the lodge on her own.

At the rate he was going, he wouldn't be moving out and setting up housekeeping anytime soon so it was probably moot.

The image of the woman on the third floor, the one who was here with her dad and brother, came to mind. Long shiny brown hair, big brown eyes, great smile, equally great curves. And it wasn't hard to tell she cared about her dad. He wondered if she had a boyfriend.

He remembered his conversation with the guys at Zelda's. Rob was right. There was no point in starting something with a guest. They never stayed. Home was somewhere else.

The phone rang and he picked up. "Icicle Creek Lodge."

"Hey, bro."

At the sound of his brother's voice Eric felt the usual mix of love and irritation. "You'd better not be calling to say you're not coming home for Christmas." Mom never pushed but he knew she looked forward to having Brandon home for the holidays.

"Of course I'm coming. What kind of jerk do you think I am?"

A spoiled one. But whose fault was that? Brandon was the baby of the family, good-looking, charming and popular. Growing up, everyone had adored him, including his big brother, who'd protected him from jealous school-yard bullies and gotten him hooked on skiing. That had been a mistake. The sport became consuming. Brandon had done it all, from becoming an instructor to doing ski patrol. At one point he'd even dreamed of the Winter Olympics. He'd been good, but not good enough. Still, the addiction held, and it seemed he was always off somewhere, looking for new thrills. Or new women.

Meanwhile, big bro held down the fort here. Not that he minded doing that. He felt about the lodge the way Brandon felt about skiing. Still, it would be nice if his brother could be content with skiing the Cascades and staying around to help more. Mom wasn't getting any younger.

"Then what's up?" Eric asked.

"I just wanted to let you know I probably won't get in until late Christmas Eve."

"I hope you're staying through Christmas Day."

"Ha, ha. I'm staying through New Year's, so make sure you get us a table at Zelda's for New Year's Eve."

Happiness won out over irritation and Eric smiled. The little pissant was going to stick around for a while. That would make Mom happy. It would make him happy, too. Brandon could help in the dining room on Christmas Day, and once the holiday guests had left they'd hit the slopes, hang out, take Mom to dinner. It would be good to have Brandon home for longer than a couple of days. Unless...

"You bringing anyone?"

"No," his brother said grumpily.

Even better. That meant they'd actually see something of him.

"The women here are all, I don't know, shallow."

Eric remembered the last woman his brother had brought home. She'd been a piece of work. "Well, we've got new people moving to town all the time. Maybe you'll find some action here."

"I'm planning on it. Don't forget to make that reservation, bro. See you soon."

"Yeah, see you," Eric said, and hung up, still smiling. Mom might not get any romance under the mistletoe, but she'd have both her sons home for Christmas and that would be the next best thing.

And knowing Brandon he'd meet some little honey to hang around with.

Damn. Eric wished *he* was going to get some action. Too bad he was too old to believe in Santa. He'd ask the guy to give him a girlfriend for Christmas.

As Olivia walked through her living room, past the family tree decorated with ornaments from Christmases past, she was able to remind herself that she had a good life. Not ideal. Ideal would have included her husband, George, but he'd succumbed to a heart attack while out hiking with a group of friends. At least he'd died doing something he enjoyed. Small comfort, but better than none at all. She entered her bedroom and opened the door to the closet she'd stuffed with clothes. George would have been happy to see her helping strangers in need, she told herself. There, in the far corner, a hint of red plaid peeked out from behind a summer dress that she hadn't worn in years.

The dress was now two (okay, three) sizes too small but it was so pretty she kept it in the vain hope that she'd someday fit into it again. Could happen. If she stopped baking. If she had her lips sewn shut. Every time she saw that dress she wished she was forty pounds lighter and fifteen years younger. And that she wasn't a widow.

Never mind that now. She pulled out the shirt and then slid a few more hangers down the rack until she got to the pants, an old pair of khakis. She took them out and examined them. They looked as though they might fit Mr. Claussen. Maybe they'd be a little snug, but men didn't seem to mind letting their bellies hang over their britches.

Clothes in hand, she emerged from the apartment to find her son checking in a well-dressed couple in their late sixties. The Spikes, she concluded. The man was tall with salt-and-pepper hair. His wife was slender with silver hair and she dripped expensive jewelry. She was taking in the lodge with a jaded eye and a tolerant smile. Slumming for the holidays.

Just wait till you taste my cooking, Olivia thought as she passed them with a smile and a nod. A couple of minutes later, she was knocking on Mr. Claussen's door. His daughter opened it and, seeing the clothes on Olivia's arm, smiled at her as if she'd come bearing gold, frankincense and myrrh. "You found something. Thank you so much."

"I hope they'll fit," Olivia said, handing over the precious bundle.

Now Mr. Claussen was at the door, too. Oh, yes, he was a dead ringer for Santa with his husky build and round face and that handsome beard. "That's very kind of you," he said as his daughter passed them over to him.

"It would be a shame if you couldn't come down and enjoy our piano concert," Olivia said. "These were my late husband's and, well, it makes me happy seeing them put to such good use."

"Your late husband's," he repeated. "Are you sure you want to lend them to a stranger?"

"People don't usually remain strangers in Icicle Falls," Olivia said. "Anyway, they've sat in the closet long enough. I know my George would have been happy to help Santa," she couldn't resist adding with a smile. "Do you think they'll fit?"

He held up the shirt and then checked the pant size. "I think so. My elves and I thank you," he said, putting an arm around his daughter's shoulders.

"Yes, we do," the young woman seconded.

She was so sweet, just the kind of daughter Olivia would have wanted. Not that she had any complaints about her boys, of course. It would, however, be nice if they'd both settle down and give her some daughters-in-law, and maybe a couple of grandchildren.

"Okay, Daddy, hurry up and change so we can go take a walk in the snow and look at the Christmas lights downtown," said the daughter as she stepped out into the hallway.

Her father nodded. "Dylan and I will meet you in your room," he said, and shut the door.

"Thanks again for helping us out," she said to Olivia.

"That's what we're here for," Olivia said. "If there's anything else you need, just let me know." She'd be more than happy to help the gentleman with whatever he wanted.

As she went back down to the lobby she wondered what had happened to Mrs. Santa. Was Santa in the market for a replacement?

What a silly, unrealistic thought, she scolded herself. *As if, at your age and your weight, you're going to find someone new.* She was no beauty like her friend Muriel Sterling, who'd never gone long without a man in her life. Even though Muriel was now a widow for the second time, her old friend Arnie was constantly taking her to dinner. And if she didn't wind up marrying Arnie, some other man would come along. Other than one short-lived flame, no one had come along for Olivia after George died.

But she'd been fine on her own. She'd known love and she had two wonderful sons. What more did a woman need?

She thought of the mistletoe she'd hung up around the lodge and sighed. There was definitely something lacking in her life.

Chances were slim she was going to get it, though. Right now it was time to set out the Christmas cookies for her guests. And steal a couple for herself. If a woman couldn't have sex anymore, she could at least have cookies.

James was just about to go next door to Brooke's room when his cell phone rang. It was his sister Georgia, not a call he could ignore and stay out of trouble.

"How do you like your surprise?" she asked.

"You knew about this?"

"I did, and I told Brooke I thought it was a great idea. You needed to get out of that house before you started growing moss."

"Is that so?" Had his whole family been discussing him?

She ignored his offended tone of voice. "So, what's the town like? What have you done so far?"

"Not much yet. I've been waiting for clothes."

"Nobody packed you any?"

"It's a long story," he said, deciding to save his son's reputation. "But we're good to go now."

"What's on the agenda for tonight?"

"I know Brooke's anxious to get out and see the town, and then there's a concert here at the lodge."

"It sounds lovely. Did she tell you? We were supposed to join you. I'm so disappointed my other half got this nasty bug. It simply won't go away. Maybe next year, though. Maybe we'll start a new family tradition," she said cheerfully.

"Maybe," James said, and couldn't help thinking how much he'd loved the old family traditions. But those days were gone, and all the wishing in the world wouldn't bring them back. Suddenly the last thing he wanted was to wander around this town and take in all its happy holiday sights and sounds. But Brooke was trying so hard to make him happy. He couldn't disappoint her. "Well, sis, I should get going or my daughter will be banging on the door, wanting to know what's taking me so long."

"You have a wonderful time. We'll get together in the new year."

The new year, he thought as he ended the call. There was nothing it could bring him that would make his life better.

Bad attitude, he chided himself. Life was what you made it. Faith had said that often enough. She'd be very disappointed in this new, negative James. "I'm gonna try," he said out loud. Then he said it again, like a mantra. "I'm gonna try." And that was all any man could do.

Olivia was arranging cookies on a platter when her protégée, Bailey Sterling-Black, stopped by, carrying a plate of goodies.

"I thought you might like to taste my latest creation," Bailey said. "Eggnog scones."

Olivia took the plate. "They look yummy. Let's sample them. Come on in and have a cup of tea."

Bailey stamped the snow off her boots and then entered, removing them at the door. "It always looks so pretty in here."

"I bet it looks pretty over at your house, too," said Olivia as she went to the kitchen to heat water.

Bailey had recently gotten married and was now enjoying her first Christmas with her husband, Todd Black. Together they owned two very different establishments: the Man Cave, a seedy tavern and favorite hangout of the men in town, and Tea Time, a tea shop that sold all manner of teapots and accoutrements and served afternoon tea.

"Well, we got the outside lights up and our tree, and that is about it. I shot my wad decorating the tea shop," Bailey confessed.

"And it's gorgeous with all those deep rose and gold decorations."

"Well, that's all thanks to Lupine Floral," Bailey said modestly as she joined Olivia in the kitchen. "Those guys are great."

"I think you can give yourself some credit," Olivia said. Bailey had truly found her niche. She'd returned to Icicle Falls after her LA catering business had failed and, after a crisis of confidence, had reinvented herself and opened the tea shop. The place had instantly become popular and soon customers had to make a reservation a week in advance if they were to have any hope of securing a table. As the December calendar moved closer to Christmas, that week in advance had turned into two. With families visiting from out of town and kids getting out of school, demand grew. It seemed that every mother and daughter in town wanted to visit Tea Time and enjoy holiday teas served from Fitz and Floyd Santa teapots and eat special Christmas cookies and scones on fine china plates.

Bailey saw the half-filled platter sitting on Olivia's counter. "Oh, you're busy getting ready for tonight. I should leave."

"Nonsense," said Olivia. "I have plenty of time before the concert starts. I was simply being efficient."

"I'll help you." Bailey stepped up to the sink and washed her hands, then got busy arranging cookies on the platter.

Olivia had known the Sterling sisters all their lives, but she had to admit Bailey had always been her favorite, probably because they shared a love of all things culinary. For a moment Olivia found herself wishing selfishly that Bailey and her younger son had made a permanent connection. Or Eric, for that matter. It was really a shame no one did arranged marriages in America.

But Bailey was wildly happy with Todd Black, reformed bad boy. True love, it roamed where it willed. Once again, she thought of that mistletoe hanging all around the lodge, of feminine parts long neglected. Did anything down there even work anymore?

And what good did it do to ask that question? "Let's try those scones, shall we?"

Chapter Seven

Silver Bells

John Truman wandered around downtown Icicle Falls, staring at the sights like a kid in a candy shop. Man, this town really knew how to market itself. Holland, being in advertising, would be impressed. Icicle Falls proclaimed itself a Bavarian village, and the town made sure that was exactly what it looked like, from the frescoed buildings with their window boxes to the signage. Of course, the mountain backdrop didn't hurt, either. He could almost believe he was in Oberammergau or some such place.

Except for the Salvation Army bell ringer standing next to her kettle over by the gazebo in the town square. As far as John was concerned, that was pure USA. But it was also pure Christmas, along with the canned Christmas music being piped through the speakers mounted near the bandstand.

The little outdoor ice rink was filled with people of all ages clad in winter wear and colorful hats and scarves, enjoying themselves. He could picture Holland and him skating on it, hand in hand. He hoped they'd have time to fit that in.

The shops were closed but local artists and street vendors were still doing a brisk business in the town square. He wandered over that way, lured by the smell of roasting nuts.

He'd passed booths selling everything from candles to jewelry and was studying the framed mountain meadow photographs by a local artist when Missy and her children came into sight. It'd be rude to turn his back and pretend he hadn't seen them. He smiled and waved, and Missy smiled and waved back. On seeing him, the kids raced ahead of her.

Carlos reached him first but it was Lalla who spoke first. "Mommy's going to buy us nuts," she announced.

"That's an excellent idea," John said. Those nuts did smell enticing. He'd gotten sidetracked looking at the art, but now would be a good time to buy some.

Missy had caught up with the kids. "Isn't this the most fabulous place?" she said to John.

"Yeah, I have to admit, it's pretty impressive," he said.

"Let's get our nuts, Mommy." Lalla tugged on her mother's coat.

"Let me get them," John offered.

"That's okay, I've got money," Missy said.

"Yeah, but it's almost Christmas. I need to score more points with Santa," John joked.

"There's no such thing as Santa," Carlos informed him.

"Dude, how do you know?" John countered.

Carlos kicked at a little pile of snow. "He never brings me what I want."

"Maybe that's because Santa knows we can't have a dog where we live," said his mother.

"I hate where we live," Carlos grumbled.

"Well, how about those nuts?" John said, moving over to where the vendor was roasting different kinds of nuts. John pointed to the almonds in cinnamon and sugar. "We'll take four," he said, and soon he and Missy and her kids were eating warm nuts from small white paper bags.

"Thanks," she said. "That was really nice of you."

"Hey, it's Christmas. If a guy can't buy someone a treat at Christmas, when can he?"

"I suspect you're nice all the time," Missy said.

Was she flirting with him? That wouldn't be good.

He was about to deny it when she added, "I bet your girlfriend is really nice, too."

Was that the right word to describe Holland? Probably not. Clever? Hot? Fun? Fascinating? Oh, yeah. But nice? No.

Nice was the proverbial freckle-faced girl next door who wore cutoff jeans and went barefoot and brought you home-baked cookies. Holland wore designer jeans and spent a small fortune on shoes. And she never baked. But she had other talents. She had flair. She'd helped him decorate his apartment and thanks to her it looked…freakin' impressive. Every man wanted her and John always felt like a rock star when she left the club with him. She had an edge to her and she brought a kind of excitement into his life that he hadn't experienced with any other woman. "Oh, yeah, Holland is something else."

Sometimes he wondered what she saw in him. He was an average guy earning an average salary. (Holland actually made more than he did.) He wasn't ever going to be a famous writer or musician or even a company CEO.

And that was okay with him. All he wanted was to buy a house with a yard someday, one where he could mow the lawn and throw Super Bowl parties. Have a couple of kids. Maybe do some good deeds once in a while, like helping Habitat for Humanity. Just have an average, happy life. With Holland. Except with Holland it would be average seasoned with a dash of excitement.

Missy nodded, taking in what he'd said. The kids began darting from booth to booth and she followed them.

John fell into step with her. "What about you? Have you got a boyfriend?"

Her expression went from wistful to unhappy. She shook her head. "Hard to find someone who wants to take on two kids."

"Their dads aren't in the picture?"

"No. Carlos's dad died."

John blinked in shock. "Gosh, I'm sorry."

"He was a good guy," Missy said with a sigh.

"Uh, what about Lalla's dad?"

Missy frowned. "It's complicated. I can't say I wish I'd never met him, though, 'cause I got Lalla out of the deal. My kids are the best thing that ever happened to me."

Aside from her children, it didn't sound as if very many good things had happened to her. "They're great kids," John said.

"They are. They deserve better than what I'm giving them," she said softly.

She obviously didn't have a lot of money, but her kids seemed happy, especially right now. "Hey, you're giving them a super Christmas," John pointed out.

She smiled at that. "They are having fun. I saved all year for this," she said proudly.

"What do you do?"

"I'm a hairstylist."

"Yeah? I should tell Holland. Where do you work?"

Now she didn't look quite so proud. Her gaze dropped to the ground. "I work at Style Savings."

He didn't know one of those places from the other. There was a salon not far from his place in Belltown and he went there for his haircuts. But Holland was a more frequent salon visitor. It seemed she was always going to hers.

"Where's that?" he asked Missy. Maybe Holland could give her some business.

She told him the area and he realized Holland would not be going to that location to give anyone any business. He nodded and wished he could think of something to say.

"I won't always be there," Missy said as if reading his mind. "I'm good, and I'm planning to move up to a high-end salon."

He glanced at her clothes. He was no expert on women's apparel, but he'd been with Holland long enough to recognize the difference between cheap and expensive. He hoped Missy had some classy outfits she could wear to interviews at those high-end salons. When it came to clothes, women could be snobs.

"I *will* get there," she insisted. "It's just a matter of time. All I need is a break."

"I'm sure you'll get it," John said.

"The sooner, the better. I've about had it with some of the people who come into our place."

"Yeah?"

"Oh, yeah." And with that she told him about her customers earlier that day—Mrs. Steele, the old witch who'd walked off without paying, and the mad groper.

"And you like what you do, huh?" he teased.

"I do. I mean, I know I'm not healing sick kids or keeping the streets safe or even making big money, but I help women look their best and feel good about themselves."

"Well, that's more than I can say." Crunching numbers wasn't exactly brokering world peace.

"What do you do?" Missy asked.

"I'm an accountant. Pretty boring."

"Pretty hard." She wrinkled her nose. "I suck at math."

John grinned. "That's why there're people like me."

The vendors were starting to close up for the night now. "I guess it's time to go back to the lodge," Missy said. "Anyway, I don't want to miss the piano concert. I've never stayed anyplace where they had a free concert. The kids are gonna love this." She sent him a shy glance. "Are you going to hang around for the concert?"

It was either that or go up to the room alone and wish Holland was with him. "Yeah, I think I will."

The sky was dark but the town was still lit from head to toe with Christmas bling to illuminate their walk back. And once they left downtown, they still had old-fashioned streetlights to get them to Icicle Creek Drive.

There were streetlights on that road, too, but not so many that they blocked the view of a clear, starry sky. "Wow," Missy said, looking up at the stars. "You sure don't see that in the city."

"You sure don't," John agreed. "Hey, guys. There's the Big Dipper."

"I don't see a dripper," Lalla said.

John knelt behind her and pointed. "See? Follow the lines. It looks like a long-handled cup."

"I see it!" Carlos cried.

And then, so did Missy. "Wow," she breathed.

"And there's the Little Dipper," he said, moving his hand to show the outline of the constellation.

The kids were properly impressed. So was Missy. "I remember looking at pictures of those in books when I was in school," she was saying, head still thrown back, "but I could never find it in the sky."

"You don't get a sky like this in the city," John said.

You don't get a life like this in the city, Missy thought.

They strolled companionably down Holly Road to the lodge, Missy with her hands stuffed in her pockets for warmth, the kids running on ahead. "You can wear my gloves if you want," John said.

She shook her head. "I'm fine, but you can bet the first thing I'm gonna do tomorrow is find a place that sells mittens."

Once back at the lodge, the fact that she was missing gloves didn't stop Missy from flopping down onto the lawn with her kids and making snow angels. She giggled. "Aren't you gonna make one?" she asked John.

"Snow angels are easy," Carlos told him, and immediately demonstrated.

Making snow angels wasn't something John would do with Holland. She was simply too…sophisticated for that sort of thing. So was he, really, but what the hey. He hadn't done it since he was a kid and he found it freeing to fall onto the snow and flap his arms and legs back and forth.

"Now, that's a serious snow angel," Missy said after he'd gotten up.

Yeah, he'd been good at snow angels when he was

a kid. Good at building snow forts, too. If Holland wasn't coming up the next day, he would've offered to help Carlos build one. Every boy needed someone to build a snow fort with. And to show him how to write in the snow with his pee. Totally gross but an important guy winter sport.

Who did guy stuff with little Carlos? There had to be a grandpa or an uncle or someone. "So how come you guys are here all by yourselves?" John asked as they made their way up the steps of the lodge. "Do your parents live out of state or something?"

She bit her lip. "It was only my mom and me, and she's dead now."

"Oh, man. I'm sorry," he said. So Missy Monroe really was on her own.

"It's okay," she said brightly. "We're having fun. Who knows? Maybe we'll come up here every Christmas."

He could sure see himself coming up here every Christmas with his wife, and then later a couple of kids.

They walked inside the lodge to find that several people had made themselves at home on the sofa and chairs and by the fireplace hearth. As they all chatted with one another, the woman who'd checked him and Missy in was circulating, carrying a big platter of Christmas cookies.

"Cookies!" Carlos took off at a run, Lalla in hot pursuit.

A skinny old woman with long gray hair, wearing black pants and a red sweater, looked up and frowned in disapproval.

"Just walk," Missy called, and hurried after her son.

Too late. Carlos had already managed to trample the old lady's toes in his haste to get to the cookies. She let out a yelp and glared first at him and then at his mother, who quickly began apologizing.

John followed at a more leisurely pace and decided he wasn't in any hurry to have kids, after all.

Olivia appreciated everyone who spent time (and money) at the lodge, but some she appreciated more than others. The cranky old bat who was now muttering that kids should be in bed after a certain hour was not going to make Olivia's list of favorite guests.

The young mother blushed as she removed her children's coats, and Olivia gave her a pat on the shoulder and a red napkin. "Every child gets excited at Christmas."

"Thanks," the young woman said gratefully.

"Try one of the sugar cookies," Olivia urged, and her embarrassed guest selected one in the shape of a star. "Monroe, right?" Olivia asked. She worked hard to remember the names of her guests.

The young woman nodded. "Missy."

"Now, there's a cute name. What do you do, Missy?"

"I'm a hairstylist," Missy said.

"Figures," snorted the cranky woman in the armchair. "The blue hair was a dead giveaway," she said to her friend, who was seated next to her, barely bothering to lower her voice. "She looks like a Smurf."

"You're showing your age, Jane," her friend hissed. "All the young girls these days are coloring their hair like that."

"I know," Jane retorted. "But if you ask me, it's ridiculous."

"I think it's fun," Olivia said to Missy, and slipped Carlos another cookie before moving on to where Mr. Claussen and his family were seated. Lalla, her tiara firmly in place, was Olivia's shadow, moving along behind her.

"How did you enjoy your visit to town?" she asked the family as she distributed red napkins to hold their cookies.

"Very much," the man replied. "As you can see, the clothes worked fine."

She'd thought they would. Mr. Claussen was a big, burly man, just as her George had been.

"I'm glad." She proffered the platter of cookies and he took one shaped like a Santa. "Now, why am I not surprised to see that you took a Santa?"

"We Santas have to stick together," he said.

"Are you Santa?" Lalla asked eagerly.

Olivia could tell from his expression that the man regretted his slip. But he smiled at the little girl and said, "Now, if I was Santa I'd be wearing my red suit, wouldn't I?"

Lalla nodded slowly.

"And Santa doesn't have time to sit around and

eat cookies. He's too busy loading his sleigh with toys for good boys and girls."

"I've been good," Lalla said.

"I'm sure you have," said Mr. Claussen.

"Maybe Santa will bring me a grandma for Christmas," she continued.

"Well, he'll bring you something," her mother said.

There was no grandma in the picture, that was obvious. Otherwise, this young woman and her children wouldn't be here alone, and surely the children would've had nicer clothes. They would if *she* were their grandma.

"And Carlos wants a dog," Lalla finished. "Except Santa won't bring him one 'cause he hasn't been good. He hit me yesterday."

Her brother glared at her. "Santa never brings me what I want. There's no such thing, anyway."

"Is, too!" Lalla cried.

"Which cookies do you like best?" Mr. Claussen's daughter asked Lalla.

It was a clever distraction and it worked. "Santa," Lalla crowed, and Olivia gave her another one.

"These are great," said the Claussen son after downing half a frosted Christmas tree in one bite.

"Have another," Olivia urged, and he grinned and took two more off the plate.

His sister frowned in disgust. "Oink."

That made Lalla laugh, but it didn't faze the Claussen brother. He merely grinned again. "Hey, you're probably dieting so I'm eating your share."

"There's plenty," Olivia said, holding out the plate to his sister.

"No, thank you," she said.

"I'll have hers," said Mr. Claussen, helping himself to a snowball cookie. "By the way, I'm James."

"James," Olivia repeated. It was a good, solid name and it fit the man.

"I figure if I'm going to be borrowing clothes, we should be on a first-name basis," he said. "My daughter is Brooke and this is my son, Dylan."

"I'm Lalla," the little girl piped up. "I'm named after a princess."

"You make a very pretty princess," Brooke complimented her.

The princess looked as though she was outgrowing her jeans. They were at the high-water mark. She was probably having a growth spurt. "Can I have another cookie?" she asked.

"You've had enough for tonight," said her mother, which made Lalla pout and flop down on the floor.

Missy pretended not to see the protest.

Olivia swallowed a smile and introduced herself properly to the Claussen family.

"We were wondering, is this a family-run B and B?" Brooke asked.

"It is," Olivia replied. "My husband and I built it when the boys were young. He'd be thrilled to see how well it's done."

"Everything's lovely," Brooke said.

"Thank you. We're proud of our lodge, and we

couldn't have picked a better place for it than Icicle Falls."

"It's so charming in town, especially with all the lights," Brooke said.

"It is," Olivia agreed. "Of course, it's beautiful up here in the summer, too, when all the window boxes are filled with flowers, but I have to say Christmas is my favorite time of year in Icicle Falls."

"Christmas was my wife's favorite holiday," James said, and suddenly his smile fell away.

His son set aside his second cookie and his daughter got teary-eyed.

Oh, dear. "Is this your first Christmas without her?" Olivia guessed.

"We lost her last Christmas Eve," James said. "It had been a long time coming," he added, as if he thought that was somehow supposed to make it easier.

Olivia had never bought the rationalization that losing someone after a long battle with illness was actually a relief to the bereaved. Loss was loss. She ached for this poor, brave man and his family, trying so hard to redeem the holidays. Horrible to lose a loved one at any time, but having to endure that loss during a season of celebration had to be even worse. The parties and laughter would feel like a mockery.

"I'm so sorry. I know how painful it is to lose a spouse," she told James.

He nodded and sighed deeply. It was with obvious effort that he kept the conversation going, asking, "Did you lose your husband?"

She nodded. "Yes, it's been fourteen years and I still miss him every day. But it's a blessing to have your children. I don't know what I would've done without my boys after I lost George."

James smiled at his son and put an arm around his daughter's shoulders. "Same here. I've got great kids."

"I can see that," Olivia said. "I hope you'll all be able to create some new memories while you're up here."

"We intend to," Brooke said in a tone of voice that dared the spirit of Christmas not to cooperate. It was easy to see that this year she was in charge.

Every parent needed a steady child to lean on in hard times. For Olivia it had been her older son, Eric. For James it would be his daughter, who obviously adored him.

Olivia was suddenly aware of John Truman at her elbow. "I heard you guys talking about Santa and, uh, I was wondering. Is there a guy here who has a Santa suit? Lalla claims she saw him."

Olivia shot a look at James Claussen, who subtly shook his head. "Well, if there is, I think he's probably off duty now."

Disappointed, John nodded and went to sit by the fire, but James smiled gratefully at her. She smiled back.

She would've liked to linger and talk more with James and his children, but a new family had just come down and she needed to speak with them. Anyway, Charlie Dicks was there now, shedding his overcoat, which meant the concert would soon begin.

Charlie was the high school music teacher. He'd been divorced for several years and to fill his time he gave piano lessons on the side and, during the holidays, offered nightly concerts on the baby grand piano here in the lodge. The piano had been her parents' and they'd given it to her when Eric started taking piano lessons in third grade. He'd quit by fourth grade, more interested in fishing with his father than practicing scales. She didn't play very well herself, but she hated to see it sit neglected in the corner. Charlie didn't charge much and the concerts added a festive touch.

It was difficult to visit with her guests when the piano was being played, though. Darn. Because she found herself wanting to drift back to the Claussens and visit with them some more. Well, mostly with James.

With the new arrivals welcomed and seated, she moved on, offering cookies to the Spikes, the well-dressed older couple. She couldn't resist asking how they liked their room.

"It's lovely," said Mrs. Spike.

The expression on the woman's face when they'd checked in had telegraphed her thoughts. *Small town, hokey little lodge. Where's the nearest Hilton?* But Olivia had known Mrs. Spike would be won over. This was a special place that could delight even the most jaded traveler.

"The view out our window is breathtaking,"

Mrs. Spike continued. She smiled at her husband. "I'm glad Frank suggested coming here. It makes a nice change."

Olivia's gaze strayed to the Claussen family. *A nice change.* She hoped the Claussens would experience that.

Her final family was the Williamses, a forty-something pair with two teenage daughters in tow, and once she'd served them she was done. The cookies were distributed and the guests welcomed. Time to fade into the background and let everyone enjoy the concert.

Anyway, she had company coming. Her friends would be here in a few minutes for eggnog and cookies and a gift exchange.

Her longtime friends Muriel Sterling-Wittman and Pat Wilder were the first to arrive. The three had known one another since they were girls, had all grown up in Icicle Falls. The town had changed a lot since then, and so had their lives. Even when they'd all become busy raising their families and starting businesses, they'd still managed to stay connected.

Olivia had withdrawn into herself when her husband died, but Pat had eventually rescued her, organizing a widows' group for herself, Olivia and Dot Morrison, who'd lost her second husband. It hadn't been something they'd advertised. She hadn't even told Muriel about it. There'd been no point, really. Muriel had gone from happily married to widowed to happily married again faster than the speed of light.

But when Muriel lost her second husband, they'd pulled her in, too, and now they all shared a bond nothing could break, the bond of hard times survived together. These women were her closest friends, and she knew she could count on them to be there for her no matter what, just as she would be for them. They'd seen one another's businesses thrive and one another's children grow up. Olivia had helped launch Muriel's daughter Bailey in her new business, the tea shop on Lavender Lane.

Now the women entered Olivia's private living quarters, carrying presents and surrounded by the scents of fresh mountain air and Gloria Vanderbilt perfume. "I smell something good," Pat said.

"Rum cake," Olivia told her.

"Yum," said Pat. "Nobody bakes like you. Well, except for Bailey," she added, smiling at Muriel.

"She learned from the best," Muriel said, hugging Olivia. As always, she looked beautiful and perfectly put together in a black wool coat with black gloves and a faux-fur black hat on her head. Shedding the coat revealed a tasteful black cashmere sweater and fitted jeans, accented with a simple gold bracelet, earrings and tiny gold chain with a gold *M* dangling from the end of it.

Pat was equally glamorous in her slacks and expensive boots and the dark green sweater that set off her auburn hair and fair skin so well. She'd accented her outfit with a scarf and simple gold hoop earrings.

Olivia was only wearing a plain red sweater that didn't do much to hide her extra pounds, and a pair of slacks with an elastic waistband (a girl's best friend). Not for the first time she vowed to go on a diet come the new year so she could look more like her friends. Although even if she lost thirty pounds, she'd never look as glamorous as Muriel and Pat. But then, she'd never been as glamorous as they were and she'd certainly never been as slender. Still, a woman could hope. If she lost weight she'd get them to take her shopping.

They'd just put their presents under her little tree when the last member of their group arrived. "Remind me again why I live here," Dot Morrison said in her husky voice as she walked in.

Unlike Muriel and Pat, Dot didn't smell like fresh air and perfume. She smelled like an ashtray. Dot didn't have to worry about losing weight. Dying of cancer, yes, but not losing weight. She had her own unique style. Tonight she wore a stocking cap over her gray bob and a big white parka over jeans. She took off the parka and Olivia saw that she'd found a new holiday sweatshirt. This one was white and bore a picture of the cartoon character Maxine, Dot's alter ego. Underneath it, red lettering said Dear Santa, Define Good.

Olivia thought Dot's sweatshirts were tacky and refused to encourage her by commenting.

Pat, however, couldn't resist. "I see you're making a new fashion statement."

Dot smoothed down the sweatshirt and smiled. "Tilda got this for me."

"Well, it's you," said Pat.

"As if anyone should brag about being bad," Olivia muttered.

"Hey, we all have to be good at something," Dot retorted.

Actually, Dot was good at a lot of things. She was a sharp businesswoman and her restaurant, Pancake Haus, was always packed. She also beat Olivia at Scrabble on a regular basis.

"You probably had to bribe Santa to bring you anything when you were a kid," Olivia joked.

Dot's snarky smile faded just a little. "Well, let me tell you, I don't remember ever getting much from Santa." Olivia felt guilty that what had been intended as a joke had fallen flat. A moment of sad silence fell on the group until Dot perked up, saying, "Except the year I got pregnant with Tilda. Now, that was some Christmas."

Pat raised the goblet Olivia had just filled with eggnog. "That's the kind of Christmas we like to drink to." She took a sip and then removed the glove from her left hand. "I got a nice present this year myself."

"Well, well," Dot said with a grin. "About time Ed made an honest woman out of you."

"It's absolutely beautiful," Muriel said, bending

over her friend's hand to inspect the diamond ring glittering on her third finger.

"Congratulations," Olivia said, ignoring the green-eyed demon at the back of her mind chanting, *Unfair, unfair.*

There was nothing unfair about Pat finding love once more after spending so many years on her own. She was a kind and beautiful woman.

Who was getting to have sex again.

Sex, sex, I want sex, protested the demon.

"Have you set a date?" Muriel asked.

"We're thinking May. The pass will be clear and his kids can all come up for Maifest."

"That sounds wonderful," Muriel said. "Do any of them know yet?"

Pat shook her head. "We're going to make the rounds and tell the kids living in Seattle on Christmas Day. Although my Isabel knows."

"You can't keep things like that from your daughter," Muriel said.

"Well, good on ya," said Dot. "I'm ready to be a bridesmaid." She struck a dramatic pose.

Pat chuckled. "You'll have to fight his daughter and mine for that privilege."

How much fun would it be, getting married to some wonderful man? Olivia thought. Maybe she should look into online dating.

"Olivia?"

Muriel's gentle voice yanked Olivia back to the present. "Where were you just now?" she asked.

"I was thinking how nice it would be to have someone," Olivia said wistfully. "I miss sex."

"Oh, brother," Dot groaned. "Get a vibrator, for crying out loud. It's a lot less hassle than breaking in a husband."

"I know what you mean, Liv," Muriel said, paying no attention to Dot. Muffin the cat had made an appearance and was now rubbing against Muriel's legs. "It's not just the sex," she said as she picked up the cat and draped Muffin over her shoulder. "It's the closeness that comes with it. It's those little hugs in the kitchen, and cuddling in front of the fire on a cold evening. The companionship. That's what I miss most."

"You could have all the companionship you wanted, Muriel," Dot pointed out. "You always have a string of men following you around."

"But not the right one," Muriel said. "I had two wonderful men. That's more than most women ever get."

"You can say that again," Dot responded, serious now.

"What about Henry Figg?" Muriel asked Olivia.

Henry had been hanging around the lodge the past few months, but Olivia knew why. "He's only looking for a live-in cook." If he'd wanted anything else he'd have done more than show up for Sunday brunch. He spent his Friday and Saturday nights lounging around the Man Cave, drinking beer with his buddies.

"Ugh," said Dot in disgust. "She can do better than that. Even I could do better than that."

"Well, Olivia, maybe we need to take you to see Santa," Pat said lightly.

"Maybe," Olivia agreed. She could think of a certain Santa with a lap that was just the right size…

Chapter Eight

Cold December Night

The pianist finished his concert with "Jingle Bells," encouraging the guests to sing along. Singing a Christmas song together obviously created some kind of bond because people lingered even after the pianist had packed up and left. James watched as his fellow guests visited with each other. Everyone was friendly and open to mingling with everyone else. All except the two young Williams girls, who were busy texting.

Missy Monroe, who'd been seated nearby, introduced herself to James and his family while her son wandered over to duck under the piano and check out the view from beneath.

"Is the cookie grandma coming back?" Lalla asked.

"I don't think so, but we'll probably see her tomorrow," Missy said.

Lalla heaved a sigh, then went to join her brother under the piano.

"She wants a grandma in the worst way," Missy said. "Wouldn't you know? Something I can't possibly give her."

"It sounds like your son wants a dog. That should be easier," James said. Every kid should have a dog.

Missy frowned. "I'd love to give him one, and I'd love a dog myself, but there's the Entwhistle factor."

"The Entwhistle factor?" Brooke repeated.

"My landlady in Seattle. She has a no-dog policy." Missy frowned. "Too noisy, too messy. I wish I could find a way to convince her that we'd clean up after it. But she's old and kind of frail. I think maybe she's afraid of dogs, too."

"That sucks," Dylan said. "Every kid should have a dog," he added, echoing James's thought.

"You're right." Missy nodded. "I had one when I was a kid. Well, until my mom decided we couldn't afford him and gave him away."

"That *really* sucks," Dylan said, shocked.

Missy shrugged. "Yeah. The truth is, I want a dog as much as Carlos. And once I get a better job and we can afford to move, we'll get one," she said with determination.

Meanwhile, though, her kid had given up on Santa. It was always kind of sad when kids stopped believing. It was especially sad when disappointment fueled that unbelief.

"Oh, boy," Missy said, looking over to where her kids were now crawling in circles under and around the piano, the giggles getting louder. "I think I'd better pull the plug on the fun and games and get them up to our room before anybody says anything."

James glanced at the two older women. The plump one was smiling fondly but the skinny, gray-haired one was scowling in disapproval. Leaving the gathering was probably a good plan.

"Nice talking with you," Missy said politely, and hurried to collect her children.

"No dog," Dylan said with a shake of his head. "That's just wrong."

James agreed. He watched as Missy's children scampered up the stairs, with her running after them. There was something about that young woman that made him want to champion her. He didn't know her story but she was obviously a single mom. Probably working hard to give her kids everything she could. Too bad she didn't have a place that allowed pets. But sometimes life wasn't fair and there were some things even Santa couldn't fix.

James caught sight of his daughter thoughtfully eyeing the young man who was sitting over by the fireplace. Good. Brooke needed someone in her life. This man seemed pleasant enough. Odd that he was up here by himself.

James was about to approve of her starting a conversation with the guy when she said to him, "I'm curious. Why were you asking if there's someone up here with a Santa suit?"

Oh, no. What was she up to?

The other women all turned to eavesdrop and

the young man's cheeks became red. "I was just wondering."

"Is there some special reason you were wondering?" Brooke persisted.

"Honey, I'm sure he doesn't want to discuss that with everyone here," James said, now hoping to end the conversation.

The guy's cheeks were still red but he quickly recovered and, with the besotted smile of a man in love, announced, "My girlfriend's coming up tomorrow. I'm going to propose at dinner."

This was met with female sighs and murmurs of "How sweet."

Oh, boy. James had enough years of experience under his belt to know where this was going.

Sure enough. "I was hoping I could get Santa to give her the ring."

"That's a great idea," Brooke said enthusiastically. Then she looked pointedly at James.

He wanted a break from his alter ego. No way was he donning that red suit again, not even for young love. "Well, son, she might be just as happy getting the ring someplace more private."

The guy's face fell. "I guess. I just thought it would be…you know, special. I want to make this as memorable as possible."

"*That* would've been memorable," said the plump older lady who'd introduced herself as Vera.

"These days you have to make a big deal out of proposing," said Dylan, who wasn't even dating anyone at the moment.

My son, the romance expert.

But James kept his mouth firmly shut and the subject was dropped. The Williams family went to the lower level, which housed a workout room, a Ping-Pong table and a small indoor swimming pool, and the older ladies helped themselves to more cookies. The other guests began to make their way to their rooms.

"Daddy," Brooke urged in a low voice as the young man started to leave.

"Brooke, no," he said firmly. "Santa's taking a break."

"But think how special it would be for them," she pleaded. "You could really make their Christmas."

He didn't want to make anyone's Christmas. He just wanted to get through his. "If I showed up as Santa to deliver that ring, the children would expect something." Like a dog.

"We could find something for them," Brooke said. "Come on, Daddy. Your suit's here. Why waste it?"

"Dylan, how about you put on the suit?" he tried.

His son looked at him as if James had asked him to strip naked and run around the lodge with Christmas ornaments hanging from his ears. "Oh, no. That's not my thing."

Well, it wasn't James's thing, either. Not at the moment, anyway.

"Daddy, just for a few minutes. Think what a wonderful memory you'd be giving that couple."

He sighed heavily. Brooke would keep after him

until he gave in. Might as well do it now. And as she said, it was only a few minutes of forcing out some ho-ho-hos and scattering around a few presents. Just one more time in the old suit, and then he could pack it in. "Okay, I'll go talk to him."

She beamed at him as if he were a saint. "Daddy, you're the best."

He was far from that, but he never liked to disappoint his daughter. Anyway, he knew what a big deal it was to pop the question.

He remembered how much effort he'd put into proposing to Faith way back when. He'd taken her for a drive around the city to look at Christmas lights and had brought along special cupcakes from their favorite local bakery. He'd nestled the ring in the frosting of her cupcake. Of course, he'd gotten frosting all over the ring but Faith hadn't cared. She'd been thrilled and touched by his creativity. In fact, she'd bragged about it to all her friends.

Every man wanted his woman to brag about him. So, okay, he'd give this one bragging rights. James caught up with him at the foot of the staircase. "So, young man, you need a special delivery for that engagement ring?"

The guy looked at him as though James was about to hand him the winning Lotto ticket. "Yeah."

"What's your name, son?"

"John Truman."

James held out his hand and they shook. "I'm James Claussen, and I've got a Santa suit."

"Yeah?" John said hopefully.

"Slip me the ring before dinner tomorrow and I'll make your delivery for you."

John Truman pumped his hand hard enough to separate his arm from his shoulder. "Oh, man, thanks. This is gonna be awesome."

The young man's optimism infused James with a little of that Christmas spirit he'd been missing and he found himself smiling. Okay, for true love Santa could pull out the stops.

"Are you going to do it?" Brooke asked when he rejoined her and Dylan.

"Yes," James said, feigning reluctance. It wouldn't do to let his daughter think she'd won such an easy victory. A man had his pride, after all.

"I'm glad," she said. "Imagine how you'll make their Christmas. Of course, now we really need to do something for the other people, too."

"I don't see why," Dylan muttered.

"You can't have Santa show up when there are children present and not have gifts for them. They'd be so disappointed. And the adults will want to get in on the fun, too. I bet those two older ladies would love some fancy soap."

Dylan looked suspiciously at his sister. "Does this mean we're gonna waste the whole day tomorrow shopping?"

"Don't worry. We're here through Christmas. There'll still be time for skiing," she assured him.

"Good," Dylan said with a nod, "'cause the guys don't want to be stuck in a bunch of shops all day. Right, Dad?"

His son enjoyed being active, and James didn't want to disappoint either him or his daughter. "I'm sure we can work it all in."

Brooke seconded that. "Of course we can," she said. "How hard will it be to pick up a few presents?"

A few? Had she seen the size of this lodge? There were probably people staying here who hadn't even been in the lobby for the concert.

But James kept his mouth shut. Thanks to his pension from Boeing and some careful investments, he had the money and this was the time of year to spend it, making people happy.

"I'll get a list of the guests tomorrow morning," Brooke said.

"I'll go with you only if you don't spend hours picking stuff out," Dylan told her.

She gave him a look that no doubt made her kindergarteners shake in their shoes. "I can be efficient."

That she could.

"Okay," Dylan said, in a voice that dared her to be anything but. "Come on, let's go check out that Ping-Pong table downstairs. Whoever loses to Dad has to pay for lunch tomorrow."

"That means we'll be splitting the bill," Brooke said.

James smiled. She was right about that. Their old man could still play the game.

But not as long as he once could. After an hour James was pooped and ready to go back to his room, stretch out on the bed and see what he could find on TV. "You kids go along and have fun. I'll catch up with you in the morning."

"Are you sure?" asked Brooke, who seemed determined not to leave his side for a moment.

"I'm sure," he said. "I bet there's some hip nightspot just waiting for you two."

"I heard Zelda's restaurant has a great bar," Dylan said to his sister. "Let's go."

"Have fun," James said, and sent them on their way. The night was still young and they deserved to enjoy themselves.

When the kids were gone, he flopped onto his bed with the remote control and began to channel surf. There really wasn't much on. Reruns of old TV shows he couldn't less about, a sappy movie, the kind Faith used to love.

Their favorite thing to do on a Friday night had been to snuggle on the couch with a big bowl of popcorn and watch some classic love story. As far as James was concerned, nothing could match their own love story.

He hadn't found her until he was in his mid-thirties. He'd pretty much given up on meeting his perfect woman. "There's no such thing," his mother kept telling him. "You wait too long and you won't find anyone."

But his mom had been wrong. He'd gone to Children's Hospital to visit a friend's daughter who was struggling through chemo. It was the first time he'd ever donned the Santa suit, but seeing the girl's grin when he entered her room had hooked him on playing Santa. He'd been leaving the room, ho-ho-ho-ing as he went, and had almost mowed down a cute little nurse in the process. That nurse had been Faith. He'd gotten her number and called her the next day, and they'd made a date to go see *It's a Wonderful Life*, which was showing at a theater in Seattle's University District.

"I love stories with happy endings," she'd said, teary-eyed, and he'd known their story was going to have a happy ending, too.

It had until she got sick.

He changed channels quickly. Nothing appealed to him. Neither did sitting in his room alone.

He put his shoes back on and wandered down to the lobby. No one was at the reception desk and he hesitated to ring the bell. What excuse could he give other than that he was lonely and TV was a poor substitute for a wife? He didn't want to look pathetic.

He was about to go back up the stairs when he remembered Brooke talking about getting a list of the people staying at the lodge. He could do that. It would also give him an excuse to talk to Olivia. Not that he wanted to replace Faith. No one could. But he needed… Well, besides the obvious, he needed interaction with someone his own age, someone who knew what you were talking about when you mentioned Lesley Gore or the Turtles.

Still he hesitated. Maybe Olivia Wallace was busy. Maybe he should go back to his room and do some more channel surfing.

Oh, what the heck. He rang the bell on the counter.

A moment later the door marked Private opened and out she stepped.

"Sorry to bother you," he said, although the smile on her face and the pink on her cheeks told him she wasn't.

"You're not bothering me in the least. What can I do for you?"

"I was hoping you could help me out with a list of your guests." She looked uncomfortable and he hurried on. "I don't need a lot of details, just sort of a shopping list. The reason I'm asking is because I've been drafted to play Santa at dinner tomorrow night and deliver an engagement ring for John Truman."

She smiled at him in delight. "Oh, how lovely!"

"Well, my daughter and I thought that since Santa's making an appearance he should have gifts for the other guests, as well."

"Oh, my," she said. "That's a bit of an outlay."

"We're not talking expensive, just some token presents to open. And a few things for the kiddos."

"That's terribly nice of you."

"'Tis the season." And even if he wasn't exactly in a jolly mood, it didn't mean he couldn't take a few minutes to put a smile on other people's faces. "Between you and me, I think that young mother and her children could use some extra pampering."

"Oh, you're so right," she said, "and I'm sure that for Santa we can come up with some sort of list that won't compromise our guests' privacy."

Feminine laughter drifted out from that door

marked Private. "You have company," James said. "I can get it in the morning."

She looked over her shoulder and then back at him, as if trying to come to some sort of conclusion. "I do have some friends here, but they'll be leaving soon. Could I call your room when they're gone? Perhaps you'd enjoy some peppermint schnapps in the lobby."

Perhaps he would. "Sure."

She smiled and nodded and then went back to her friends. And James returned to his room, whistling as he climbed the stairs.

"I could not do what you do," Dot said when Olivia rejoined them. "You never have a minute to yourself."

Oh, yes, she did. Sometimes more than she wanted. "I don't mind."

"Was it someone with a complaint?" Dot asked. "If so, just point us to him. We'll stab the sucker with a holly bough."

"Nothing like that," Olivia said, and proceeded to tell them about her resident Santa.

"He and his family seem awfully nice," Muriel said.

Dot raised a gray eyebrow at Olivia. "And you say he's a widower?"

Was it suddenly warm in here? "Yes."

"Well, well," Dot said. "Looks like a merry Christmas for Olivia."

"He's just a guest," Olivia said firmly.

But Dot persisted. "He sounds like a catch to me. If you don't want him, send him my way."

"This from the woman who, only a little while ago, was saying what a hassle it is to train a husband?" Pat teased.

"Who said anything about a husband?" Dot retorted. "I might be in the market for a boy toy."

"I think James has too much principle to be a boy toy," Olivia said. "In fact, I wonder if he's the kind of man who had that one great love and won't allow himself another."

"Unless you can convince him it's not a bad thing to go around a second time," Dot said. "God knows my second time was better than the first."

Going around a second time? What would that be like? Olivia was more than ready to find out.

James practically dived for the phone when it rang and said an eager hello.

"James? It's Olivia. I have that list if you're still up for meeting."

"Sure," he said. "I'll be right down."

He got to the front lobby to find it deserted except for their hostess. She was seated in one of the armchairs facing the fireplace, where a cozy fire still crackled. On the coffee table sat a sheet of paper, as well as two small liqueur glasses and a bottle of peppermint schnapps.

Peppermint schnapps, a charming lodge, a fire in the fireplace—Faith would have loved this, James thought in a moment of melancholy, and sadness began to pull a dark curtain around him.

But then Olivia smiled at him and the curtain parted just a little. He smiled back. "Thanks for going along with this."

"Our guests are going to love it," she said. She was still wearing the Christmas red sweater and the dark slacks she'd worn earlier but he noticed that she'd added some sparkly red earrings to her outfit and he caught a whiff of perfume that reminded him of his wife's rose garden in summer.

"I sure hadn't planned on putting that suit on again," he said as he settled into the chair next to hers.

"Does it get old?" she asked, handing him a little glass of schnapps.

"Only lately. I haven't been in the mood much." Feeling briefly disloyal, he took a sip. He shouldn't be here drinking peppermint schnapps with some other woman. What was he thinking?

A conversation with his wife came back vividly. Faith had taken his hand one afternoon when it was just the two of them, her in bed, him sitting beside her on a chair, and said, "James, you have to promise me that you'll live your life after I'm gone."

"I won't have a life after you're gone," he'd said miserably.

"Yes, you will. Life goes on. Mine will go on, you know that. But not in this body and not with you."

Not with you. That was the problem. Living without Faith was no life at all. "My wife was sick for a long time. Maybe I should've been prepared to lose her, but…" How did a person prepare for something like that? "Every morning I wake up and ask myself, 'Why get up?'" he confessed to Olivia. Great. Here he was, baring his soul to someone he'd just met. He downed the last of the schnapps in one gulp.

"I felt that way," Olivia said. "It was spring when I lost George. I'd hear the birds singing and want to shoot them. And I love birds." She sighed and picked up the bottle of schnapps, raised it inquiringly.

James held out his glass and she refilled it. Down went another shot. Now his sinuses were entirely cleared. If only this stuff could burn the pain out of his heart.

"Of course, I had my sons," Olivia continued. "And that gave me something to live for."

James nodded.

"And I have friends who helped get me through."

"I think you women have us men beat there," James said. Oh, he had his fishing buddies, but they never sat around and talked about their feelings. Other than some awkward moments at Faith's funeral, they preferred to steer away from unsettling emotional scenes. And he didn't blame them. He was the same way.

"Well, it's important to have girlfriends you can talk to," she said. "But sometimes it's even better to talk to someone with a voice lower than yours," she added, and this time when she smiled he noticed that she had dimples.

"You're a good woman, Olivia," he said.

That made her blush. "Oh, I don't know about that." Now her schnapps had disappeared and he picked up the bottle and refilled both their glasses.

"Thank you," she said, and hiccuped.

Then she giggled and James chuckled and the ache in his chest subsided. Coming up here to Icicle Falls had been an inspired idea. What a smart daughter he had.

The bar at Zelda's was a holiday beehive, humming with Christmas cheer and rampant hormones. It was obviously *the* place to be in this town, since it was packed. Brooke and Dylan had snagged the last available table and yet people still were coming in, a parade of the town's young and beautiful, the men in jeans and T-shirts, the women in clingy dresses or jeans paired with pretty tops and lots of bling. Some had come in groups but most were paired up. Paired up or not, everyone knew everyone else. People stopped by tables to chat, waved at friends. Men sauntered over to tables where groups of girlfriends sat and pulled up chairs.

Looking around her, Brooke felt like the girl at the dance who wasn't getting a boy. She hadn't felt like that since middle school. She took another sip of her drink, something the cocktail waitress had recommended called a Chocolate Kiss.

Well, a chocolate kiss was better than no kiss, she supposed.

Oh, who was she kidding? She was more than ready for a real kiss. Ever since she'd broken up with

Mark two years ago, her life had been sadly lacking in hot, sexy kisses. Other than her dad and her brother, it had been sadly lacking in men, period. There sure weren't any single ones at her school. The faculty was mostly populated by women, and the two token men who worked there were married and middle-aged. There wasn't so much as one lonely divorced father in this year's crop of parents. As for online dating? Oh, shudder. She was still recovering from her meet-up with Ralph Turner, with his garlic breath, big hairy hands and not-so-subtle hints that they go back to his place and hook up. Ugh.

The bar had a respectable dance floor considering the size of the room, and a small stage at one end. A band consisting of two guitar players, a bass player and a drummer had set up on the small stage and were starting to bang out a fast rock song. Several people got out on the floor and began to dance.

It had been a long time since she'd done that. "Come on," she urged her brother. "Let's get out there."

He rolled his eyes. "I'm not dancing with my sister."

"Oh, come on," she begged. "You used to."

"I was ten. You were twelve. You made me."

"What if I buy you another beer?"

He heaved a long-suffering sigh. "Okay, fine."

But they were barely out on the floor when she discovered the real reason for his cooperation. Three girlfriends had taken to the floor and he was smiling at the one with red hair and showing off his moves. And she was smiling right back. Well, brotherly loyalty only went so far.

The song ended and Brooke was halfway to their table when she realized her brother hadn't followed. Instead, he'd made his way over to chat with the three women. Now a new song was starting, and yep, there he went out onto the dance floor with the redhead.

"Thanks, bro," Brooke muttered. "Just what I wanted, to be stuck here all by myself."

"Now, that wasn't very nice of your date to go and leave a pretty lady like you all alone," said a voice at her elbow.

She looked up and saw a drool-worthy man wearing jeans and a cowboy shirt smiling down at her. Lean but well muscled, ruggedly attractive. Okay, Dylan could stay away as long as he wanted. "He's my brother. I guess one dance with his sister was about all he could handle."

"Hell, there's plenty of guys here who'll dance with you."

Like him? That'd work.

"My name's Billy Williams. Everybody calls me Bill Will."

"I'm Brooke Claussen."

"Well, hi there, Brooke. Wanna come on over and join us?" He gestured to a table on the other side of the dance floor where another man and a couple of women were sitting.

Neither woman was sending her what she'd describe as a friendly smile. In fact, one of them, a blonde in jeans, a tight red top and a Santa hat looked as if she wouldn't mind breaking a beer bottle over Brooke's head.

"You know, I think I'll pass but thanks for the offer."

"Well, okay, but if you change your mind come on over."

Brooke watched as he sauntered off and settled in next to Santa Blonde, who scowled at him. He took a swig from his beer bottle and laid a hand on her arm and she yanked it away. Naughty or Nice? It wasn't hard to tell which category the friendly Billy fell into, at least in Santa Blonde's opinion.

Brooke sipped her drink, watching the dancers and wishing she had the nerve to ask some man if he wanted to dance. But she'd spent too much time with five-year-olds. She'd lost her edge. She sat back in the chair, crossed one leg over the other and swung it back and forth. There, that should send out the signal that she wanted to dance.

Nobody got the signal. Everyone here was too busy partying with friends.

Okay, enough of trying to pretend she was having fun. She finished her drink and got up just as the song was ending.

"Hey, where are you going?" Dylan called, walking up to the table with the redhead in tow.

"I'm going back to the lodge to check on Daddy."

"He's fine," Dylan said. "Anyway, what about that beer you were gonna buy me?"

"I'll buy you a beer," the redhead volunteered, smiling up at him.

Dylan grinned at her. "How about I buy you a drink instead?"

"Okay," she said happily.

Well, someone was going to get kissed under the mistletoe tonight. Actually, the way Dylan's new pal was looking at him, Brooke suspected they wouldn't waste time searching for mistletoe.

"See you at the lodge," she said.

"Don't wait up," he responded, still grinning.

The band started another song and more people poured onto the dance floor now, the magic of booze convincing them all that they could be on *Dancing with the Stars*. Brooke left with the strains of "Love Shack" ringing in her ears.

Outside the restaurant the music became muted, and once she'd gone a block it was only a memory. Now quiet conversations floated past her like snowflakes as fellow visitors to town gazed in shop windows or strolled along enjoying the frosty air and the Christmas lights. The rooftops of the Bavarian-style buildings were frosted with snow and the multi-colored lights made her think of gumdrops. Hansel and Gretel houses.

Passing by the town square she paused to admire the gigantic fir tree dressed up in colored lights for the holidays. Nearby was a gazebo strung with golden twinkle lights, and farther off was the skating rink, also ringed with lights. A few people were still skating on it. She could see a cart set up on one side and the smell of roasting nuts wafted over toward her. She stood for a moment, watching the skaters, wishing she was out there gliding along the ice, holding hands with someone. Maybe she should go back on the internet. Every man out there couldn't be a Ralph Turner. She wanted to find the kind of true love her father and mother had. There was still time. After all, her parents hadn't met until they were in their thirties. She was only twenty-nine. Yeah, she had time.

Meanwhile, she'd be there for her father, help him get through this difficult Christmas. She picked up her pace and hurried back to the lodge. She'd brought some homemade caramel corn, his favorite, which was waiting in her room. If he was still awake, they could enjoy a bedtime snack.

The inn was quiet as she went up the sweeping front steps. Most of the guests were probably out enjoying the town's nightlife or getting in one final whirl around the skating rink before it closed. She walked in the front door and was greeted by the sound of a woman's laughter. And under it, like a bass counterpart, came a man's chuckle. In the lobby, two pairs of legs stretched out from the wingback chairs in front of the fireplace. Two faces smiled in profile. Her father was awake, all right, and he wasn't alone. Brooke stopped, wide-eyed with shock. This picture was wrong! Why was Olivia Wallace here? What was she doing with him?

Whatever it was, she shouldn't be doing it. It had only been a year since her mother had died. Daddy was not available. Brooke's jaw clenched tightly and she narrowed her eyes. Somebody needed to set this woman straight, and that somebody was going to be her.

Chapter Nine

Frosty the Snowman

"Daddy, why are you still up?"

James turned his head to see his daughter approaching, smiling at him as if he were a naughty child. Or some doddering old coot who needed watching every minute. And he was neither.

"I just brought your father a list of the people staying here. For your shopping tomorrow," Olivia explained. "This is awfully sweet of you," she said, giving Brooke a warm smile.

The one his daughter gave Olivia in return was decidedly lukewarm. "Well, we should probably get to bed," she said to James. "We've got a busy day tomorrow."

"You run ahead, angel," he told her. "I'll come on up in a little bit."

Brooke didn't run anywhere. Instead, she shrugged and fell into a chair on the other side of the coffee table. "Come to think of it, I'm not that sleepy."

"Would you care for some peppermint schnapps?" Olivia offered. "I can fetch another glass."

"Oh, no, thanks," Brooke said. "I had a drink at Zelda's."

Olivia nodded. "Some of those can pack a wallop."

"It wasn't that strong," Brooke said, choosing to be argumentative. "So, how long have you owned this place?"

"Eighteen years," Olivia said. "It was just starting to take off when my husband died."

"That must have been hard," James said. "Trying to keep the business going while you're grieving…"

"It was. But I had good friends who got me through. And, of course, my sons have been a big help around here, especially my older son, Eric."

"Well, you've all done a great job with the place. Mom would've loved it here, wouldn't she, Daddy?" Brooke said, inviting Faith's ghost to the party.

Suddenly, James wasn't having such a good time anymore. "You know, that schnapps is making me sleepy. I think I'll turn in."

Olivia looked momentarily disappointed but she quickly covered it with a smile. "Of course. I enjoyed visiting with you, James."

"Same here," he said. "For a minute there I almost forgot…" *That my whole world ended last Christmas.* He didn't finish the sentence. There was no sense ruining another person's holiday mood.

He forced himself to stand. "Thanks for the drinks, Olivia."

"My pleasure," she said. "I'll see you both to-morrow."

But not alone, not if his daughter can help it, Olivia thought as father and daughter walked up the stairs to their rooms. Brooke Claussen was her father's self-appointed bodyguard, making sure no other woman got close enough to step into her mother's shoes.

Olivia's boys had gone through a similar phase. Eric had been convinced that Manny Esposito was a fortune hunter, out to marry her so he could get his hands on the lodge. She'd had to remind Eric that she was a grown-up, in charge of her own life, especially her love life, and twenty-year-old sons didn't get to have a say in who their mother went to dinner with.

Manny hadn't lasted long, anyway. Eric had been too obnoxious to him and Brandon had been a lippy little pain. Manny had moved on. He'd found a rich widow with a ranch in Ellensburg and moved away from Icicle Falls. So maybe Eric had been right. Still, that mistake had been hers to make. And Ms. Brooke would have to learn the same thing about her papa.

But James had been a widower only for a year, and the loss was still a raw wound. For both him and his children. Olivia knew she needed to respect that.

But, oh, how she'd liked talking with him. And how she wished Brooke hadn't shown up when she had. If she hadn't come along, they'd probably still be in the lobby talking.

"You already have two wonderful men in your life," she lectured herself. However, the day would come when they'd fall in love, and then they'd be gone, too. Well, Brandon for sure. He would never return to Icicle Falls to live. Maybe Eric would stay, though. He'd been so involved with running the lodge that the place had seeped into his blood. Hopefully, he'd find a woman who wanted to share the life of an innkeeper, one who'd always wanted a mother as much as Olivia had wanted a daughter. If he didn't, if he married someone who wanted to live in the city…

She decided not to think about that. Anyway, it was time to go to the kitchen and put together her French toast casserole for morning. And maybe have a cookie. Life was generally better with a cookie.

John's nose woke him up in the morning and urged him to get to the dining room ASAP. He could smell something *really* delicious.

He arrived to find several people already at their tables. He saw a new couple who hadn't been in the lobby the night before, holding hands across the table. They looked about his age and the wife had a growing baby bump. John smiled. That would be him and Holland someday. The Williamses and their teen girls were seated at a far table, the mom sipping coffee and admiring the view of the mountains out the window, the dad reading the morning paper and the two girls texting, ignoring the vases of flowers on the tables, the pine paneling and the paintings of various German castles hanging on the walls. The Spikes were done with their breakfasts and down to finishing their coffee, while the two old women, Jane and Vera, were eating some sort of bread casserole and bacon. Missy Monroe and her kids were sitting at a table over by the window and she was waving at him.

He waved back. It would be rude not to go sit with them.

"Is that what I'm smelling," he greeted her, pointing to her plate.

She nodded. "French toast casserole. Olivia promised me the recipe if I keep it a secret."

"Whoa, pretty nice," John said. "Don't you normally have to pay for the chef's special recipes at a restaurant?"

Now Missy looked panicked. "Oh, gosh. Do you think she's gonna charge me?"

John plopped onto a seat. "Nah. Otherwise, she would've said. I just meant it was pretty generous of her. Hey, guys," he said to the kids.

"Hi, John!" Carlos said eagerly. "Want to help me build a snow fort today?"

"I want to build a snow fort," Lalla declared.

"Snow forts are for boys," Carlos informed her.

"Uh-uh." Lalla shook her head, frowning. "I want to build a snow fort with John and Carlos," she said to her mother.

"The three of us will build a snow fort," Missy

said, "but John has someone coming today and he'll be busy."

"You will?" The face Carlos turned to John plainly begged, "Say it ain't so."

"Sorry, buddy," John said. "But I tell you what. Before my girlfriend gets here I'll help you with the foundation. How's that?"

Carlos nodded. "Okay." At his mother's pointed glance, he added, "Thanks, John."

"Me, too," Lalla piped up. "I want to help."

"You can go do something else," Carlos told her, and that started the sibling battle all over again.

Missy finally settled it by suggesting that she and Lalla make a big snowman to watch over the fort, which solved the problem.

"Let's go." Carlos slid off his seat, his breakfast forgotten.

"Let's give John a chance to eat first," Missy said. "And that'll give us a chance to finish, too. Building snow forts and snowmen is hard work, so we need energy."

A few minutes later, a high school girl came out of the kitchen and pointed John in the direction of a side table housing pitchers of juice as well as a big bowl of fruit salad and another huge bowl holding small containers of yogurt packed in ice, then promised to be right back with the rest of his breakfast.

Breakfast consisted of scrambled eggs and the very thing that had awakened John's nose that morning. John didn't waste any time digging into the breakfast casserole when it arrived. "Oh, man, that's good," he said, savoring the taste of cinnamon, butter and brown sugar.

"Tell me about it," Missy said.

"Would you like another serving?" their waitress asked. "Mrs. Wallace always makes plenty."

"Oh, yeah." Missy handed over her plate.

John was surprised. "You're not on a diet?" Okay, that hadn't come out exactly the way he'd intended. "I mean, I've never dated a girl who wasn't on one."

Missy shrugged. "I don't believe in diets. They're too hard to stick to. Anyway, eating's too much fun."

"You got that right," John said, forking up another mouthful of the French toast casserole. "And anyway, you don't look like you need to go on one."

She smiled. "Thanks."

"Holland diets a lot." And he was sharing this because? "But she looks great. Uh, not that you don't." Where was he going with this? He decided that wherever it was, he needed to end the trip. He stuffed a piece of bacon in his mouth to shut himself up.

Now their waitress was back with a second helping for Missy. "Thanks," she told the girl. "This stuff is the best."

She dug in and they let the kids carry the conversation, which consisted of snowmen and snowball fights. "I can sing 'Frosty the Snowman,'" Lalla announced, and then proceeded to serenade them.

The kid didn't have a bad voice, but she did have a pitch problem. John smiled politely and tried not to wince. "That was nice," her mother said before she could launch into a second verse, "but you know what? I'm going to finish my breakfast before you finish yours."

Lalla went back to eating. Lalla's mom was pretty clever.

"So, what have you got planned for when your girlfriend gets here?" Missy asked John.

Only the perfect day, that was all. "Well, first a sleigh ride, then I have reservations for lunch at Schwangau, that fancy restaurant in town. If there's time, I want to take her skating at the ice rink over in the park. Then shopping. And the Christmas carol sing."

"And after that, dinner here at the lodge," Missy said. From the expression on her face you'd have thought they'd be giving away diamond earrings. "A big Christmas Eve dinner with special Christmas china. I saw the picture on the website."

His family did that every year, but she made it sound like something unique. Maybe it was for her. John decided not to share anything specific about his family's typical Christmas Eve.

"What does your family do for Christmas every year?" she asked.

"Oh, you know, the usual," he said vaguely, not wanting to embarrass her by going into detail.

"I'd like to hear what that is," she said wistfully.

"Santa comes to our house on Christmas Eve," Lalla offered, and took a big drink of juice.

"Yeah? He comes to our house, too," John said.

"There is no Santa," Carlos insisted yet again.

"There's always Santa if you believe," John told him.

"Well, I don't." Carlos shoved away his plate of half-eaten food.

"You're going to feel pretty silly when Santa leaves you a present," his mother said.

"He won't leave me what I want," grumbled the child.

Missy ignored him. "So, what does your family do at Christmas?" she asked John, returning to the subject of family tradition.

He shrugged as though it was no big deal. "Christmas Eve we have a potluck. Aunts and uncles and cousins come over and bring salads and snacks, and my mom cooks up a big pot of clam chowder and makes garlic bread."

"That sounds like fun," Missy said.

"It is," he admitted. "My mom's kind of pissed that I won't be there this year, but since I'm proposing to Holland, I wanted to make it special. Anyway, we'll go see both my parents and hers later on Christmas Day, show off the ring. I've got it with me." He lowered his voice. "I'm going to give it to Mr. Claussen as soon as I'm done eating. You know, to present it to her."

"Can I see it?" Missy asked.

"Sure." He'd put real thought into picking out the perfect ring for Holland. It had to be affordable but rich-looking, something unique and special. He pulled out the ring box and opened it, revealing a

ring with a square of pink and white diamonds done
in fourteen-karat white gold. Little diamonds edged
the band.

"Wow, that's gorgeous," Missy breathed.

"You think she'll like it?" he asked eagerly.

"She'd be crazy not to. Your Holland is one lucky
lady."

"No, I'm one lucky guy. I guess I'll take this over
to Mr. Claussen right now," he said, and walked over
to where the Claussen family was eating breakfast.
After a quick greeting, he handed over his treasure.

"Can we see it?" asked Brooke.

He nodded. He never got tired of looking at it.
He sure hoped Holland would feel the same way.
Well, if she didn't like it, they could always take it
back and get one she did like. But the way Brooke
Claussen was admiring it confirmed to him that he
had darned good taste.

"It's gorgeous," Brooke said, echoing Missy's
comment. "She'll love it. And what a surprise when
Santa gives it to her."

John smiled. Yes, this had been a great idea. Now,
if Holland would just hurry up and get here. He
thanked James Claussen again and went back to
his breakfast, feeling like a kid waiting for Christmas morning.

James, Brooke and Dylan were finishing their
breakfast when Olivia came out of the kitchen to
make the rounds and visit with her guests. She
started with the Spikes, who were seated several

tables away. Good, Brooke thought. Maybe the boys would be done eating before Olivia reached their table and they could get out the door. She suspected the woman would be more than happy to monopolize her father's entire morning, and there was no time for that. After all, they did have a busy day ahead. And even if they hadn't Brooke would've found something they needed to do…away from the lodge and Olivia.

Dylan had already finished his second helping, but suddenly Daddy slowed down, stirring his coffee over and over, dawdling his way through the rest of his casserole. Brooke began to feel antsy.

"Maybe we should get going," she suggested.

"We've got lots of time, angel," her father said.

"I wonder if there's any more of that casserole kicking around," Dylan said.

"You've had two servings," Brooke pointed out. At this rate they'd never get out of here.

"So? It's good." He signaled the waitress and asked if there was any left.

"I think so," she said. "I'll go see."

"Bring one for my sister, too, please."

"No, that's okay," Brooke said quickly. That casserole had hardly been low-cal. She might as well have slapped it right on her hips. She looked at her brother in disgust. "At this rate you're going to end up weighing three hundred pounds."

"Hey, I'm a growing boy." He patted his firm middle. "Anyway, I'll work it off at the gym next week."

"I'll probably never get it off," Daddy said, "but darn, that was good."

"Yeah," Dylan agreed. "If this is breakfast, I can't wait to see what dinner's like. I haven't eaten this well since…" He swallowed the rest of his sentence and stared at his cup, then slugged down the last of his coffee as if he could wash away memories of their mother.

Mom had been a wonderful cook and they'd shared family Sunday dinners even after Brooke and Dylan had moved out. Holidays had always been a mother-daughter bake-fest. It had felt all wrong making the boys' favorite cookies without Mom. Brooke found herself blinking furiously, trying to dam up the tears.

The waitress returned with one more piece of French toast casserole for Dylan just as Olivia approached their table. "How was your breakfast?" she asked, smiling at all of them.

As if she didn't know it was good. Fishing for compliments. Rather pathetic, if you asked Brooke.

"Well, I've had seconds and my son's on his third piece of that casserole," her father said.

Olivia beamed at them. "I'm so glad you enjoyed it. I really love to cook for other people."

"So did my mother," Brooke said. Olivia's smile slipped toward the South Pole.

"Would you like to join us?" Daddy asked.

"She probably has to do things in the kitchen," Brooke said.

"Oh, that can wait." Olivia sat down. "So, I imagine that after this, you folks are off to do some Santa shopping."

Daddy nodded. "Yep."

Missy Monroe and her children walked toward them just then. Well, Missy walked. The little girl, Lalla, was skipping behind her brother, who was off to the races.

"Good morning," Missy said.

"We're going to make a snowman," Lalla stopped to inform Brooke. "You want to help us?"

"Oh, that sounds like fun," Brooke said. "But I have to do some errands for Santa."

That made the girl jump up and down and clap her hands. "Santa! I want a grandma," she said, still jumping.

"Well, I'm not sure that's Santa's specialty," Brooke said. "But I know he'll bring you something wonderful."

Meanwhile, Carlos was already out the door. "Come on, Lalla," her mother urged. "Let's go put our coats on. Bye, you guys. Have a great day."

"What on earth are we going to get those kids?" her father asked, watching them go. "And that's not a rhetorical question."

"The little boy wants a dog," Olivia said.

"Yeah." Dylan nodded. "But they've got...what did she call it?"

"The Entwhistle factor," Brooke replied. "She has a landlady who doesn't want dogs."

"Too bad. But a dog would be an easier feat than a grandma, that's for sure," Daddy said.

"Oh, I don't know," Olivia said thoughtfully. "I wouldn't mind becoming an honorary grandma. At the rate my boys are going, it may be as close as I'll ever get." An honorary grandma. Olivia Wallace was a kindhearted woman, Brooke had to admit. And yes, she could certainly cook. If Mom had lived they probably would've become friends.

For a moment Brooke felt bad about her attitude toward Olivia Wallace. But only for a moment. Yes, the woman could cook, and yes, she was kind, but she was also…predatory. Daddy, still bereaved, Mom's ashes barely cool, and here she was, inserting herself into their family party, fishing for compliments on her cooking.

"You think you could do something with the kid?" her father was asking. "Some sort of grandmotherly thing?"

"I'll bet Lalla would enjoy baking cookies and maybe reading a Christmas story tomorrow. There'll be time. They don't leave until the day after Christmas. In fact, most of our guests will be here through then. Including you folks, right?"

"That's right," Daddy said, and the two exchanged smiles.

"But you'll want time with your own family," Brooke said.

"We'll have time together. Anyway, my boys are pretty independent. My younger son probably won't even make it here before late Christmas Eve. He lives in Wyoming and it's a long drive."

Not arrive until the day was almost over? That

shocked Brooke. Who wouldn't want to be with his family at Christmas?

"It's hard for him to get away," Olivia explained. "He's seeing someone. Again."

The way she said that gave Brooke the impression that *someones* came and went fairly frequently in her younger son's life. "Anyway, I can definitely find some time for Lalla."

"Then that takes care of her," Daddy said cheerfully. "I'm afraid the boy will be a problem." He shook his head. "Too bad. He's so young to have given up on Santa."

"That's grim," Dylan said. "I believed in Santa until I was twelve."

Brooke raised a teasing eyebrow. "Twelve? How about fourteen?"

"Hey, I was just milking it then," her brother said with a grin.

"Animals are expensive," Daddy said, returning to the subject at hand. "Even if Missy could have a dog where she lives, it wouldn't be right to saddle her with the expenses of shots and food and all the other things a dog needs."

"What if we gave her money for all that, got her veterinary insurance?" Dylan suggested.

Her brother was as generous as her father. Brooke smiled in approval. "I'd contribute to that."

"Me, too," Olivia said.

"I'm not sure." Daddy rubbed his chin. "We don't actually know anything about her."

"I was just visiting with her," said Olivia, "and

one thing I do know. Besides the fact that there's no dad in the picture, the poor girl's mother is dead and she's raising those children on her own. I think she's had some tough knocks."

"All the more reason to do something really big for her," Dylan said. "The kid wants a dog. Let's give him one. Every kid should have a dog."

Dylan's right, thought Brooke, remembering the two yellow Labs they'd had growing up. The last one, Honey, had died shortly before Mom's cancer came back. Brooke had toyed with getting her father a dog this year, but when she'd hinted at it he'd told her firmly, "No. I don't want to be around death anymore, not even a dog's." And that had been that.

"You're forgetting about the landlady," Daddy said.

"I wonder if she'd relent if someone paid her a damage deposit," Brooke mused.

"Most landlords want a pretty hefty deposit," Olivia said.

"I just keep seeing that little boy's face when he said there's no such thing as Santa." Brooke sighed. "A dog would make his Christmas."

"Hey, a dog would make his *life*," Dylan proclaimed.

"And Missy seems just as keen on having one," Brooke recalled from their earlier conversation.

"Well, there's nothing we can do in that department," Daddy said. "As for getting in touch with her landlady… We have no idea where she lives."

Inspiration struck. "But we do know her landlady's name," Brooke said. "How many Entwhistles can there be in Seattle?"

Dylan was already searching on his phone. "Eight," he announced. "And one of them's gotta be our little old lady." He began punching in numbers on his phone. A moment later he had his first Entwhistle. "Hi. I'm looking for Mrs. Entwhistle. Oh, okay, sorry."

"No Mrs. Entwhistle?" Brooke asked.

"Only a Mister." Dylan went on to the next number and got a crabby woman who informed him that she was single and demanded to know what he was selling.

"What are you planning to do if you find her?" Daddy asked as Dylan moved on to his third Entwhistle.

"Give the phone to Santa and let him take it from there," Dylan said with a grin.

Her father's face turned pale. "What am I supposed to say to this woman?"

"Tell her you're Santa and if she doesn't let Missy's kid have a dog you'll run her over with a reindeer. Hi. Mrs. Entwhistle?…Uh, how old are you?…No, this isn't an obscene phone call…No, I don't want to know what you're wearing. I just want to know if you're old." Dylan made a face. "She hung up on me."

Brooke rolled her eyes. "I wonder why."

"Guys, I think we need to come up with something else for Carlos," Daddy said.

Too late. Dylan had a new Entwhistle on the phone. "Mrs. Entwhistle?…Do you have a renter named Missy Monroe?…You do? Great…No, no, she's not in trouble. I'm a friend of hers and some of us want to get her something special for Christmas… Yeah, she's a great woman…Uh-huh…Yeah, it's a bummer that she's on her own…No, I'm not a boyfriend. Here, let me put my dad on. He can tell you what we're cooking up." Dylan handed the phone to his father. "Okay, Dad, close the deal."

Everyone at the table was looking at James as if he really was Santa Claus and could work holiday magic. Oh, boy. Sweat broke out on his brow.

He took the phone. "Mrs. Entwhistle?"

"Yes," said a shaky voice.

"Merry Christmas. My name is James Claussen."

"And you want to do something for Missy."

"Actually, my whole family is in on the surprise," James said. "And some other friends, too," he added, glancing at Olivia.

"Well, I think that's lovely," Mrs. Entwhistle said, "but I don't understand why you're calling me."

His kids and Olivia were all leaning in, watching him intently. Now his armpits were damp and he could feel sweat trickling down his back. "You see, we need your permission before we can get the present we have in mind for Missy and her family."

"Oh?" The shaky voice was suddenly infused with steel.

Oh, boy. "I understand you have concerns regarding your renter owning a dog."

"Oh, dogs. No dogs," Mrs. Entwhistle said. "They're messy. And noisy."

"Well, they can be, which is why so many landlords charge a damage deposit."

"I just couldn't have a dog digging up my yard," Mrs. Entwhistle said, and James could almost see her shuddering.

"A well-trained dog wouldn't do that. That's why we'd be paying for obedience training." Okay, where had *that* come from? In for a penny, in for a pound, James decided. "And, of course, I'll pay whatever the going rate is for a pet deposit."

"My friend Wilma charges five hundred dollars," said Mrs. Entwhistle. Her voice was getting stronger by the minute.

That seemed a little steep to James.

He was about to say so when Mrs. Entwhistle continued. "I shouldn't do this. I'll regret it. But…"

She seemed to be saying, *Jump in and make your offer.* What the heck. It was only money and he couldn't take it with him. "Well, I'll be happy to pay that," James said. Although *happy* probably wasn't the most accurate word. "And really, dogs make a nice addition to a family. They also discourage vandals and robbers."

"Oh, I never thought of that."

Probably because she'd be able to take on a burglar single-handed. She'd probably hold him hostage and demand he pay a damage deposit. "If the dog does more than five hundred dollars' worth of damage…"

He didn't need a crystal ball to see who'd be on the hook for it. "How about when I come by to pay you the damage deposit, I give you my phone number? That way if there's a problem you can call me."

"That is an excellent idea, and it would make me feel so much better about this," she said, her voice reverting to its former frail state.

No good deed goes unpunished, James thought as he completed his arrangements with Mrs. Entwhistle. This was crazy and extravagant and reckless. And just the sort of thing Santa should do.

"You're a very kind man," Mrs. Entwhistle said before ending the call. "Missy is a lucky young woman to have you in her life."

"Thank you," James said. And if this dog thing didn't work out, he'd have more than Missy in his life. He'd have a dog, too. And Missy wouldn't be feeling so lucky. But he assured himself that it would work out now that the landlady was on board. "Looks like we're good to go," he told the others.

"She'll be thrilled," Olivia said.

"Daddy, you're brilliant," Brooke praised him. Was that what you called it when a man offered to pay a hefty pet deposit to someone he didn't know for someone he'd just met? No, if he was brilliant he'd have found a way to stop this holiday madness.

But then he wouldn't be feeling so darned happy.

Now that everything was squared away with the landlady, Brooke was anxious to make this happen.

"Is there an animal shelter around here somewhere?" she asked Olivia.

"There is. It's on the edge of town and off toward Sleeping Lady Mountain. Why don't I show you the way," Olivia proposed. "I've got time before I have to start dinner."

No ulterior motive there. "Oh, we don't want to bother you," Brooke said. "You must have things you need to do." Didn't she have dishes to wash or…something?

"It's no bother."

That apparently decided it. Daddy slapped his thighs and stood up. "Let's go."

Was this woman going to tag along with them all day?

"Can you give me twenty minutes to put everything to rights in the kitchen?" Olivia asked her father.

No.

"Sure," he said.

"Wonderful. I'll meet you all in the lobby."

"Great," Daddy said.

Great, thought Brooke, and frowned.

"So, what's your problem?" Dylan asked twenty minutes later as they waited in the lobby for their father and Olivia to join them.

"What do you mean?"

"You know what I mean. I saw the snotty look on your face when Olivia offered to come with us."

"I did not have a snotty look!" Brooke protested.

"Yeah, you did." He shoved his hands into his

jeans front pockets and rocked back on his heels, clearly enjoying his moment of superiority.

"Well, if I did, I didn't mean to," she said stiffly.

"And I saw how you tried to talk her out of coming."

Since when were men so observant? "I did not," she lied.

"Look, if Dad wants to hang out with her, so what? What do you care?"

"*So what?* Are you kidding? Mom's only been gone a year! Daddy doesn't need some man-hungry woman sweeping in and getting her hooks into him. I don't care if she *can* cook."

"Hey, he's lonely."

"And he's vulnerable. And she's—"

"My mother," said a voice at Brooke's elbow.

Chapter Ten

The Most Wonderful Time of the Year

Brooke gave a start and turned to see the man who'd been working the reception desk the day before. He was still as good-looking as before but he seemed taller.

Maybe that was because she was suddenly feeling rather small. The sizzle of embarrassment rose from her neck to the roots of her hair.

"Any man would be lucky to have my mom," he said.

Olivia's son, of course. She should have guessed. The sizzle grew hotter.

Still… "I'm sure that's true, but right now my father doesn't need a woman in his life," she said defensively. "My mother just died a year ago. Anyway, he has a daughter to take care of him."

Now the man practically sneered at her. "No offense but there are some needs a daughter can't fill."

Brooke's face flamed with a fresh infusion of

embarrassment and Dylan laughed. She scowled at him.

He was ignoring her, though, thrusting out his hand. "I'm Dylan Claussen. This is my sister, Brooke, the warden," he added, making Brooke fume.

She was not a warden. She was simply watching out for their father's interests. And their mother's memory.

"Eric Wallace," said the man, giving Brooke a smile as cold as an icicle.

She lifted her chin. No smile for him. If he could do icicles, she could effect an entire ice cave.

Their father had joined them and was introducing himself to Eric Wallace when Olivia arrived. "Eric," she said, looking adoringly at her son. "Are you going to join us?"

No, not him, too.

"Any objections?" he asked Brooke.

"Of course not," her father answered for her. "The more, the merrier, right?" he said, placing one arm around her shoulders.

She smiled weakly, then caught sight of Eric Wallace's gloating expression and dropped the smile.

Missy Monroe was coming down the stairs now, her kids racing ahead of her. The little girl managed to fall down the last three steps, landing on her hands with a thud and a noisy howl. Eric picked her up and set her on her feet.

"Thanks," Missy said. "They're excited to get out and play in the snow."

"I don't blame them." He winked cheerfully at the kids. "Have fun, guys."

"We're going to make a snowman," Lalla said loudly. "But first we have to go buy Mommy some mittens on accounta she forgot hers," Lalla finished with a long-suffering sigh.

"You know, I think we have some in our lost and found that no one ever claimed," said Olivia. "Let me check before you go buying any."

"Oh, wow, that would be great." Missy smiled at the assembled group. "You all off to go shopping?"

"You could say that," Dylan said, grinning widely.

"Come *on*, Mom, let's go," Carlos implored, obviously eager to get out in the snow.

"In a minute," she said.

"Grown-ups always take so long, don't they?" Brooke said to the boy. "I'll play rock, paper, scissors with you while we're waiting."

"What's that?" Carlos asked.

"Don't do it," Dylan cautioned. "She's psychic. She'll beat you every time."

The game kept Carlos entertained until Olivia returned, carrying a pair of red mittens that looked hand-knit. "These should fit."

They did, and Missy barely had them on before the kids were towing her toward the door. "Thank you," she called over her shoulder. "See you later."

And here came John Truman, all bundled up. "Come on, John," Carlos called.

"I love to see young people having a good time,"

Olivia said happily. "This is such a wonderful season."

Yes, it was. Even with the sad memories attached, Christmas was still Brooke's favorite holiday. And she supposed she should be glad her father was enjoying himself. Still, it upset her that he could so quickly forget about Mom and latch onto another woman. As if all their years together didn't matter. Mom was the love of his life. How many times had he said that? How could he so easily forget the love of his life to hang around with someone new?

"We should take Eric's Land Rover," Olivia suggested. "If we find a dog, we'll need a way to transport it home."

"We can take Brooke's SUV and follow you," Dylan said.

"Sounds like a plan." Daddy followed Olivia into the Land Rover, leaving his daughter and son to fend for themselves.

"She's taking over, like...some kind of alien invasion," Brooke muttered.

"No, she's not," Dylan said in a tone of voice that made Brooke feel as if she was five.

"She is, too!" Why couldn't anyone but her see this? Olivia Wallace was like a giant eraser, rubbing out their mother's image.

"Hey, we wanted him to have a good Christmas. Remember?" Dylan said as they got into Brooke's SUV. "He's having fun, so what the heck?"

What the heck? "He's rushing into friendship with some woman he's just met! It's...it's disloyal."

Disloyal or not, it was happening, and all Brooke could do was fret and fume as Olivia and her father walked through the animal shelter, debating over the right kind of dog for a little boy.

The animals were housed in a small single-story house. But this house was decorated with posters sporting sayings such as Find a New Best Friend and Wag More, Bark Less. Beyond the reception area, a big room with a long counter and file cabinets standing behind it like sentinels, they had found the cat room, currently empty of kittens.

"Cats don't come into heat until the beginning of February and then go out in October," explained Dr. Wolfe, the local vet who was volunteering that day. "That's why we have no kittens at Christmas."

"Just as well we're on the hunt for a dog," Daddy said.

"Well, we're a little sparse on dogs at the moment, too," Dr. Wolfe told him, "but we have a couple of good ones who sure could use homes."

The dog area had fourteen large cages but only three of them were occupied. And now Daddy and Olivia were debating the benefits of big and woofy over small and yappy. Eric was with them, and Brooke watched as he bent in front of one of the cages and held his hand out to a mutt that was barking and wagging his tail.

"Hey, boy," he said, and the dog jumped and barked. "This one sure is friendly."

He was also the doofiest-looking dog ever, resembling Clifford the Big Red Dog of children's book fame.

"He's rather big," said Olivia, who was leaning toward a Chihuahua trembling against the far wall of the cage.

"What do you think, Brooke?" her father asked.

She thought that Eric Wallace had a very nice butt. *Oh, no,* she scolded herself, *down, girl.* She was not interested in Eric Wallace. He came with a man-hunting mama. Anyway, they'd gotten off on the wrong foot. He wouldn't be any more interested in her than she was in him.

Except part of her *was* interested. The man had certainly stirred up her sedentary hormones. But just about anything in pants would do that. She spent most of her time with five-year-olds, so her hormones were easily stirred.

She told them to cool it and approached the cage with the Clifford clone. He barked again, then jumped up and put his paws on the door, tail still wagging, tongue hanging out. *Pick me, pick me!*

"It's gotta be this guy," Dylan said, and the dog barked in agreement.

"He does have a lot of personality," Brooke said.

"He's a friendly one," Dr. Wolfe agreed. "But he'll need some obedience training."

"What's his story?" Olivia asked.

"Dot Morrison found him hanging around Pancake Haus earlier this month. I think somebody dumped him."

"You mean just left him?" Brooke asked, horrified. What kind of person would do a thing like that?

Dr. Wolfe frowned. "People move, or decide they don't want an animal, so they drive to a neighboring town and dump him. Or her."

"That's terrible," Brooke said. A new thought occurred. What if, for some reason, Missy Monroe didn't want this dog? Would it wind up back here? She looked at her father. The wistful smile on his face gave her the answer to that question. Clifford the Second would have a new home for Christmas, if not with Missy and her kids, then with Daddy.

"I'd want this dog if I was a kid," Dylan said. "Hey, I want this dog *now*."

Clifford the Second would definitely not be homeless.

"Well, he is sweet," Olivia conceded. "How old is he?"

"I'd say somewhere between eight and ten months," said Dr. Wolfe. "He's already been neutered and I gave him his shots."

"We'll take him," Daddy said.

Dr. Wolfe nodded approvingly. "You might consider putting in a microchip."

Obedience training, microchips—the costs for this good deed were mounting.

But her father didn't blink. "Great idea," he said.

Another expense came to mind. "Daddy, what if Mrs. Entwhistle doesn't have a fenced yard?" Brooke asked as they followed Dr. Wolfe to the office to fill out pet adoption papers. The dog could run out into the street and get hit by a car.

"Yeah, I should have asked. But don't worry. I'll take care of it."

Generous as usual. This was one of the reasons she loved her father so much. He was as close to a real-life Santa as any man could get. "Daddy, you're really something."

"That's me," he joked. "Now, how about you help me out and take care of letting Missy in on Santa's surprise? And be sure to tell her we've cleared this with her landlady."

"I can do that," Brooke said.

"Thanks," he said, and smiled broadly.

Brooke had no problem with doing what her father had asked, but she wasn't going to let him foot the bill for pet deposits and fences and heaven knew what else. She'd take money out of her savings if she had to. Fifteen minutes later, the adoption paperwork was filled out. Dr. Wolfe became concerned and nearly stopped the deal when he learned the dog was going to be a gift. "That sort of thing often doesn't work out."

"Don't worry," Daddy assured him. "If the dog doesn't work out with our friends, he'll have a home with me, and I've had dogs all my life. And I've got a big fenced yard."

"And if you don't want him, I do," Dylan said.

"I don't think this dog is going to wind up homeless." Olivia smiled at the vet.

"I guess not," he said, smiling back.

And so with the papers completed and a hefty donation made, the dog was theirs. Well, technically Daddy's. And the mutt was happy to be out of doggy jail. He nearly knocked Olivia over jumping up on her, and if Eric hadn't grabbed his collar he would've been out the door.

"We're going to have to buy a leash for him," Daddy said.

"And dog food," Dylan threw in.

"And a dog dish and some chew toys," Brooke added. So much for buying inexpensive, token gifts for Santa to give out. But it would be worth every penny when they saw the expression on the little boy's face. "Plus I think we need to get a big green ribbon to tie around his neck."

"I think we need to buy Missy a year's supply of dog food," her father said. "This guy's going to eat like a horse."

"Hi, ho, Silver," joked Olivia. "Well, let's get him home. By way of Safeway," she told her son. "We can pick up a leash and dog food there."

Brooke was about to say goodbye and suggest a run to Wenatchee for some pants and a shirt for her father when he said, "I'll come with you and pay for it."

Olivia shook her head. "Oh, no. We'll get the bill for that. I want to help with the pet deposit, too."

"We can talk about it at the store," Daddy said genially.

So now they were going to the store together.

"We'll come, too." Brooke was determined not to let her father out of her sight.

"Okay," Olivia said. "But you must let us pay for half. After that, we can take the dog back to the lodge and watch him while you get some more clothes and the rest of your presents."

Brooke nodded curtly. The sooner they got her father out of Mr. Wallace's clothes, the better. It would be one less connection to Olivia.

"That's very kind of you," Daddy said.

"Don't mention it."

All right, we won't, thought Brooke. "We'd better buy our supplies so you can get Clifford back to the lodge," she said with a polite smile.

Eric fell in step with her as they left the animal shelter. "Clifford?"

"He reminds me of the big red dog in those children's books."

He smiled. "That's what I was thinking, too."

He did have a nice smile. And maybe she was a bit too…vigilant. "About earlier today. I didn't mean to insult your mother."

He stiffened.

"But really, it's too soon for my father."

"I get that," Eric said. "And I felt the same way after my dad died. Chased off more than one man."

"I'm not chasing anyone away," Brooke protested, even though that wasn't true. But it *was* too soon.

"The thing is, our parents are grown-ups. They don't need to ask our permission if they want to see someone."

She'd only just met this guy and he was lecturing her? She frowned.

"My mom's not out to replace yours, any more than your dad's out to replace mine."

"We're not ready. He's not ready," she said, correcting herself.

Eric nodded. "Sometimes things happen whether we're ready or not."

Okay, she'd had quite enough of Mr. Dr. Phil. "Well, thanks for your input," she said, her words frosty, and marched to her SUV. "I don't like that man," she told Dylan as they climbed in.

"Why? He seems fine to me."

"He's a know-it-all."

"Ha! A bigger know-it-all than my sister?"

"You're not funny."

He seemed to think he was. He was still chuckling when they pulled up in front of the Safeway.

She scowled at him.

"Think I'll go in with Dad and the Wallaces," Dylan said, "before you lock me up, warden."

"Ha, ha," she said, and hurried to her father's side.

It turned out Olivia wasn't just going in to help select a leash. She wanted to pick up a few grocery items.

"We can get the dog supplies while you're doing that," Brooke told her. Maybe, if they were lucky, Olivia would meet some man in the produce department.

"That's okay. I'm on it," Eric said. "I'll get the dog stuff."

"Well, then, shall we go see what they have in the way of candy canes?" Daddy asked Brooke. "Santa can't show up tonight without candy canes."

That worked for her. She squeezed her father's arm as they walked along. "Mom would have loved this adventure."

"Yes, she would have," her father said. For the first time in a long time he didn't look as though he wanted to cry.

That was good but… *Please, Daddy, don't rush into anything. You don't even know this woman.*

John and Carlos had begun construction on the snow fort when Holland called to tell John she was on her way.

"You finally awake?" he'd teased.

"It's Christmas Eve, John. I don't want to get up at eight in the morning on my day off."

He'd almost said, "Not even to be with me?" but then thought better of it. Holland had an acerbic sense of humor, which she might have been tempted to use, and in light of everything he was planning it wouldn't have sat well with him. Instead, he said, "I'll see you when you get here."

The snow fort was nearly finished and there was still no sign of Holland. The hours sure dragged when you were waiting for someone you loved. When she finally arrived, it would be time for lunch. And that would mess up his itinerary, since he'd booked the sleigh ride for earlier. But that was okay, he told himself. He could be flexible. It was all good.

That was more than he'd been able to say a few months earlier. They'd broken up in August after what he'd considered to be a stupid fight. "You're so lame sometimes," she'd said.

What was lame about wanting a night in, just the two of them? He'd wanted to spend some quality time together instead of going out to a noisy bar. Weren't women supposed to be into that?

She *was* into quality time, she'd insisted, but not cheap time. "You never want to do anything that costs money," she'd accused him.

"That's not true," he'd argued. Only the night before, he'd taken her to an expensive Seattle restaurant where they'd gotten small servings of food for big prices. Talk about a waste of money. And he'd spent plenty on her when they were first together. But now he wanted to save for bigger things, like memorable vacations, maybe even a house. If it was up to Holland, they'd blow every cent they had on clothes and dinners out and overpriced lattes.

In addition to accusing him of being cheap, she'd then claimed that he didn't want to have any fun. Well, he was having fun now.

"This is gonna be the best fort ever," Carlos said as he packed another handful of snow on top of their growing wall.

"Yeah, it is," John agreed. Someday he was coming back here with a kid of his own and building another snow fort. He and Holland had talked about kids once. She wanted them, down the road, of course. Well, yeah. Down the road. They had plenty of time.

"Our snowman's gonna be really big," Lalla called from the other side of the yard.

"Not bigger than our fort," Carlos yelled, packing on more snow. "Right, John?"

"Right," John said.

Lalla tried again. "Snowmans are better than forts," she yelled back. "Right, Mommy?"

"Are not," Carlos retorted. "Right, John?"

"Uh, right," John said.

Their mother cleverly kept out of the argument.

After that, the snow fort team worked in silence, while Lalla and Missy kept up a conversation with their snowman. They'd been busy with construction for about ten minutes when Carlos quietly asked John, "Do you believe in Santa?"

"Sure," John said. "Everybody should believe in Santa. That's part of what makes Christmas special."

Carlos fell silent again, digesting this. A few minutes later he spoke again. "I asked Santa for a dad once. I had a dad for a while but he didn't stay."

Lalla's father, John guessed. Oh, crap. He was in over his head here. "Well, uh, maybe Santa's working on finding you a better one."

Carlos made a face.

"Anyway, I'm not sure dads are his thing. He's more into toys."

"I don't want toys. I want a dad. Or a dog."

"Hey, toys are cool," John said. That was probably what the kid's mother had bought him.

"They ain't a dog."

Well, that was true. John had always gotten what he'd asked for from Santa. He'd also had a dog growing up and, even more important, a dad.

He wished he could think of something wise to say to Carlos, but all he could come up with was, "Yeah, you're right. They're not." Poor kid. John hoped Christmas morning wouldn't be too much of a disappointment.

The Monroe kids were playing on the front lawn when Eric and Olivia and the dog arrived at the inn. What a wonderful surprise this was going to be for those children, Olivia thought gleefully. "Pull around back, dear, so Carlos won't see," she said, and they slid by unnoticed with their big surprise.

"Can you handle getting him inside while I unload the other stuff?" Eric asked.

"Of course."

"The leash is in the bag in the backseat, along with the toys and the dog dish," Eric said.

She nodded and leaned over, removing the leash from the bag. Then she walked around to the back and opened it. "Here we are, boy."

Before she could even grab the dog's collar he was out of the vehicle and bounding off in the snow. "Oh, no! Come back! Here, boy!"

Boy had no intention of coming back. With a

wail Olivia started running after the dog, slipping and sliding in the snow.

Eric was past her in a shot.

This, as far as the dog was concerned, was a highly entertaining game. He stood for a moment, watching Eric approach. Then, just when Eric was almost within range, he dodged and raced off. And now he was heading for the front yard.

"Get him before he rounds the corner," Olivia cried, waving the leash. She was doing well until she slipped and went down in the snow on her backside. Ugh.

Eric didn't have time to help the fallen. He raced around the corner after the dog, sliding and barely keeping upright. Now the animal saw the kids. Oh, boy.

"A dog!" shouted Carlos. "Here, boy!"

The dog loped over to Carlos, jumping on him and knocking him backward into his snow fort, pushing him through the wall. He landed with an "Oof," and Lalla let out a squeal of laughter.

Here's your present, kid. Surprise. Eric picked up his pace and dived for the dog, who once more managed to dodge him, and Eric wound up making contact with the snow fort instead. Damn, but a wall of snow was hard on the nose.

"I've got him," John Truman said, taking off after the beast, who'd now moved on to greet the little girl. She, too, went down, along with her snowman, and came up crying. Missy tried to catch the dog's collar and fell face-first in the snow, tripping John, who had almost closed in. And meanwhile, the animal was off again like a shot.

Now Eric and the dog were doing a lap around the lodge. Oh, yeah, this was fun. Nothing he liked better than doing laps behind a dog butt. "Come here, damn it," he growled.

"Aarf!" replied the dog, which, translated, probably meant "Bite me, sucker."

Okay, here came Mom from the other direction, ready to head the animal off. Great. The thing would knock her over and break her arm. "Mom, get out of the way!" Eric called.

"No!" She crouched in front of the animal like a sumo wrestler in drag.

Oh, crap.

But then, to Eric's astonishment, she threw herself on top of the animal, taking it down.

The dog let out a yelp and struggled to get free, but his mom was now channeling John Wayne. Like a cowboy roping a steer, she held the dog down, got the leash on his collar and struggled to her feet, the runaway finally stopped.

"Ha! Gotcha," she said triumphantly.

Acknowledging defeat, the dog sat on his haunches and looked up at her, panting, tongue lolling.

"Not bad," Eric said in between gasps for air.

She smiled. "You just have to show them who's master." And with that she led the dog into the lodge.

Everything was fine until they got into their living room and their four-footed guest saw Muffin the cat. Muffin hissed, leaped from the top of the couch, where she'd been reigning supreme until the canine invader had arrived, and bolted across the room. The dog raced after her, pulling the leash right out of Mom's hand, and the animals began doing the four-legged version of the Indianapolis 500 around the living room, over chairs, on the couch, under the dining room table. Oh, yeah, and there went the lamp.

"Stop!" Mom shouted. "Oh, Eric, do something."

Once in the kitchen the cat jumped from the floor to the counter, and then to the top of the fridge. The dog stalled out, front paws on the counter, and barked like crazy.

Eric grabbed his leash and pulled him down, saying, "Okay, dude, party's over."

His mother fell onto the rocking chair. "My goodness. I haven't had that much exercise since…well, I don't know when. Dr. Wolfe was right. We're going to have to pay for obedience school for this animal."

"Meanwhile, we should find some dog tranquilizers," Eric said.

"Maybe you can call Dr. Wolfe and get some suggestions for how we can get him whipped into shape for tonight."

"Dog training in one afternoon?"

"Have you got a better idea?"

"Yeah. Get the kid a stuffed dog."

"Where did that dog come from?" Carlos asked.

Missy noted his bright eyes and eager expression. What she'd gotten him wasn't going to cut it. And how did you explain to a kid that you couldn't afford a dog even if the landlady would let you have one? Especially a dog that big. That dog probably ate more than both her kids put together, would probably eat its dog food and half of what was in the fridge and then eat the fridge for dessert.

Once she got a job at a high-end salon they could move. And then they could get a dog. Meanwhile, though, they'd have to stay dogless.

"I'm sure he belongs to someone," she said, making her son frown. "Maybe a friend of Mrs. Wallace."

"That was a mean dog," Lalla whimpered.

"Aw, he's just playful," John told her.

"I wish he was mine," Carlos said wistfully.

"Hey, we should get our fort fixed before the bad guys get in," John said, picking up a handful of snow.

It was enough to distract Carlos, and Missy smiled gratefully at their new friend. He sure was a nice guy. For a moment she found herself wishing he didn't have a girlfriend coming up, that he wasn't about to get engaged. That he could be cloned. Sigh.

Finally the wall was done, and Carlos lobbed a snowball at his sister from behind it. When she rewarded his effort with a squeal of outrage, he laughed and threw another. That made her run screaming to her mom, and they hid behind their snowman.

"We'll get you," Missy called, and threw a snowball in the general direction of Fort Manly Man.

"Yeah, we'll get you," echoed Lalla, imbued with sudden bravery.

Of course, the boys had the advantage, and Lalla soon got tired of hiding behind the snowman and whined to go inside.

"Oh, come on. Don't be a sissy," Carlos yelled.

"I'm cold," Lalla said. "I'm going inside."

"Come on, Lalla. Don't go," her brother pleaded. He came out from around the wall of his fort. "I'll let you hit me."

That gave Lalla renewed strength and soon the children were pursuing each other around the lawn, throwing snowballs.

Missy was laughing at them when something hit her in the back. She turned to see John grinning.

"Gotcha," he said.

"Oh, yeah?" She formed a snowball even as he danced away.

Giggling, she ran after him. John came to a sudden halt and she took full advantage and threw her snowball at him. Of course she missed. But he didn't turn around to taunt her. Instead, she realized he was looking at the attractive, size-two blonde with the fancy jacket and jeans walking around the front of a car that was a lot newer than hers.

"Holland," John said, all smiles. "About time you got here."

So this was the girlfriend. Of course she had to have a model's face—full lips, a delicate nose, blue eyes, great cheekbones and, to top it all off, a high-end haircut and highlights. It was wrong not to like people you hadn't even met, but Missy sure felt inclined to. The woman was probably nice, too, which would make it *really* wrong to dislike her.

She looked over at Missy, who suddenly felt like the queen of cheap in her bargain Goodwill jacket and borrowed mittens. The woman didn't smile. Instead, she lifted one perfect eyebrow in disdain. Okay, Missy hated her.

She turned her back on Missy but her words carried. "I see you've been busy this morning."

"Just killing time," John said, hurrying over and kissing her.

Killing time. Thanks.

Now he seemed to remember Missy and the kids. "Oh, hey, Holland, this is Missy Monroe, Carlos and Lalla."

"I'm named after a princess," Lalla told the newcomer.

"That's nice," said Holland, smiling at Lalla. Her smile chilled considerably when she looked at Missy again.

"Come on, John," Carlos urged. "Let's play some more."

"Sorry, dude, my girlfriend's here now. I'm gonna have to say goodbye. See you guys at dinner. Have fun today."

"Good meeting you," Holland said politely if not warmly.

"You, too," Missy lied. "You guys have fun."

Not that John was paying attention. He was too busy now, getting Holland's suitcase out of the

trunk and walking her up the front walk. His words
floated back to Missy. "Isn't this place cool?"

"What's it like inside?" asked Holland, obviously
not ready to be impressed.

"Even better. Wait till you see our room, babe.
It's got a fireplace. I have a ton of stuff planned for
today."

Missy stood listening and frowning until their
voices were just a murmur. She knew the type of
woman this Holland was. A Mrs. Steele. Not as old
as Missy's nightmare customer but no less bitchy.
Poor John Truman.

A whack in the head with a snowball brought
Missy out of her reverie. She yelped and turned to
scowl at her son.

"Sorry," he muttered.

"How about not aiming for the head, okay?" she
said grumpily. But she knew it wasn't really the
snowball that had gotten to her. And yep, she for
sure hated Holland.

Chapter Eleven

Happy Holidays

John walked Holland into the lobby, expecting to hear her rave over its old-world charm, the baby grand in the corner, the elaborately carved banister on the staircase, decorated with greens. The big sleigh filled with presents. Instead, she asked, "Who was that woman?"

"What woman?"

She frowned at him as if he were an idiot. "The one you were playing with in the snow."

"Oh, her." John had already moved on mentally to being with Holland. He shifted gears. "She brought her kids up here for Christmas. Anyway, I thought we'd start with lunch at Schwangau."

"You just met her?"

Switching gears again. "Yeah."

Holland raised an eyebrow.

She couldn't be jealous of some poor single mom and her kids, could she? "What?"

"You seemed pretty friendly, is all."

"Hey, I made friends while I was here. What did you want me to do, sit in my room until you got around to coming up?" This wasn't exactly the way to begin a romantic holiday, but she was ticking him off.

"No," she said stiffly.

"I'm not interested in her if that's what you're thinking."

"Okay, fine. I just thought it was kind of weird. I mean, last night you were begging me to come up when I had to work late, and this morning you're hanging out with some…woman."

This had all the makings of a stupid fight, and he didn't want to fight. He wanted to have fun. "Come on, babe," he said, wrapping his arms around her. "This isn't how I want to start our holiday."

Just then the two older women were coming down the stairs. "Oh, John," said Vera, the plump one, "I see your sweetie has arrived."

"You know them, too?" Holland asked under her breath.

"What can I say? I met everybody."

"You're a lucky girl," Jane said, and Vera patted Holland on the shoulder as they walked past.

"Hear that?" John teased. "You're a lucky girl."

She just shook her head. "Let's see the room."

Thankfully, the room passed inspection. "Wow," Holland said, looking around. "It's really charming." She stood by the window and looked out at the mountains. "Great view."

"I did good, huh?" he said, coming to stand behind her and slipping his arms around her waist.

She turned to smile at him. "Yeah, you did." Suddenly something rather like guilt crossed her face.

Of course, now she felt bad that she hadn't been willing to come up with him the night before. Good.

But he was willing to forgive and forget. "It's okay," he said, and kissed the side of her face. "You're here now, and that's all that matters. We're gonna have a great time."

"John." She bit her lip.

"What?" Where was the smile? "What's wrong?"

She shook her head. "Nothing. It was sweet of you to plan this."

"Hey, I know how to have fun," he told her. "This is going to be a weekend to remember."

She smiled. "I saw some great shops when I drove through town. Let's go check them out."

"We will," he promised. "But first I have something lined up for us. Something you'll love, and—"

"John, you're not going to take over and *plan* this whole weekend, are you?"

He blinked in surprise. Wasn't that a romantic thing to do? "What do you mean?"

"I mean, I want to go shopping."

"Oh. Well, okay. We can do that other thing later." A sleigh ride would be just as romantic after lunch.

So off they went to the little downtown, and she dragged him from shop to shop. They bought white-chocolate rose truffles at the Sweet Dreams Choco-

lates gift shop. They dismembered gingerbread boys
purchased at Gingerbread Haus. She insisted on buying him a Cat in the Hat stovepipe hat at a shop called
the Mad Hatter, informing him that he looked cute in
it. He wore it for a while to humor her, even though
he felt like a dork. She bought her mother a scented
candle at a shop that overflowed with household
decorations. And that was just the beginning. She
bought a souvenir tree ornament at the Christmas
shop, and at Bubbles she purchased something that
looked like a pink snowball, which she explained was
a "bath bomb." Further explanation was required before he finally got it. Overpriced scented bath gunk.
Okay. The packages began to multiply as she bought
scarves, shoes and jewelry. Pretty soon John was
loaded up like a pack mule.

"This is fun, isn't it?" She slipped her arm through
his as they left a store that sold Northwest food spe-
cialties, with a selection of hot sauces for her dad.

He wouldn't go so far as to say this was "fun,"
but he didn't mind it. Still, there were so many other
things to do. He hoped she didn't want to spend the
whole day shopping. He checked the time on his
cell phone. "Ready for lunch? Wait till you see the
place where we're eating."

Holland was properly impressed with the dark
wood paneling and fancy table settings at Schwangau,
and was happy to let John order them a bottle of
gewürztraminer. "This is good," she said after her
first sip. "Oh, that's what we should do next. I want
to hit that wine shop."

He nodded. "Then after that I've got something else I want us to do."

"Wine shop first," she insisted.

And all the shops surrounding it, probably.

It wasn't that John didn't want her to enjoy picking up souvenirs, but spending sprees tended to bother him. Not just because of the wasted money. Sometimes it seemed that Holland focused too much on *stuff*.

Of course, a lot of that stuff, like clothes and jewelry, she put on herself, and he sure didn't mind the way she looked.

After lunch they went to the wine shop, which offered a wine tasting. There went another forty minutes. As they came out, Holland pointed to a place that sold antiques. "Oh, I should check this out."

"You're not really interested in old stuff," he reminded her.

"But some of the things in that window are cute."

John sighed heavily.

She looked at him, eyebrows lowering. "What?"

"Nothing," he said with a shrug. "It's just that I had this surprise planned and—"

She held up a hand and in an exasperated voice said, "Okay, fine. Whatever."

What kind of reaction was that when a guy said he had a surprise for you? He frowned. "Jeez, Holland. I went to a lot of trouble so you'd have fun."

"I *am* having fun," she assured him. "I'm sorry. We should do something you want to do now."

"It's not something I want to do for *me*. It's something I want to do for you." And he'd already called twice and changed the time they'd be there.

She smiled at him and kissed his cheek. "You're sweet."

Her words warmed his heart.

Until she added, "Sweet, but controlling."

"I'm not being controlling," he muttered. Planning a Christmas getaway so everything went smoothly was not controlling.

"Whatever," she said again, linking arms with him.

"And I actually had to reserve a time for this thing I want us to do."

"Okay, John, I get it," she said. "I get it. I'm sure that what you've got planned will be impressive."

It would be. She'd see.

They returned to the lodge to drop off their purchases and were nearly trampled by Missy's kids running down the stairs.

"Hey, John!" Carlos shouted. "We're going skating. Are you gonna come with us?"

Holland frowned. "That's not what you had planned, is it?" she said under her breath.

Before he could answer, Missy had joined them. "He's busy, Carlos," she said. She studied the load of packages. "Looks like you guys found all kinds of stuff."

Holland didn't bother to confirm the obvious. Instead, she managed a tight smile and continued up the stairs.

Missy watched her go, looking a little sad. "Next

time I come up here, I'm going to make sure I bring more spending money."

"We didn't buy anything that exciting," John told her. Except that, dorky or not, he did like his Cat in the Hat stovepipe hat. Probably because Holland had bought it for him.

Missy shrugged and smiled. "Oh, well. These guys break everything, anyway."

Carlos and Lalla were now both at the lobby door. "Come on, Mom," Carlos said, already leaning against the door and pushing his way out.

"Guess I'd better get going," she said, hurrying down the stairs. "I've never skated before. Hope I don't break my butt."

Never skated before, not even as a kid? That was sad. John suspected much of Missy's life had been subpar.

"John," Holland called impatiently, and he put all thoughts of Missy out of his mind and hurried up the stairs.

Missy scowled as she followed the kids down the front walk. John Truman's girlfriend was a bitch. Self-centered, superior. Spoiled. She probably never tipped her hairstylist. It wouldn't occur to her that the stylist might have kids to support, bills to pay. She would, of course, figure that the stylist, like the poor woman who did her nails and the cocktail waitress who brought her drinks at whatever fancy club she haunted, only existed to serve her.

You're not being fair, she lectured herself. *You don't even know the woman.*

But Missy knew her type. John's girlfriend was the kind who, growing up, would never have been caught eating lunch in the school cafeteria with the likes of Missy Monroe. Holland What's-Her-Name would never have been caught eating in the school cafeteria, period. She'd have gone off campus with the other too-cool-for-school kids to eat her lunch. And whatever high school she'd gone to, guaranteed it was nowhere near Missy's neighborhood. Holland would've gotten her education with kids who'd come from homes with as much money as hers. And, like her, they now took the people who dressed and styled them and waited on them for granted. And looked down on those people's kids just as Holland had done with Carlos on the stairs.

Missy ground her teeth. Holland could hook up with a movie star, a rock star, Spider-Man, whoever, but she'd never produce a kid as great as Carlos.

They were almost at the skating rink when they ran into Mr. Claussen and his son and daughter. All three were heavily laden with shopping bags, and for one jealous moment Missy wished she could afford to spend money like all the other tourists. She didn't dare even go into the shops. If she did she'd be tempted to blow her money on something dumb like an Icicle Falls sweatshirt or some fancy bubble bath. She had enough money to buy the kids a treat at the ice rink and some gingerbread cookies and a couple of cheap souvenirs, and that was about it. *Next year,* she promised herself.

And the thought of how next Christmas was going to be so much better made it easy to smile and wave.

"We're going skating," Lalla told Brooke Claussen.

"I haven't been skating in ages," Brooke said.

"You could come with us," Lalla offered.

Brooke thanked her. "I'd love to, but Santa still has some work for me to do."

"Santa's coming tonight!" Lalla cried, jumping up and down, making her cornrows bob.

"He sure is," Brooke said, giving Missy a smile that seemed almost conspiratorial.

Missy smiled back, unsure what sort of nonverbal message she'd just been sent.

"Missy, could I talk to you for a minute?" Brooke asked, moving them away from the kids.

Missy nodded as Lalla began to tell the men all about their upcoming skating adventure and Carlos picked up a handful of slush.

"I wanted to give you a heads-up that Santa is going to show up at dinner tonight," Brooke began, "and—"

She was drowned out by a howl of pain from Lalla.

Missy whirled around to see her daughter in tears and holding her head, Mr. Claussen and Dylan bending over her while Carlos stood with his hands in his coat pocket, looking sullen.

"He hit me with a snowball," Lalla wailed. "Right here." She pointed to the side of her head.

Missy took her son by the arm and turned him to face her. He preferred to study his toes. She gave his arm a shake. "What did I say about not aiming for people's heads?"

"Sorry," he said defensively.

They were blocking the sidewalk, people moving around them, some frowning, probably in disapproval of her children's behavior. And there were the Claussens standing nearby, looking awkward.

"I think my son has a snowball fixation," she said, trying to make light of Carlos's naughty behavior and her own embarrassment. She picked up the crying Lalla and commanded her son to follow her. When they got to the skating rink they were going to have a serious conversation about the dangers of hard-packed snowballs. "We'll see you back at the lodge," she called to the Claussens, and led her children away, Lalla still milking her injury for all it was worth and crying at the top of her lungs. "Okay, enough," Missy said as she trudged down the street. "You're not hurt that bad."

"Carlos is *mean*," Lalla cried. "Santa's not going to bring him anything."

"I wasn't trying to hit her in the head."

"There, see?" Missy told her daughter. "Santa knows what's in every child's heart."

"Will he find us?" Lalla asked.

Missy thought of what Brooke had said. "Oh, yes."

"Will he bring me a grandma?"

"No." Carlos scowled, staring at the ground. "And he won't bring me a dog, either."

"But I bet he'll have something for you," Missy said. "And whatever he brings or doesn't bring, it doesn't matter because we're having fun. We're together and that's the most important thing. Don't you guys ever forget that."

"We won't," Lalla promised solemnly, and wrapped her arms around Missy's neck.

A moment later a small hand slipped inside hers, and she looked down to see her son looking up at her, tears in his eyes. "I didn't mean to hurt her."

"I know you didn't," she said. She gave his hand a squeeze and felt her own heart tighten. He deserved so much more than he was getting for Christmas.

"Did you get a chance to tell her?" Dylan asked Brooke as they watched Missy march her children off down the street.

Brooke shook her head. "If Lalla's brother could have held off his assassination attempt for about ten more seconds we'd have been good to go."

"Don't worry," her father said. "One of us is bound to see her later this afternoon. Or you can tell her at dinner."

"I can hardly wait to see the look on her face." Brooke smiled, excited about their plan. "She's going to be *so* surprised."

"That's part of the fun of Christmas," Daddy said, his eyes twinkling.

Oh, yes, getting her father in touch with his inner Santa had been a good idea. This was going to be a wonderful Christmas Eve…as long as they could steer clear of Olivia Wallace, man-eater.

"Surprise!" John said as he and Holland drove through the entrance to Currier's Tree Farm.

She took in the farmhouse decorated for the holidays and the Christmas tree in the front yard, the big barn, the rustic split-rail fence. Then she studied the horses, all decked out with jingle bells, attached to a sleigh festooned with greens and ribbons and—oh, yeah, success!—smiled. "A sleigh ride?"

"Yep." The minute he'd visited the website, he'd known they absolutely had to do this. Currier's land stretched way beyond the tree farm, which displayed every imaginable kind of Christmas tree. John could just picture the two of them swooshing along under snowy boughs and past frozen streams.

They were greeted by a lean, gray-haired man who looked as though he'd stepped right out of some old John Wayne cowboy movie. "Hello there," he called. "You John?"

"Yep," John called back.

The man came over to him in big cowboy strides. He took John's hand in his giant paw and gave it a viselike squeeze and a good shaking.

"Thanks for letting me book a later time," John said, trying not to wince.

"You got lucky. We had a cancellation. Otherwise, you'd have been up the creek, young fella. The sleigh rides stop after this. We got family coming for Christmas Eve dinner, and I have to get out the extra table and chairs." The man smiled at Holland and pointed to a little refreshment stand. "Got hot cider and to-go cups over there if you want something for the ride."

Once they had their cider, the old man was back, wearing a heavy winter coat and a red muffler. They climbed into the sleigh and he handed them a thick plaid blanket for their laps. Then he jumped up on the box, took the reins and gave the horses' rumps a gentle slap. "Walk on, girls."

The sleigh lurched and then slid across the crusty snow and they were off. Holland snuggled next to John and took a sip of her hot cider. "This is great," he said.

"Yeah, it is," Holland agreed, and he felt so proud of himself it was all he could do not to puff out his chest.

Oh, yeah, this had been a super idea.

They were soon on a trail edging along the tree farm, the horses trotting and making the bells on their harnesses jingle. John had paid a pretty penny for this ride, but seeing how happy Holland was made it worth every cent.

"Where are you kids from?" asked their escort.

"Seattle," John said.

The old man nodded. "Nice city, Seattle. If you like cities. Me, I like mountain air and small towns."

"How much do places go for up here?" John

asked, admiring a huge log house perched farther up the mountain.

"They're not cheap. People know the value of what they've got," their driver replied.

"Wouldn't you like to have a house up here?" John said to Holland. "Maybe get a cabin, come up and go cross-country skiing."

She wrinkled her nose. "That sounds like way too much work. And boring."

"Seriously? Look at the scenery."

"It's just trees, John."

Just trees and snow and beautiful mountains. Who *wouldn't* want to live in a place like this? Well, Holland, apparently…

"What's there to do around here?" she asked the driver.

His shoulders lifted in a shrug. "Lots of hiking, fishing, river sports."

"How about, like, clubs?" she persisted.

"Clubs?"

"You know. Places to go at night."

"Oh, that. Well, there's always a good country band playing over at the Red Barn."

John glanced over to see Holland rolling her eyes. "Any place else to dance?" she asked.

"Zelda's has a bar. I think there's a dance floor in there. The wife and I don't go in for that kind of thing much, so I'm not up on all the hot spots."

"There probably aren't any," Holland said with a sneer in her voice.

Okay, so it looked as if they wouldn't be buying

a cabin up here. But they could come and visit. He could already see them celebrating their first anniversary in Icicle Falls. She was obviously feeling it, too, because she snuggled closer.

"I'm getting cold," she said.

"I'll warm you up," John said, and drew her closer against him. This was exactly how he'd envisioned it would be.

"Let's go back and get a drink at that Zelda's," she said.

"You got twenty more minutes on the meter," the old man said.

"Twenty more minutes?" Holland echoed. "I'll be a Popsicle."

And so that was the end of the sleigh ride. It had been *almost* as he'd envisioned.

But hey, if a woman was cold, she was cold. They'd had the experience; that was what counted. They'd stop by Zelda's on the way back to the lodge and have a cozy drink. And then it would be time for dinner and the big surprise. Oh, yeah. Everything was going according to plan.

Chapter Twelve

Have Yourself a Merry Little Christmas

Back in town, people of all ages were enjoying themselves. Adults laden with packages paused to visit in the town square, while children chased one another with snowballs and rode plastic sleds down the hill between the downtown park and the skating rink.

"It looks like something out of an old movie," Holland observed as they drove along Center Street past the downtown park with the gazebo and the little ice rink.

John took that as a sign. "Let's check out the rink," he said, pulling into a parking spot.

"I just got warm," she protested.

"You'll stay warm skating," he said in a cajoling tone.

"I haven't been ice skating since I was in Blue Birds."

"What the heck is a Blue Bird?"

"You know, Camp Fire Girls? The ones who sell the candy," she elaborated.

"Oh, yeah. Love those mints. I bet you were a cute Camp Fire Girl."

"I was."

That was Holland, no false modesty. "So, come on," he urged. "Once around the rink. Then we'll go have drinks at Zelda's."

"Oh, all right. I can tell you're dying to do this."

"Hey, we need the whole Icicle Falls experience, don't we?"

She sighed. "I guess."

Her enthusiasm was underwhelming. When had Holland turned into a stick-in-the-mud? *Never mind,* John told himself. Once they were on the ice she'd have a blast.

They walked up the little hill to the ice rink. He could see Missy and her kids out there, wobbling around. She spotted him, waved and went down on her butt, then came up laughing.

Holland had seen Missy go down. Now she said, "I don't know about this, John. I don't want to get hurt."

"You won't," he blithely assured her. "I'll hang on to you."

"Do you know how to skate?" she asked dubiously.

"Of course," he lied. "Well, roller-skating," he amended. "I used to go every Saturday. This can't be that much harder."

Yes, it could, he decided once he had his skates

on. Same principle as roller-skating, but darn, it wasn't so easy balancing on that thin blade. Still, John was confident he'd get the hang of it pretty quickly. "Come on," he called, motioning for Holland to join him on the ice.

She wobbled her way onto the rink and promptly went down with a squeak. Before John could even get to her, some guy in jeans, a parka and a cowboy hat was helping her up. John didn't like the flirty smile she gave this clown.

John arrived on the scene just as the guy put an arm around her and asked, "You okay?"

"I'm fine," she said, and thanked the stranger.

"Anytime," he said. And then, seeing John's frown, he skated off.

As soon as the guy was gone, she dropped her smile and said to John, "If I go down one more time, we're out of here."

"Got it," he said with a nod. "But you won't. It'll all come back to you. Now, take a nice, long glide," he coaxed, then demonstrated. "Like this." *Not bad,* he thought, pleased with himself.

She followed suit and managed to stay upright. "I did it," she said, smiling again.

"I knew you could." He held out his hand and she took it, and they cautiously began to make their way around the rink.

More experienced skaters zipped past them. In the middle of the rink a woman was practicing some fancy twirls. A little boy wearing a Santa hat chased a little girl in jeans and a pink parka. Off to the side of the rink someone was selling roasted chestnuts. John inhaled, suddenly hungry.

Behind them he heard childish laughter and then a cry of panic. He turned to see Missy's kids barreling toward them. Carlos had obviously been chasing Lalla, but she'd fallen down, and now he'd tripped over her and lost his balance, and here he came, arms windmilling.

"Look out!" John said to Holland, and tried to pull her out of the way.

But it was too late. Holland turned just in time to see Carlos sliding into her legs. She crashed to the ice with a shriek, bringing John down, too, turning them all into a heap of arms and leg.

And now here was Missy, struggling to skate up to them. "Oh, my gosh. Are you okay?" she asked Holland.

"No, I'm not okay," Holland snapped, tears in her eyes. "I think my wrist is broken."

Oh, no. This couldn't be happening, not when everything had been going so well. John scrambled to his feet. "Here, babe, take my hand."

"Let me help," Missy said, coming to her other side.

"I'm fine," she said, throwing off Missy's hand and sending her flying backward onto her butt. "Is there a doctor in this stupid town? Oooh, it hurts."

"I'm so sorry," Missy said to John as she got laboriously to her feet. "Carlos, I told you not to chase your sister. Now, you guys apologize," she said sternly.

"Sorry," both children mumbled, heads hanging.

Holland waved away their apologies. "Get me out of here," she said between gritted teeth.

Now the guy who'd picked Holland up the first time she fell was back. "Here, let *me* help," he offered, taking her arm and skating her confidently over to the bench where they'd left their shoes, leaving John to follow behind.

"I'm so sorry," Missy said to him. She couldn't seem to stop apologizing.

"Hey, stuff like this happens," he reassured her. She nodded, but her expression was doubtful.

Once at the bench he knelt at Holland's feet to remove her skates. Or rather skate. The other guy already had one off.

Holland looked accusingly at John. "We should've just gone to Zelda's like I wanted."

"Sorry," John said. "We'll get you to the doctor for some pain pills and you'll feel better."

"I would've felt fine if I hadn't fallen," she snapped. "We should get this x-rayed. I want to make sure it's not broken." The very thought of having a broken wrist was enough to bring tears to her eyes.

"Oh, babe…" John hurried out of his rental skates and into his boots. "Here, I'll go return our skates and we'll be out of here."

"I can do that for you," the stranger told him.

"Thanks," John said.

"Your best bet is to go straight to the hospital,"

their Good Samaritan went on. "It ain't much but the docs are all good. They'll get you fixed up."

"Thank you," Holland said, managing a weak smile.

John escorted her to the car, telling her how sorry he was the entire time.

"It's okay," she said. "Except I wish we'd just gone to that Zelda's."

Man, oh, man, so did he.

Missy felt a stab of jealousy as she watched John Truman escort his girlfriend back to their car. That woman was such a drama queen. And she sure didn't deserve her man.

Some women had all the luck. Great hair, great figures, great boyfriends. Holland What's-Her-Name probably had a perfect home growing up, too, with a perfect mother who was still married to Holland's father. The mother probably drank only mineral water. Or a glass of white wine when she went out with the girls. And at this time of year she undoubtedly had pictures hanging on the wall of Holland all dressed up and sitting on Santa's lap.

Missy had gotten to see Santa once. She still remembered it. She'd been six and she'd cried because under the beard the guy looked a lot like her mother's boyfriend who yelled a lot.

"I can't believe I paid good money for you to sit there and cry," her mother had said, hauling her out of the department store. Good old Mom, with her boozy breath and her string of men and her attempts to get it right as a parent. Somehow, like the visit to Santa, Mom never quite succeeded.

And here was Missy, following in Mom's footsteps.

Not in everything, she corrected herself. Not with the booze, that was for sure. Missy never drank anything stronger than soda pop. But the men? Sigh. She'd certainly failed in *that* department. She tried to imagine being with a man like John Truman.

She suspected there weren't many men like him, though. He was the kind of guy who was in a class all by himself, and he sure deserved a better girlfriend than the one he had.

Like you? Yeah, right.

The Claussen family finally returned to the lodge late in the afternoon with a change of clothes for James and several bags filled with gifts for the guests, plus wrapping supplies.

"That's a lot of stuff," Dylan observed, looking at the pile on Brooke's bed.

"It's going to be so much fun watching everyone open their presents," Brooke said. "And I can't believe we lucked out and found this great velveteen bag in that Christmas store. It'll be perfect for holding everything. So, guys, I don't suppose you'd like to help me wrap all this," she said even though she knew the answer.

"You don't suppose right," her brother said. "That's a girl's job."

Brooke shook her head at him. "Thanks a lot."

"Hey, I helped pay for it. That's help enough. I did my part." He turned to their father. "Dad, want to play some Ping-Pong?"

"Unfair," Brooke said in mock protest. "You guys get to go off and play Ping-Pong while I have to stay here and wrap?"

"Whose idea was it to buy out every store in town?"

"We can stay," her father offered. "Help with some of the wrapping."

She shooed them out the door. "Never mind. I've seen the kind of wrapping you guys do."

"See, Dad? It pays to be incompetent," Dylan said. "Come and find us when you're done," he added, and rumpled Brooke's hair as he moved toward the door.

"Are you okay with doing this, angel?" Daddy asked. He seemed reluctant to leave her on her own.

"Of course she is," her brother answered for her. "She loves doing this kind of stuff."

It was true. She did. "I'll be fine," she told her father. "Anyway, you should enjoy your break while you can. Come dinnertime you'll be busy."

Her father made a face.

"You're going to love it," she said, and gave him a kiss on the cheek. "I'll find you guys as soon as I'm done."

"Come on, Dad," Dylan urged. "The Ping-Pong table's waiting."

"Okay, if you're that anxious for a beating," Daddy said, and clapped Dylan on the back. "Let me just change out of these borrowed duds and then you're in for a whipping."

"I don't think so," Dylan retorted. "My can of whup-ass is bigger than yours."

"So you say."

Brooke watched fondly as father and son left the room, still teasing each other as they went. Getting away from sad memories, making new ones—yes, this *had* been a positively inspired idea. She smiled as she set to work wrapping fancy little soaps in pink tissue paper. In addition to bath goodies for all the ladies and the teenage girls, they'd found a bargain on novelty Christmas ties for the men. Brooke had gone all out for Missy and her family, getting a box of imported glass tree ornaments for Missy and a classic board game for each of her kids. Of course, the big presents would be the dog and then the grandma for a day.

It was sweet of Olivia Wallace to play grandma to little Lalla. The woman really was nice.

But not what the Claussen family needed. They needed to come together, learn how to go forward with only her mother's memory. And that memory deserved to be honored, not pushed aside in favor of someone new.

Brooke realized she was strangling the little package she was wrapping. She took a deep breath and loosened her hold on the ribbon. *Oh, Mom, why aren't you here with us?* Her mother had been much too young to die. She was supposed to live until she was ninety, not be gone by sixty-two.

Brooke shook off the sad thought. *New memories,* she reminded herself. Her mother wouldn't want them to be sad. Still, how could she not be? "I miss you," she murmured.

Suddenly her quaint room felt lonely. Maybe this would be a good time to find Missy and tell her about the dog. She hurried through her gift-wrapping, stuffed Santa's sack with all the pretty packages and then left to search for the future proud owner of a big red dog.

She went downstairs to the reception desk to get Missy's room number, but when she rang the bell no one showed up. That was odd. Usually there was someone manning the desk. Well, Missy and her kids probably weren't in the room, anyway. She looked out the front door to see if they were on the lawn, playing in the snow. The only one there was the snowman Missy and Lalla had made earlier that day.

She went down to the lower level and checked the pool. No one in there. She was on her way back to the main floor when she encountered Eric Wallace coming down the hall with the dog straining at the leash. "I see the dog's taking you for a walk," she said, unable to resist teasing him.

"That's about it. So much for watching the desk. This guy is a full-time job. Sit," he commanded, and gave the leash a firm pull.

The dog got the message and dropped to his haunches and sat, tongue hanging out.

"That's impressive," Brooke said.

"We're making progress. I think we'll be okay by tonight as long as he doesn't catch sight of my mom's cat."

"I can hardly wait to see Carlos's face," Brooke said. "This is going to be a wonderful Christmas Eve dinner."

"Every Christmas Eve dinner at Icicle Creek Lodge is," Eric said. "My mom goes all out. But having Santa there, that's really going to be great," he added.

The dog whined and stood, eager to get moving again.

"Yeah, I know," Eric said. "He wants another walk. This is our third time out," he explained to Brooke.

"Kind of like having kids," she said.

"Except kids know how to use the bathroom," he said. He looked at her thoughtfully for a moment, then asked, "You want to walk with us? The lodge has some of the best views in town right out back."

Going for a walk in the snow did sound romantic. But she didn't want to be romantic with Eric Wallace. Well, in a way she did, but getting too chummy with him would just encourage her father to get chummy with Eric's mom. "I should find Missy. I've been looking all over for her."

"She's probably still in town. Five minutes. Don't leave me alone with this brute."

It would be rude to refuse. "All right," she said. "Just let me get my coat."

He nodded. "We'll meet you out on the back patio."

Five minutes later, Brooke joined Eric on the large patio that extended beyond the dining room. A few tables and chairs had been left out, and off to one side she saw a fire pit surrounded by chairs. Glass windows ran the length of the dining room and the curtains were open so she could see inside. The tables were set with linen tablecloths and Spode holiday china, and crystal glassware glowed in the lamplight. The main buffet table sported a huge holiday arrangement; all the other tables held smaller versions of it.

"It looks so elegant in there," she said as they made their way across the patio.

"Christmas is my mom's favorite holiday."

"Ours, too," Brooke said. They walked past the outdoor pool, which was deserted and waiting for the return of warm weather, and strolled through a garden area. "I bet this is beautiful in the summer."

He nodded. "Yeah, it is. But I like it in winter, too."

It was like a fairyland. The trees were strung with white twinkle lights. Snowflakes began to float down, dancing in and out of the light. "Did you put up all the lights yourself?" Brooke asked.

He nodded again. "But it was my mom's idea. She's always thinking of ways we can improve the place."

Was he trying to put in a good word for his mother? "I guess that keeps you busy."

He shrugged. "I don't mind. She's a great mom and I'm happy to do anything that makes her happy."

More extolling his mother's virtues. "Are you trying to sell me on your mother?"

They turned down a trail now, ducking under snow-laden tree boughs. "I don't have to sell anyone on her," he said, his voice taking on a sharp edge. "Everybody loves her and for good reason. She's got a big heart."

Okay, this was getting awkward. "I'm sure she does." What to say now? "Look, I'm sorry we got off on the wrong foot. I never meant to insult your mom. But you've been down this road. You know what a disaster it can be for people—especially people who've lost a spouse—to jump into new relationships when they're not ready."

He nodded and waited while the dog sniffed at a bush. "I also know that nobody gets to decide for someone else when they're ready."

It was getting cold out here. She pulled her coat collar more tightly around her neck. "Do you always lecture your guests?"

"Is that what you think I'm doing?" he countered.

"It's pretty obvious."

"I wouldn't presume to tell someone how to live her life."

Late afternoon winter darkness had swallowed most of the daylight now, so it was hard to read his expression. But she was getting his underlying message loud and clear. And she didn't want it.

"I guess I'll go back in," she said. "Thanks for showing me around."

"My pleasure," he said.

He was a good man, responsible and kind. If only he'd been just another guest here. She would've gone farther down that path with him and seen where it led.

Eric watched Brooke scurry back to the lodge, shoulders hunched. "That went well, doncha think?" he said to the dog.

His four-legged companion ignored him, moving forward to sniff at a snow-clad huckleberry bush.

"I must be the world's biggest idiot," he mused. What was wrong with him? Why was he setting himself up as a shrink, running around lecturing someone else on how to handle her parent? Who made *him* Dr. Phil?

More to the point, why was he always picking women he had a snowball's chance in hell of ending up with? Maybe he was a masochist. Had to be. Otherwise, why would he have suggested a walk to Brooke?

She was a guest, just someone passing through. And someone determined that her father and his mother not enjoy so much as a minute of holiday romance. He got it, of course, understood that overprotectiveness. But seeing it aimed at his mother didn't sit well.

Too bad he and Brooke hadn't met under different circumstances. He had a feeling they would have hit it off. She was exactly the kind of caring woman he'd been looking for. And she was easy on the eyes. But she sure wasn't easy on his mom, and that wasn't going to cut it.

"Come on, boy," he said, tugging on the dog's leash. "We've had enough."

Back inside the lodge Brooke saw her brother coming through the lobby. "Where's Daddy?"

Dylan nodded in the direction of the dining room. "Dad wanted a break. He stopped by the kitchen to talk to Olivia about Santa's appearance later."

Why was he talking to Olivia and not her? *She* was the one he should be conferring with. She was Santa's helper. She was…jealous? Surely she couldn't be that petty.

"You done wrapping presents?" Dylan asked.

She nodded. "I was just trying to find Missy. I think she's still in town."

"I bet that place is a zoo right about now," Dylan said. "Come on, let's go play some Ping-Pong before dinner."

"In a minute," she said, and started for the kitchen. "I'd better go see what's going on tonight." Of course her father didn't need her help with something he'd been doing his entire adult life. But she didn't like the idea of him having a quiet tête-à-tête with Olivia Wallace.

Dylan caught her arm. "I think they've got it under control. Come on, sis. The game room's empty."

"I'm going to check on Daddy first."

Her brother frowned. "Cut him some slack, will ya? We're up here to enjoy ourselves."

"I'm not trying to stop Daddy from enjoying himself!" she protested.

"He doesn't need you shadowing him everywhere he goes."

"I'm not," she said, freeing her arm. "We're supposed to be up here having fun as a *family*."

"That's right. So let's play Ping-Pong," he said, grabbing her again and steering her toward the lower level.

She wriggled out of his grasp. "You go on down. I'll be there in a minute. I have to put away my coat." And she could do that by way of the kitchen.

Her brother wasn't fooled by the old coat ploy. He shook his head but moved in the direction of the bottom floor game room. "Don't be all day."

She ditched her coat in her room and then went in search of her father. She found he'd migrated from the kitchen and was now parked at a table in the dining room with Olivia Wallace, drinking a cup of coffee. "Daddy, I've been looking everywhere for you."

He smiled at her. "Well, hello there, angel. Are all our presents wrapped?"

She took a third seat at the table. "Wrapped and ready to deliver."

"Great," her father said jovially. There was a new energy in his voice. Brooke would have congratulated herself on the fact that she'd talked him into playing Santa up here, but seeing the way he was looking at Olivia Wallace she knew she couldn't take credit for his good mood. Sadness settled over her. It should have been her mother sitting at the table with them.

"Would you like a cup of coffee?" Olivia asked her.

"No, thanks. I just came to talk to Daddy about tonight."

"I'd say we're about as prepared as we can be," her father said. "I'll slip out right after the main course and Santa will make his appearance during dessert."

"When are you going to give Carlos his dog?" Brooke asked.

"We'll save that for the end," Olivia replied. "My son will be waiting out on the patio with him. Normally, we don't allow dogs in the dining room unless they're service dogs, but for tonight we'll make an exception. That's a very sweet dog."

"Doesn't sound like your cat thinks so," her father said, and the two smiled at each other.

They were already becoming friends, swapping stories.

"We're going to save the engagement ring until last," he continued.

"The grand finale," Olivia added. "It's so exciting to be celebrating not only Christmas but true love, as well." She and Daddy exchanged smiles so warm that Olivia's cheeks grew pink.

"Everything okay, Brooke?" her father asked, and she realized she was frowning.

"Oh, yes, fine."

"Well," Olivia said, "I'd better get back to work." She stood, and Daddy stood, too, the perfect gentleman. "I'll look forward to seeing you both later this evening."

Her father stared after her, like a teenage boy with a crush. With the uncharitable feelings swirling inside her, Brooke felt like the Grinch.

Even worse, she could feel the beginnings of a migraine stealing up on her. She'd been clenching her jaw.

"Are you okay, angel?" Daddy asked, looking at her in concern.

"I think I'm getting a headache," she admitted.

"Not a migraine, I hope."

She shrugged. "I'd better go take a pill and lie down for a little while." So much for getting to see the tree-lighting ceremony. Her only consolation was the knowledge that at least Olivia would be busy in the kitchen and out of their hair.

Her father put an arm around her. "Come on. I'll walk you to your room."

Olivia felt her smile fading as she returned to the kitchen. Interested as she was in James Claussen, much as she enjoyed his company, this wasn't going to go where she'd hoped it would. His daughter didn't want her in their lives and was going to bar the door; that was plain to see.

She wished there was something she could do to win Brooke over, to show her that she wasn't out to replace her mother, but she didn't know what. Oh, children were so hard to deal with! Once they got taller than their parents, they suddenly thought they were in charge.

Eric entered the kitchen just as she banged a pot onto the stove. "Whoa, I guess I'd better leave before you start throwing knives around. What's wrong?"

"Nothing." Nothing she was going to tell her son about, anyway.

"That's some nothing," he said.

"Don't mind me, dear. I'm just having a moment." She'd had her share of moments on Christmas Eve in the past, but she'd always pulled herself out of them. There was too much to be grateful for and she refused to wallow around in self-pity. She pinned a smile on her face. "I'm fine."

He looked at her dubiously.

"Did you want a cup of coffee? A snack?"

He shook his head. "Nope. I came in to see if there's anything you need me to do before I go camp out at the reception desk."

Thinking how blessed she was to have such a good son made it easy to turn her smile into something genuine. "No, Margaret got all the prep work done for me earlier this afternoon. Everything's under control here." Including her emotions.

"Okay," he said.

Fresh snow was falling, and he'd probably rather be out doing a quick run around the property on his cross-country skis. But she'd given her front desk staff the day off, which meant extra work for her and Eric. He never complained, though.

He did so much around the lodge, and she knew he loved the place. But sometimes she wondered— would he have remained here if his father hadn't died?

This was hardly the time for a serious discussion when she had Christmas Eve dinner to prepare, but the question tumbled out, anyway. "Sweetheart, would you still be here if your father had lived?"

He blinked in surprise. "What kind of question is *that*?"

She leaned against the stove and studied him. He was an attractive young man, his eyes serious behind the glasses. Even as a child, he'd often worn that same serious expression, contemplating a book or looking out the window at the snow. Once, when he was about five, she'd asked him what he was thinking and he'd replied, "I'm wondering what the mountains would be like if there was never snow." He could have become a scientist, a doctor, any number of things. Instead, he'd taken business classes and helped her run the lodge. They had a limited staff and did most of the work themselves.

"I sometimes worry that I tied you down here," she said.

He sighed loudly, as if she'd said the most ridiculous thing in the world. "What makes you say that?"

"You could have done anything."

"I *am* doing something. I'm helping you run the

best lodge in the state." He came over and hugged her. "I like it here."

"Do you really?"

"Of course." He kissed her cheek. "I'll see you later." And then he was gone.

And she had a big meal to prepare for her guests. But as she worked, she kept thinking about her oh-so-responsible older son. He was heavily invested in running the lodge and someday it would be his. Well, and Brandon's if he wanted a share in it. But she hated the thought of him here alone, always observing other people's lives with no life of his own. He needed someone.

"Oh, Lord," she prayed, "there must be a nice girl somewhere out there for my son. Help him find her." She was giving up on herself, but Eric was young and had his whole life before him. Seeing him happy would be the best Christmas present she could ask for. "In the new year," she added, deciding she'd better make her request more specific.

Yes, if Eric could find someone and be happy, then she could be happy. She resolutely pushed the image of James Claussen's smiling face from her mind. The next generation was what mattered, not the longings of a woman well past her prime.

And yet there was James again, refusing to be ignored. "Oh, brother," she muttered. It was foolish to fall in love at her age but she was well on her way. Still, how could a woman not fall for a real live Santa?

Chapter Thirteen

Merry Christmas, Darling

John was relieved to learn that Holland's wrist wasn't broken. Still, the sprain was enough to ruin the holiday mood, even once she got some painkillers inside her, even after he'd run to the local drugstore and picked up an ice pack. Now she sat on their bed, propped up with pillows, the TV tuned to reruns of *House Hunters*.

"Are you sure you don't feel like going out to the Christmas Eve ceremony?" he asked. "It might make you feel better."

"I feel fine right here," she said. Her cell phone rang. She checked caller ID, then ignored the call, tossing the phone onto the nightstand.

"Who was that?"

"Just someone from work."

"On Christmas Eve?"

"Most people have to work on Christmas Eve, John."

He bristled at her condescending tone of voice. "A lot of people get Christmas Eve off."

"And the rest of us have to specially ask for it off."

From her tone of voice, he could tell she was wishing she hadn't asked for the day off, hadn't come up here.

He sat on the edge of the bed. "I'm sorry you fell."

"Me, too. If only those bratty kids weren't staying here."

What happened at the ice rink had been an accident, but John decided this wasn't the time to mention that. Instead, he took her hand.

"You should go to the Christmas Eve thing," she said.

"Without you?" What would be the point of that?

"You can take pictures."

"No, this is our romantic weekend together. I'm not leaving you," he said. He scooted over and put an arm around her.

"I know you want to go. Anyway, you'll be bored stiff hanging around the room."

"I could never be bored with you," John insisted.

"You could today. I just want to take a nap."

By herself, without him. He got that message pretty clearly. "Oh. Well, okay."

"Just go to the tree lighting," she said. "I'll rest here and be fine by dinner."

He nodded and got off the bed, and she immediately spread out, pulling the coverlet over herself, focusing once more on the TV. This sure wasn't how he'd envisioned them using the bed.

Feeling dismissed and frustrated, he grabbed his coat and left the room. *Never mind,* he told himself. She'd feel better by dinner. And she'd feel really good when she saw the ring. Cheered by that thought he left the lodge and joined the crowd of holiday revelers as they surged toward the town square.

This was quite a sight. The town was lit up like a movie set, all colored lights and fat red ribbons. A brass quartet dressed in Dickensian costumes was playing "Joy to the World." People of all ages and sizes milled around, clad in parkas and mittens and knit caps. Many were nursing to-go cups, and the aroma of the coffee joined with that of roasted chestnuts and danced around his nose as he took pictures on his cell and sent them to Holland.

"It's wonderful, isn't it?" said a voice at his elbow.

He turned to see Missy Monroe smiling shyly up at him, her glasses frosted and her blue hair peeking out from underneath her cap. Next to her, the kids gazed around, enthralled.

"Yeah, it is."

"How's your girlfriend?" Missy asked. "I hope she didn't break her wrist."

"Nope. Just a sprain."

"Oh, good. I'm glad it's not broken. I guess she didn't feel like coming out, huh?"

"She's resting."

Missy nodded, taking that in. She looked so sad.

"It wasn't your fault," John said.

"It was my kids'. Same thing."

"Hey, it could've happened to anyone." He'd already told her that, but found himself repeating it, not wanting her to feel guilty.

"I know. I wish it hadn't been us, though." She put an arm around Lalla. "But they're just kids. I couldn't get too mad at them."

"Absolutely not."

"Mommy, look! There's Santa!" Lalla pointed to the gazebo. "I *told* you I saw him," she said to Carlos.

The band had finished its song, and now the town's mayor was welcoming everyone and wishing them all a merry Christmas. "And, as you can see, Santa has stopped by to join us."

"Ho, ho, ho," said the man in the red suit. "Have all you boys and girls been good this year?"

"Yes!" cried all the children in the crowd.

"Yes!" squealed Lalla, jumping up and down. Next to her, her brother frowned.

"Well, then, you can expect a visit from me later on," Santa announced. "But first, I want to hear you all sing my theme song."

That was the cue for the brass quartet to play "Santa Claus Is Coming to Town." The crowd began to sing along, including John and Missy, who hugged each of her kids. She smiled at John and he smiled back, feeling as though he was in some old-fashioned movie.

Santa made his exit and one of the local pastors

offered a prayer. The band played the introduction to "Silent Night" and once again the crowd began to sing, many people using the lighter app on their cell phones and waving them back and forth.

Holland would've said this was corny, and she would've been right. But it was also fun. And singing that old Christmas carol reminded John of the real meaning of the season, something he had to admit he'd lost track of. There was a quality about this town that made a guy stop and think, made him remember what was important in life. Once more he envisioned himself experiencing this place someday with his own kids.

But could he see Holland doing this? Hmm. Probably not.

Okay, so she sneered at small-town celebrations. So what? It was all right that they saw some things differently. A couple didn't have to have *everything* in common.

Look at his folks. His dad loved football and his mom hated it. That hadn't kept them from being happily married for forty years. Anyway, he and Holland had plenty in common. They never lacked for stuff to do on the weekend; they'd have plenty to keep them together once they were married.

The song ended and Missy said, "This is super, isn't it? Just like a Christmas movie, only it's real."

John couldn't help noticing that she didn't use the word *corny*. "Yeah, I was thinking exactly the same thing."

Missy was looking around in delight. She was so

easily pleased. The smallest activity was a big adventure. She'd probably have loved that sleigh ride.

Whoa. Where were his thoughts going? John pulled away from them in shock. *No, no,* he assured himself, *you weren't having disloyal thoughts.* It was just…an observation. And Holland would have enjoyed this ceremony. If she didn't have a sprained wrist she would've been right here with him.

"I need to get back to the lodge and see how Holland's doing," he said to Missy. *Holland, my girlfriend. The woman I'm in love with.*

Missy blinked. "Oh. Yeah. Sure. I hope she's feeling better."

"Me, too," he said, and hurried off.

He found Holland propped up in bed, drinking tea and still watching TV, her cell phone to her ear. "John's here. I've gotta go…I will," she added impatiently, and ended the call. "So, how was it?" she greeted him.

"Impressive. I sent you pictures."

She dutifully brought them up on her phone. "Wow, what a zoo. I'm glad I didn't go."

"I think you had to be there." He joined her on the bed. "How's your wrist?"

"Better, thanks to the pain pills."

"I'm glad," he said, relieved. "Dinner's in about half an hour."

She nodded. "Great. I'm starving."

That was a good sign.

Holland changed into a clingy black dress with a sexy neckline. "Zip me up?" she asked, lifting her hair and turning her back to him. Just as if they were already married, he thought and smiled.

He obliged and she did a little spin so he could get the full effect. "How do I look?"

"Incredible," he said.

"You're sweet," she told him, and gave him a kiss.

Oh, yeah, and what a kiss it was. It sealed and solidified everything in John's mind once more. For a while there, it had felt as if they'd taken a wrong turn, gotten lost in an unfamiliar neighborhood, but that feeling was gone now and they were back on familiar ground. *He* was back on familiar ground. The fancy dinner would be the perfect setup for the big moment. Suddenly he felt like a little kid on Christmas Eve, anxiously awaiting the arrival of Santa. *Oh, yeah, Truman. You knocked it out of the park this time.*

"I'm thirsty," Lalla said as Missy shepherded her children back inside the lodge after the Christmas Eve celebration downtown.

It wasn't hard to guess what had inspired her daughter's sudden thirst, and Missy led the children over to the little table at the far end of the lobby, where Olivia kept hot water, disposable cups and all manner of teas, hot chocolate and hot cider mix. It was one more treat that added to the specialness of the place. Not that she didn't buy hot chocolate mix herself, but when she did, she doled it out carefully. Here it was on tap, and the kids were having a great time taking advantage of it.

She noticed Brittany, one of the Williams girls, sprawled on the couch, frowning as she talked on her cell phone. "It's so lame up here," the girl complained.

Lame? Really?

"Mom wouldn't give me any more money."

She was lucky she had a mom.

"No, the pool is super. But it's just old people and little kids. I don't know why Mom and Dad brought us up here."

So you could have a special Christmas together?

The girl suddenly became aware of Missy standing nearby gawking at her, obviously eavesdropping, and she blushed and ended the call.

Don't say anything, Missy cautioned herself. *It's none of your business.* But she couldn't seem to stop herself. "I guess it can seem kind of boring being stuck up here without your friends."

Brittany shrugged.

"Do you usually go somewhere?"

"To my cousins'."

So that was the problem. She missed her own kind. "How come your parents decided to come up here?"

Another shrug. "They thought it would be good to do something different, just us."

Missy nodded. "I guess that would be like having to eat chocolate every day."

Brittany looked at her as if she was nuts.

"Oh. You like to eat chocolate every day?"

"Well, duh."

"Yeah, me, too. Although after a while, it's just chocolate. No big deal. I mean, if you have it every day."

Brittany was eyeing her with great suspicion now, suspecting a grown-up lecture.

"I gotta confess, I'm jealous of you," Missy confided.

"Huh? Why?"

"Because you get chocolate every day."

"No, I don't," Brittany protested.

"Yeah, you do. Or something like it. What I'm saying is that sometimes people don't appreciate what they've got when they've never been without it, you know? You have parents. And they're not drunk. And they're doing stuff for you and your sister."

Brittany's eyes got increasingly bigger as Missy talked, but she didn't say anything.

"Yeah," Missy said, looking to where her children stood, guzzling their treats, "half the time my mom spent Christmas morning sleeping off a hangover. I never even knew there were places like this when I was growing up."

Brittany bit her lip and studied her phone.

"But I guess I can see how you'd get bored. Like I said, when you've had chocolate all your life, after a while it's just chocolate. Except I wish I'd had parents like yours."

Brittany was frowning now. Missy had probably ticked her off. Lectures, like good chocolate, were wasted on teenagers. "Sorry I said anything. It really sucks when people say stuff that makes you feel bad."

"Yeah, it does," the girl muttered.

What were you thinking? Missy scolded herself. *That she'd burst into tears and thank you for wising her up?* Real life wasn't some Christmas movie where everyone learned an important lesson and came out a better person. In real life, good parents were often wasted on bratty kids, and kids like her, kids who would've given anything for a decent family, got stuck with a single mom who preferred partying over baking cookies with her daughter.

Missy cleared her throat. "Uh, guess I'll let you get back to talking on your phone."

Brittany looked as if that would be fine with her.

"Come on, guys," Missy said to the kids, "let's go to our room. But don't run," she added. "We don't want to spill on the carpet." She'd already made one mess here in the lobby. She didn't want to be responsible for any more.

On their way down to the dining room, John stopped under an archway to take advantage of the mistletoe hanging there. "Merry Christmas, babe," he said to Holland, and kissed her.

The sound of approaching children's voices had her pulling away before their lips had barely touched. He glanced up and saw Missy and her kids coming down the hall.

"Let's get to the dining room before those kids

mow me over," Holland said, striding for the elevator.

John followed her, wishing they'd had longer under the mistletoe. But never mind. After dinner they'd have plenty of time for romance, and with the ring she was getting, Holland would really be in the mood.

The dining room looked festive with all the floral arrangements on the tables and the fancy china. And the crystal winked in the candlelight. Delicious smells seeped out from the kitchen—roasting turkey and sage, brewing coffee. The guy John assumed was Olivia Wallace's son and a couple of young hirelings were putting bread baskets out on all the tables and the aroma of freshly baked rolls made John's taste buds spring a leak.

Many of the guests were already seated at tables. John smiled a greeting at the Williamses. The two older women were also seated, wearing fancy dresses and jewelry. Vera waved at John, and he waved back.

He led Holland to a table for two in a quiet corner of the room. "Turkey dinner tonight with all the trimmings, I hear," he said as they sat down.

Holland immediately dug into the bread basket. She picked up a crescent roll, pulled off a segment and popped it in her mouth. "Oh, this is yummy." She broke off a piece and fed it to him.

John smiled as he chewed, as pleased as if he'd made the roll himself. "I'm glad I found this place."

"Are you looking for compliments?" she teased.

"Well, yeah," he admitted.

"Yes, it's a fun place to visit."

He took a roll and examined it. "I could see myself living someplace like this." Then he remembered her reaction, during the sleigh ride, to his suggestion of a cabin in the mountains. "In town, I mean."

She made a face. "You've got to be kidding."

"No. What's wrong with Icicle Falls?"

She took another bite of her roll. "It's okay to visit but it's kind of...hokey. And it's so small. I'd get tired of going to the same restaurant over and over. Seeing the same people."

"Don't we do that in Seattle?" John argued. "We keep going to the same clubs, hang out with the people we work with." Well, mostly the people she worked with. And some of them weren't his favorites. Even though he and Holland were a couple, it seemed that half the time the other guys were sizing him up as competition...and he always had the impression he never came off as much of a threat.

"That's different," she insisted. "We can go somewhere different anytime we want. Anyway, Seattle's more...I don't know. More..."

"Sophisticated?" he supplied.

"Yeah. It's just classier."

Everything had to be the best with Holland. Expensive, classy. She always had to feel she drove the best, wore the best, *was* the best. Of course, there was nothing wrong with wanting to be the best, right? Across the room, Missy and her kids had joined the Spikes at their table and everyone was laughing.

Holland followed his gaze. "That woman is such a bottom-runger."

Bottom-runger. Holland used it freely to describe taxi drivers, construction workers and anyone who pissed her off. John had used it a few times himself, often when referring to one of Holland's sleazy coworkers. But it bothered him that she'd use it to describe Missy.

Granted, Missy wasn't the kind of woman either of them would have known growing up or normally hung out with. But watching her, John had to ask himself why. Why *wouldn't* they associate with the likes of Missy Monroe? She was kind, honest, hardworking. Okay, so she didn't have a high-paying job or expensive clothes. What did that matter in the long run? And so what if she didn't work in a downtown office building or move in their circle of friends? It was good to widen the circle, wasn't it? After all, a person couldn't have enough friends.

"Isn't that a little snobbish?" he chided.

Holland raised an eyebrow at him. "Well, how would you describe someone like that?"

"How about nice? Hardworking?"

Holland rolled her eyes and shook her head. "If you say so. But she looks like a loser to me and she's got bratty kids. Why would I want to hang out with someone like that?"

John frowned. Talk about making a snap judgment.

"Why are we talking about her, anyway?" Holland said, flashing a hundred-watt smile at him.

Good point. This was their night. Still, her attitude toward Missy rankled.

But that was just because she didn't really know Missy. "If you took the time to talk to her you'd probably like her."

"Maybe," Holland conceded but not very convincingly.

Everyone has faults, John reminded himself. And wasn't that what love was all about, caring for somebody in spite of his or her imperfections? Too bad Holland and Missy hadn't started off on better terms. They might even have become friends.

But that wasn't going to happen. After Christmas everyone would leave the lodge and go their separate ways. The thought made him wistful.

Of course, that was crazy. He'd just met these people. And yet so many of them felt like friends in the making, people he'd want to see more of. It had to be the town. Icicle Falls had cast a holiday spell over him.

Olivia's son arrived at their table now, setting down a carafe of wine and wishing them bon appétit.

"Thank you," Holland said sweetly, and gave John another killer smile. Oh, yeah. Merry Christmas.

He poured wine for both of them, then raised his glass to her. "Here's to a great Christmas and an even greater new year," he said.

"I'll drink to that," she said, and took a sip of her wine.

The staff made their way around the tables, serving family-style. Big bowls of mashed potatoes and stuffing appeared, followed by platters of turkey. Then there were all the trimmings—pickles and olives, cranberry relish, roasted vegetables. A veritable feast.

John took a bite of his stuffing. Oh, wow, even better than his mom's. He grinned across the table at Holland, who was forgetting her diet and now on her second dinner roll. She was obviously enjoying herself. Just wait until they got back to the room later and had champagne and those Sweet Dreams chocolates he'd picked up. By then Holland would be wearing the diamond Santa had delivered. He gave himself a mental pat on the back. *Truman, you are brilliant.*

This is what Christmas is supposed to be like, Missy told herself, watching her kids chow down on turkey and stuffing (the real thing, not the kind out of a box like Missy always made). The Spikes, her dinner companions for tonight, had been interested in her life and were encouraging when she shared her plans to make something of herself in the beauty business.

Now she heard all about their children—the daughter who had died of cancer two years earlier, and the son who had to go to Arizona to do Christmas with his in-laws this year.

"So we decided to treat ourselves this Christmas," Mrs. Spike concluded, "and see what interesting new people we might meet. And I'm so glad we did."

Did that mean she thought Missy was interesting? Missy couldn't help smiling. She'd always wanted to be, but really, it seemed she was far too busy surviving to think about being interesting.

With everyone served, Olivia Wallace had come out of the kitchen, visiting with all the guests. She made Missy's night by paying special attention to Lalla, asking her what her favorite part of the meal was, listening as Lalla described their afternoon adventures and the Santa sighting downtown.

"You never know," Olivia told Lalla. "Santa might pay us a visit tonight before he gets in his sleigh and starts making his rounds."

That was enough to make Lalla dance in her seat. "I love Santa!"

Even Carlos the skeptic was looking hopeful.

"Meanwhile," Olivia said, pulling two candy canes from the pocket of her red-and-white-striped apron, "here's a little something for you children to enjoy."

"Candy canes!" Lalla squealed.

"Thanks," Carlos added, smiling as if he'd just had a close encounter with Santa himself.

Missy was smiling, too. Sitting at the table with these friendly people, having Olivia fuss over her daughter—she could almost pretend that she was an average, middle-class girl. She didn't care what it cost. She was coming back every Christmas.

She sneaked a peek at John Truman and his girl-friend. They weren't talking very much, just concentrating on their dinner. If *she* was eating dinner with John, she'd have plenty to talk about.

She pushed away the jealous thought. Someday she'd find a man like John Truman. There had to be another one like him somewhere.

The only problem was, she didn't want a man *like* him. She wanted *him*. And she had about as much chance of getting him as her son had of getting a dog.

Chapter Fourteen

Santa Claus Is Coming to Town

After two helpings of turkey and stuffing, James was almost in a stupor but he shook himself out of it when Olivia stopped by their table.

"How was your meal?" she asked.

She smiled at everyone but her smile lingered on James. Boy, did that give him a holiday glow. A smile from Olivia Wallace was better than hot buttered rum.

"It sure beats Dad's cooking," Dylan joked.

"I think if my wife was still alive she'd have been asking for your stuffing recipe," James said. But his mention of Faith tarnished the holiday glow, and he found his smile growing weak.

Olivia laid a gentle hand on his shoulder. "I still miss George. And every year, when I make my yule log cake, I can feel him hovering over my shoulder the way he used to, hoping to snitch some frosting." She sighed. "The holidays can be hard. But I try to fill them with happy memories, and I remind myself that Christmas is all about good news—the Savior who came to give us hope."

He needed to remember that. "Faith wouldn't want us moping."

"No time for moping," Olivia said. "We're about to start serving dessert." She looked around the table. "But where's your daughter?"

"She's in her room lying down. She sometimes gets bad headaches, I'm afraid."

"Oh, the poor girl."

"I'm going to stop by her room in a little while," James said. "She took a pill this afternoon. Hopefully she'll feel well enough to come down soon."

"If not, we'll save her some food," Olivia promised. "Meanwhile, I think you'd better go find Santa," she added with a conspiratorial wink.

"I'm on my way," he said. He pointed a warning finger at his son. "And don't eat my piece of the yule log while I'm gone."

Dylan turned into the picture of innocence. "I wouldn't think of it."

"Yeah, right."

James slipped out of the dining room unobserved, just an old man probably going in search of the john. He always felt a little like Clark Kent when he went to change into his Santa suit. An average guy, nothing special.

Faith had always insisted he was special. "You have the biggest heart of any man I've ever known," she used to say. Not really, but he'd been flattered that she thought so. Still, when he came back in his Santa suit, he was a different person. Then he felt as though he could pick up the whole hurting world and carry it on his shoulders. Well, that was how he used to feel, before he lost Faith.

Tonight, however, a glimmer of the old feeling was creeping up on him. In a few minutes, he'd be back in the dining room, not as plain old James Claussen, but as Santa, the embodiment of the kindness and good cheer that Christmas held for all who believed. He began to whistle "Joy to the World" as he climbed the stairs to his room. Maybe that was what he'd needed, just a little bit of holiday hope.

He stopped by his daughter's room and tapped on the door. It took her a few minutes to answer, and when she did her hair was mussed and her face flushed, a sure sign that she'd been sleeping.

"You feeling any better?" he asked.

She nodded and rubbed her forehead. Nothing like a nap and a couple of those magic pills the doctor prescribed. "I think it helped that I caught it early. What time is it?" He told her and she sighed. "I missed dinner?"

"Not all of it. They're serving dessert now. You feel like coming down?"

"If I can wake up properly. Don't wait for me."

"I hate to see you miss all the fun, angel." This had been her idea and she'd been so excited about it. "But if you're not up for it, don't push yourself," he said hastily.

"I'll try to get down." She kissed him on the

cheek. "You'll be great, Daddy. Now you need to change and get back downstairs before everyone finishes dessert and scatters."

Good point. He nodded and hurried next door to his room.

Once there it didn't take him long to put on his Santa suit. Brooke had already stuffed the big velveteen bag full of the presents they'd purchased and left it sitting by the door. Efficient woman that his daughter was, he knew she'd have the names of all the guests printed on the gift tags. All he'd have to do was ho-ho-ho and hand them out.

He hefted the bag over his shoulder and went out the door, bubbling over with holiday cheer. Back down the stairs, across the lobby, down the hall. Now he could hear the burble of voices coming out to him from the dining room. He strode through the double doors and produced a hearty, "Ho, ho, ho."

"Santa!" cried little Lalla. She jumped from her seat and threaded her way through the tables at a run, her mother after her. "Santa, Santa!"

Too bad nobody was capturing this on film, James thought, watching the child dart toward him. She was the embodiment of the holiday in her little red dress, which, as she got closer, he saw had chocolate frosting stains on it. The cheap tiara on her head was askew and her cornrows were bouncing in all directions. Her smile lit up her entire face.

James was ready for her. He set down his bag of goodies, knelt and opened his arms wide, letting the child run into them. "Well, if it isn't Lalla Monroe," he said. "And don't you look pretty tonight."

"I knew you'd find us," she said, wrapping her arms around his neck and hugging him fiercely.

"Lalla, you're going to choke Santa," her mother cautioned.

"She's okay," James said. "Do you know what I have in my sack?" he asked the child.

"Presents!"

"That's right. I have presents for everyone here."

"Where's my grandma?" she asked, peering around the room.

"Oh, don't you worry about that," James told her. "Old Santa isn't going to let you down. But first, would you like to help me give out some presents?" She nodded eagerly and he set her down. "All right, then." He stood and slung his bag of goodies over his back again and held out a hand to the child. "Why don't you come along with me and you can give all the people here their gifts."

Lalla grinned, and her mother thanked him, then returned to her table. James positioned himself in the middle of the room and dug a present out of his sack. "Well, it looks like I have something here for Vera Winston."

Vera brought a hand to her chest in surprise.

"You didn't come sit on my lap this year," James teased, making her giggle and her friend roll her eyes. "But I have a gift for you, anyway." He gave the small present to Lalla. "Can you deliver this for Santa?"

Lalla nodded solemnly and walked over with the present.

"Thank you, Santa," said Vera. "And thank you, Lalla."

"I like helping," Lalla said.

"And, oh, look, even though I suspect your partner in crime has been a little naughty this year, Santa has something for her, too." James walked the present over and delivered it, and Jane smiled in delight.

And so it went, James making the rounds, dropping off presents with Lalla as his able assistant. Finally there were only three presents left in the sack.

James took out one of the games. It wasn't hard to tell that this one was for Lalla since Brooke had wrapped it in paper decorated with little girl angels. "Let's see what I have here. Oh, something for Lalla."

"For me?"

"You *have* been a good little girl, haven't you?"

"Oh, yes."

"Then this is for you."

She took the present and hugged it to her. "Thank you, Santa." Then her smile faltered. "I guess I didn't get a grandma."

Olivia had seated herself at a nearby table and now she came up to Lalla and slipped an arm around her. "Lalla, I'm the other half of your present. I'm going to be your grandma tomorrow and we're going to bake cookies. Would you like that?"

Lalla smiled, wide-eyed, and Olivia went back to her chair and pulled the child onto her lap.

Meanwhile, her brother sat sullenly in his seat, determined to be a tough sell. James removed the other game from his sack and walked up to Carlos. "I have something for you, too, young man."

"Thanks," the boy mumbled, and accepted the gift. No smile.

"But that's not the real present." James turned and motioned to where Eric Wallace had positioned himself outside on the patio. Eric opened one of the big glass doors and came in with the dog on a leash, a big red ribbon around his neck. The boy let out a gasp.

"I think you wanted a dog for Christmas," James said.

The words weren't even out of his mouth before Carlos was racing over to the animal. The dog caught his enthusiasm and, overjoyed, jumped on him, taking him down and licking him, the boy's delighted laughter filling the room. Meanwhile, the guests all clapped and smiled. Oh, yeah, as the old commercial said, it was a real Kodak moment.

James looked in Missy's direction, expecting a smile. No smile. Not even a hint of a smile. In fact, she seemed ready to cry. Uh-oh.

Brooke had gotten a glass of water, then sat in a chair for a few minutes, just to see how she was feeling. Well, it could be worse, that was for sure. Still, how disappointing. Christmas Eve, and what was she doing? Crawling out from the black hole of a migraine. Thank God she'd brought her pills and taken them in time. Otherwise, she wouldn't have surfaced until after Christmas Day. The worst of it was gone, but she still felt as if she'd been hit by a truck. This wasn't the kind of Christmas memory she wanted. Well, she'd go downstairs, get herself a cup of tea and watch Santa in action. That would perk her up.

Santa…presents…kids…*dog!* She'd never told Missy about the dog! Missy wouldn't know they'd gotten her landlady's permission for her to have a dog, wouldn't know that pet insurance, obedience training and a year's worth of dog food were taken care of. What would she do when she saw her son's present from Santa? What would she say to her son? Oh, this wasn't good.

Brooke bolted from her chair and dashed for the door. She hoped she got down to the dining room before Santa wound up with the Christmas equivalent of a pie in the face.

"What are you going to name your dog?" Eric Wallace asked Carlos as he handed him the leash.

"Buddy," Carlos said enthusiastically. "You like that name, boy?"

The dog barked and wagged his tail. Yep, over at that end of the dining hall it was a perfect holiday picture. Not so much where Missy was standing, though. Brooke must not have had a chance to give her the good news.

James hurried to tell her, but he wasn't fast enough. She'd already joined her son and was bending over him, talking to him, her voice low, her expression pained.

"Wait!" James called, but he was too late.

Carlos glared at his mother, then got to his feet, yanked open the glass door and ran outside, taking the dog with him. Missy rushed out after them, and the rest of the diners exchanged glances.

"Oh, dear," Vera said.

Oh, dear was right.

And now Brooke had arrived. "Oh, no," she groaned.

"Don't worry," James told her. "Your brother's on it." Sure enough, Dylan was out the door in hot pursuit, and behind him came Eric Wallace, now carrying a flashlight.

Brooke sighed heavily. "I'm so sorry. I just couldn't find her this afternoon. And then..."

"I know," James said, giving her arm a comforting pat. "It'll be okay."

"Did I miss the other presentation?" she asked, lowering her voice.

"No, you're just in time." At least that should go off without a hitch.

Oh, man. Poor Missy. Too bad John hadn't heard what everyone was planning. He could've told Mr. Claussen that Missy wasn't allowed to have dogs where she lived. Here she'd arranged this special Christmas for her kids and now it was wrecked.

"How embarrassing," Holland said. "That's why people shouldn't plan surprises for other people."

Uh-oh. "Not all surprises are bad," John argued.

"No, not all," she agreed.

"I mean, coming up here was a *good* surprise... wasn't it?"

"Yeah. Except it wasn't a total surprise. I knew we were coming." She shook her head. "I feel sorry for her, being publicly embarrassed like that."

John suspected embarrassment was the least of Missy's concerns. "I hope they can work it out." He wished there was something he could do. He'd offer to keep the dog for Missy, but his condo didn't allow dogs over thirty pounds and that one was way over the limit.

"How hard being stuck raising kids on her own," Holland said, showing her softer side and confirming to John that he had, indeed, picked the right woman. "I'd hate to be her, especially now."

And with no one to comfort her. Tidings of comfort and joy, where were they when you needed them? He wished again that he could come up with some brilliant idea. Maybe tomorrow he and Holland could put their heads together and think of something. It didn't seem fair for him to be so happy when a nice woman like Missy was so miserable. Tomorrow, for sure, they'd figure out how to help her, he vowed. It was Christmas. He wanted every-one to be as happy as he was.

Carlos was like a dart, one minute visible in the pool of light surrounding the lodge, and the next swallowed in the darkness of the woods. Frantically calling his name, Missy dashed after her son, the cold biting her arms even as parental guilt gnawed at her heart. Choosing that moment to tell Carlos they couldn't keep the dog had been dumb. She should have at least let him enjoy the animal tonight and found a way to break the bad news in the morning. Now she'd ruined his Christmas beyond repair. And, on top of that, he'd probably catch a cold running around out here in just his jeans and that lightweight red sweatshirt. Or worse. He could easily get lost. She was already half-lost herself. God help her, she was a terrible parent.

"Carlos!" she shouted. "Come back!" Of course he didn't and she could hardly blame him. Tears of reproach streamed down her cheeks. "Carlos!"

She could hear other voices calling her son now, too—Dylan Claussen's from somewhere off to her left, and Eric Wallace's.

An arc of light from an approaching flashlight searched the trees and then Eric ran past her in long-legged strides, calling over his shoulder, "Don't worry, we'll find him."

It was so dark out here in the woods. She called her son again but he didn't answer. The moments seemed to stretch into eternity. Finally she heard the dog bark. She picked up her pace, stumbling through the snow.

Relief flooded her when the arc of light from the flashlight broke through the trees and she saw Eric approaching, holding Carlos, who was now wrapped in Eric's coat, howling like a banshee and squirming to get away, the dog frolicking beside them. Missy understood that feeling. She'd had her share of times growing up when she'd wanted to run away, too.

She hurried over to them and fell in front of him, throwing her arms around him. "Baby, you can't go running off like that," she said to Carlos.

He jerked away from her. "I hate you!"

She'd said the same thing to her own mother when Mom had tied one on the Christmas Eve Missy was twelve. She'd been too old for Santa by then. But she'd still longed for the kind of traditional Christmas other people enjoyed and had tried her best to bring it about. She'd walked to the food bank, where she'd scored Christmas cookies and a ham from the friendly volunteer who knew her and her mother. She'd even found a candle at the local Goodwill store, which she'd wrapped with red ribbon and put under a tiny, scraggly tree. She'd found it at the edge of their public housing development, uprooted it and stuck it in a pail.

But Mom had never gotten around to putting anything there for her. And Mom had slept away Christmas morning. When she'd finally emerged from her bedroom she'd been hungover and cranky. And it didn't matter that they had a small ham to feast on.

Or that Mom swore she had something for Missy back in the bedroom, that she just had to remember what she'd done with it. The day was ruined.

"I hate you," Missy had snarled. "I wish you weren't my mom."

Now history was repeating itself.

No, no, no. It wasn't! She wasn't her mother, and she was working hard to give her kids a good childhood. And Christmas was *not* going to be ruined.

"Carlos, you know we can't have a dog where we live," she began.

"I hate where we live," he cried. "I hate you."

"Well, I love you," she said, "and I'm going to try my best to find a way for us to keep Buddy. Okay?" Maybe the dog could stay with her friend Miranda, just until Missy could find someplace that took pets. And that she could afford. Oh, boy. Where would that be?

Carlos looked at her, his lower lip trembling, his eyes full of hope. "For sure?"

"For sure."

He threw himself into her arms. "Thank you, Mom!"

She hugged him tightly. "You're welcome. But remember, I said I'm going to try. That's all I can do."

"It's not going to be as hard as you think to keep this dog," Eric told her as Dylan Claussen joined them.

"Oh, good," Dylan panted, "you found him. So Eric told you?" he asked Missy.

"I was just about to," said Eric.

She looked from one man to the other. "Told me what?"

"Santa talked to your landlady," Dylan explained. "She said you can have a dog. And this guy comes with pet insurance, obedience training and about fifty bags of dog food. And, if you don't have a fence, that, too."

"Or an invisible fence," Eric said. "That might be better."

She blinked. Then she tried to speak, but found it impossible. Then she burst into tears.

"Hey, it's okay," Dylan said, slipping off his coat and putting it over her shoulders.

He had no idea how incredibly okay it was. "Who did this?" she asked.

The two men exchanged grins. "Santa, of course," Dylan said.

Once the lodge was in sight, Eric gave the leash back to Carlos. "Okay, now, be firm. He needs to know who the big dog is."

Carlos took it and laughingly shoved away the friendly mutt, who was slobbering dog kisses on him.

"Take him down where the game room is, okay?" Eric said.

"Right," Carlos said happily. "Come on, boy." And then he was off, running back to the lodge, none the worse for his adventure.

"There's no way I can repay you all for this," Missy began.

"Hey, you don't repay Santa," Dylan said. "Everybody knows that. Come on, let's get back inside before we freeze our asses off."

She couldn't possibly freeze, not with the holiday glow she was feeling now.

It was hard to stay in character after what had happened with the dog, but Santa couldn't stop now, not with one more important gift to deliver. Hopefully, Dylan had that situation well in hand. Meanwhile, at least this delivery would have a positive outcome. No young man proposed publicly to a woman unless he was sure of her answer.

James forced the jovial smile back on his face and walked over to where John Truman sat with his girlfriend. "Santa still has one more present in his sack." He reached in and pulled out the black velvet ring box wrapped in red ribbon and set it on the table, next to the girlfriend.

Her eyes got big and she put a hand to her mouth. So, the boy had managed to surprise her.

John leaned forward eagerly. "Open it, Holland."

She was obviously aware of an entire dining room full of people looking on and her face turned crimson. Instead of opening the box, she shook her head and fled the table.

Stunned silence descended on the room as John stared in shock, first at the abandoned ring box and then at his departing girlfriend.

"You'd better go after her, son," James said gently.

John came to life as if someone had jabbed him

with a sprig of holly. He grabbed the ring box and sprinted out of the dining room.

Now Brooke was by James's side. "Daddy, what happened?"

"I think our young man misjudged his girlfriend's level of commitment. And I think Santa's done for the night. I'm going to go change." And with that, James took his empty bag and escaped from the dining room. *Santa has left the building.*

John caught up with Holland on the stairs. "Holland, wait!"

She kept right on going. "That was so embarrassing, John. What were you thinking?"

Was she serious? "What do you mean, what was I thinking?" Now they were in the hallway. He grasped her arm and stopped her. "I was thinking I want you to marry me. I was thinking I wanted to ask you in a really special way."

She shook her head again. "I can't marry you."

His hand fell to his side. "You…can't? I don't understand. I thought we were…"

"Dating. That's all."

"Yeah, but…" But what? He hardly knew what to say to that. "I don't get it. I thought we were serious."

"*You* were serious," she corrected him, and started for their room.

He followed her, feeling like a whipped puppy.

Once inside the room, she said, "John, I'm sorry.

I assumed we were just coming up here for some fun."

He fell onto the bed. "We were. But damn it all, Holland, I thought we were…together."

She was looking out the window, at the fireplace, her suitcase, everywhere but at him. "I don't think we're really a fit."

"You've been going out with me for how many months and you've just decided this?" Wait a minute. There had to be more to the story. "How long have you felt this way?"

She gave a one-shouldered shrug. "I don't know. Just…lately."

"Just lately, huh?" He thought of Corey Madison, one of her coworkers, who'd "just lately" been nosing around Holland. "Is there someone else?"

"No! Well…no."

"What does that mean?" His eyes narrowed. "Who were you talking to on the phone when I came back?"

"No one."

Right. "Did you really have to work late last night?"

Her cheeks were as red as Santa's hat. "Yes."

"Did you have to work *with* someone?"

"John, cut it out. I don't have to tell you every little thing I do."

"No," he said stiffly. "You don't. And obviously, you haven't been."

She gnawed her lip for a moment. Then she sighed, a big long-suffering sigh. "We should never have gotten back together. We should have stayed broken up."

He turned away from her and glared at the ring box he was still clutching. She came over to him and put a hand on his shoulder and he shrugged it off.

"I'm actually doing you a favor," she said softly.

"Thanks. That makes me feel so much better."

"I'm doing us both a favor. It's stupid to be with someone you're not totally crazy about."

"I was totally crazy about you."

There came another sigh. "I know. But I didn't feel that way back, at least not lately. I just want someone who's, I don't know, not so nice."

He looked over his shoulder at her in shock. "I'm too nice? That's why you won't marry me? Seriously, Holland?"

"I'm sorry, John. But sometimes nice is, well, boring."

"And you've been bored this weekend?"

"No, I enjoyed it. And you're sweet."

Sweet. That again. Yeah, he could see how much being *sweet* counted.

She linked an arm through his. "And I have to admit I was even a little jealous when I saw you playing in the snow with that bottom-runger."

"You know, that's a very ugly term, Holland," John said irritably.

Her eyes widened. "Well, excuse me."

"You're a snob. And that's why you're dumping me, isn't it? You think you can do better."

Her coaxing smile fell away. "Do you really want to end things like this, being mean?"

He didn't want to end things at all. "No," he said at last.

"We can still be friends, you know."

"Right," he said, refusing to look at her. Why did women say dumb shit like that?

There was a moment of painful silence, then she said, "I think I should go."

Good idea. John stood in stony silence.

"Yeah, I should definitely go," she said more firmly.

He walked over to the window and gazed out at the snowy darkness while she moved around the room, collecting her things. He heard the sound of her carry-on rolling across the carpet as she made her way to the door.

"John, I'm sorry," she said. "I really am."

He didn't trust himself to speak so he simply nodded. Then the door shut and she was gone and he was alone. He stood for a while, scowling out the window. Then he opened the champagne bottle and poured himself a glass. He turned on the fireplace and glared at the flames. *Merry Christmas. Ho, ho, ho.*

Chapter Fifteen

We Need a Little Christmas

James changed back into the clothes he'd purchased in Wenatchee earlier that day. He frowned at the Santa suit lying lifeless on the bed. He should never have let himself get talked into putting the thing back on. And he wasn't going to do it ever again. Enough was enough. He scooped it up and stuffed it in the garbage can.

Then he stretched out in the comfy armchair next to the bed and stared out the window, determined to empty his mind of the images playing over and over—Missy Monroe's upset face, her son running out into the snow. He hoped it hadn't taken too long to get the kid back inside, where it was warm. And then there was poor John Truman, who was probably in need of a therapist right about now or at least a good, strong drink. Fa-la-la.

Well, there was no sense hiding out here. James wasn't about to let a few well-laid plans going awry ruin his time with his kids. He pushed off from the chair and went back downstairs.

A few of the guests had drifted into the lobby now and the two friends, Vera and Jane, accosted him as he returned to the dining room. "That was a lovely gesture, playing Santa Claus like that," Vera told him.

"Too bad about the dog," Jane added.

"I'm afraid we didn't handle that surprise very well," James said.

"I thought I heard her tell the boy they couldn't keep it," Jane remarked.

"That's been taken care of. I actually got permission from the young woman's landlady for her to have a dog, and several of us have gone in on the expenses." Mostly him, but that was okay. He liked the spunky single mom, and helping her had been one of the things that felt right about this Christmas without his wife. This new normal...

Jane promptly fished a twenty-dollar bill from her wallet. "I'll contribute to that."

"You don't even like the girl," Vera said.

Jane pulled a frown. "I never said that. I said she looked like a Smurf."

"I want to contribute, too," Vera said, and found a ten to press into James's hand.

"That's very kind of you ladies."

"'Tis the season for giving, after all," Jane said.

"Now, if only there was something we could do for that poor young man," Vera murmured sadly.

"He's better off without that woman," Jane said.

"How do you know that?" Vera demanded.

"She frowns a lot," Jane said with a scowl. "I think we should match him up with the hairdresser."

Oh, no. No matchmaking. James wasn't getting any further involved in John Truman's affairs. He excused himself and hurried on toward the dining room.

He found Brooke babysitting Lalla, who was now hunched over a table, busy with some paper and crayons. "Have you seen John?" she asked him.

James shook his head.

"Do you think maybe you should talk to him?"

"Let's give him a chance to get over the shock of what's happened."

Most of the plates had been cleared, and he didn't see so much as a crumb of dessert. He settled for pouring himself a cup of coffee from the carafe on the table and wondered if there was any cake left.

"His girlfriend's already gone," Brooke continued. "I saw her leaving with her suitcase. Gosh, wouldn't you think he'd be sure before he asked her to marry him?"

"Sometimes people are sure because they've been seeing what they want to see."

"I'm sorry everything went so badly," she said with a sigh.

He put an arm around her. "Not everything. Everyone else loved their presents." He'd said it to console his daughter, who was looking so disappointed, but he realized he, too, needed to hear those words. In spite of things going haywire, they'd still managed to spread some holiday cheer.

At that moment Olivia joined them. "Thank you for watching our girl," she said to Brooke. "I understand you were a little under the weather. How are you feeling?"

"Much better, thanks."

"Could I bring you some food?" Olivia asked.

"Oh, no, I don't want you to go to any trouble."

"No trouble at all, my dear. I made a plate for you. I'll warm it up and be right back."

"That was nice of her," James said as Olivia hustled off.

"Yes, it was." Brooke said it almost grudgingly. She seemed to have taken a dislike to Olivia, and that was a shame because James certainly liked her.

They'd just sat down when Missy Monroe returned to the dining room, with Dylan, her face glowing with a smile worthy of a greeting card. She practically ran to their table. "The guys told me what you did. I don't know how to thank you," she said to James as her daughter scrambled into her arms, anxious to show off her picture.

"It wasn't just me. Lots of people contributed, including Jane and Vera."

Missy's eyebrows shot up. "Really?"

"Really," he said, smiling at Olivia, who was back with the plate of food for Brooke. She slid it in front of her and then, as if by unspoken agreement, everyone settled around the table.

"I'll follow you to your place with Buddy's dog

food after we check out," James said. "I can look at the fence situation while I'm there."

"We don't have a fence," Missy said. She seemed embarrassed, as if it was somehow her fault.

"Well, not to worry. I'll get that squared away with your landlady and take care of the pet deposit."

"Oh, my gosh. You have to pay a pet deposit?" Missy looked stricken.

"That's pretty standard," James said, shrugging off his generosity.

"No, that's freaking fabulous," Missy said. "No one's ever done something this kind for me. Ever." She looked around the table at everyone, her eyes sparkling with tears.

"Well, then, I'd say it's way past time," Olivia said, reaching over and giving her arm a pat.

"And if, for any reason, this doesn't work out, I'll keep the dog at my house, and you and your children can come visit," James finished.

"You really are Santa," Missy said in awe.

Not anymore. "Just one of his helpers."

"It's too bad you can't do something for that poor boy." Olivia shook her head.

"What poor boy?" Missy asked.

"Young John," Olivia said. "How awful to be publicly rejected like that."

"Rejected?" Missy repeated.

"Oh, yes, I forgot. You weren't here. I'm afraid his proposal didn't go well."

"Poor John," Missy said. "And to have it happen at Christmas."

"I can't even imagine what he must be feeling right now," Brooke said.

Losing the love of your life? James knew exactly how the kid was feeling. He suddenly became aware of his daughter looking at him. It was the same look Faith used to give him when she wanted him to do something, a look that was a mix of urging and expectation. *You absolutely must do this and I won't let you rest until you do.*

Oh, no. James drew the line at advice to the love-lorn. He shifted his gaze away from his daughter—only to find that she wasn't the only one looking at him that way. Every woman at the table wore the same expression. Here he'd thought this was a particular gift of his wife's and daughter's. Obviously, it was universal.

"James, that poor boy needs some encouragement, and you're just the man for the job," Olivia said, casting her vote of confidence.

"Absolutely." Brooke smiled, obviously happy to have an ally.

"Ladies, your concern is admirable," James said, "but in situations like this a man wants to be alone."

"But he might…do something," Missy worried.

James doubted that. "He'll be fine. He just needs time to process this."

"Can't you go help him process?" Brooke pleaded. "Dylan could go with you."

"No way," Dylan said in horror.

"Eric could go with you," Olivia offered. "I think he's downstairs with Carlos and the dog."

If the women had anything to say about it, every man in the place would be dispatched to the room of the unfortunate John Truman for a sob session and a group hug. James decided not to linger. "Okay, I'll check in on him when I go back to my room," he said, and hoped the women got the underlying message. *After that, I'm done for the night.* And he was. Suddenly, he felt tired.

"Good," Brooke said, as if that settled everything.

"Come on, sis," Dylan said, pushing away from the table. "You still owe me a game of Ping-Pong."

"Lalla, let's go find your brother and our dog." Smiling, Missy rose, too.

"You all enjoy the rest of your evening," Olivia said as the group broke up, and James found himself wondering what she was going to do now. Probably clean the kitchen. Put away the leftover cake. If there was any. Was there any?

He turned to ask and saw that she was already gathering the last of the cups and saucers. She'd be busy cleaning up and then she'd probably want to have some family time. He didn't need cake that badly.

He was about to leave when his daughter took him by the arm. "Daddy, have I told you recently what a great guy you are?"

He patted her hand. "You can stop with the flattery. I'm already doing what you ladies want."

"And what John needs," she added.

"Nobody really knows what another person needs," he said.

She looked at him thoughtfully but didn't say anything.

Once he got to John's door, he knocked, half hoping the kid wouldn't open up.

But he did. He was holding a nearly empty bottle of champagne in one hand and he gave James a tipsy smile. "Hi, Mr. Claussen." He threw the door open wide. "Come on in. Have a drink. Help me celebrate true love."

The TV was going, some action movie by the sound of it. As James came farther into the room and got a look at the screen he realized it was the old Arnold Schwarzenegger movie *True Lies*. On the bed sat a half-consumed box of chocolates.

John picked it up and offered it to James. "Want one?"

James shook his head. "No, thanks. I just stopped by to see how you're doing."

"I'm doing great," John said, falling back on the bed and sloshing champagne on himself. "Just great." And then he did what no man would willingly do if he was sober. He started crying.

James sat down on the bed and let him go at it.

"I loved her," John wailed. "I don't understand what happened."

"She wasn't the one," James said, laying a hand on his shoulder. "It's that simple. If she was, she'd have been over the moon and you two would have been drinking this together." He gently removed the bottle from John's hand and set it on the bedside table. "I understand how you feel, though. It's a sucker punch when you lose someone, a kick to the gonads."

John sniffed and nodded. "This was going to be the perfect Christmas. Tomorrow we were going to go back and show the ring to the families. Now there's nothing to show," he moaned. "What am I going to tell my parents?"

"That you haven't found the right woman yet."

John scowled. "She *was* the right woman."

"What was so right about her?"

John's eyebrows drew together. "She was…" He leaned toward James, nearly tipping himself off the bed in the process. "Hot," he finished as James rescued him.

"Okay, that's good," James said. "What else?"

"She had style, you know? And she liked to have fun. I like to have fun," he added with a scowl. "I went dancing with her every weekend."

"Did you like that?"

"Sure I did. I was with Holland."

So far James wasn't seeing much more than an infatuated young man being led around by a beautiful woman. "What other things did you like to do together?"

"Movies. We went to movies."

Movies, dancing and heat. There was a lot more to life than that. "Had you two talked about the future? Where you planned to live? If you wanted kids?"

"I want kids," John said. "I want to live in Icicle Falls." He burped loudly.

"And would your lady friend have liked that?"

"She would have. Eventually."

James nodded, taking this in.

"Everything was going so well," John lamented.

Only in his mind, James was sure. "Well, you know, sometimes things just seem to be going well. Do you think that might have been the case with you and your girlfriend?"

John scowled and shook his head vehemently. "Everything was fine. Until Corey Madison. He's a shit, but that's what she wants. You know what she told me?" John slurred. "That I'm too nice. Who breaks up with a guy 'cause he's too nice?"

A very shallow woman.

"I guess she wants…drama," John said with an exaggerated wave of his hand that made him list sideways. He struggled back up to a sitting position and frowned at the carpet. "What's wrong with women, anyway?"

"Sometimes they don't get it," James said diplomatically. "But, son, if you remember any of our conversation tomorrow, I hope you'll remember this. Things didn't work out for a reason. There's someone out there who's even better for you than the woman who turned you down, someone you're meant to be with, someone who'll take one look at that engagement ring and throw her arms around you. That's the woman you want to be with."

John ate another chocolate and nodded.

"Now, why don't you just relax and enjoy this movie," James suggested. "And I'll hang on to the rest of the champagne for you."

"We were going to drink that tonight," John mumbled, slumping back among the bed pillows.

"There'll be more opportunities for champagne in the future, don't worry," James assured him.

"My life sucks."

"Life does that sometimes," James said, and started for the door.

"Mr. Claussen," John called after him.

James turned.

"You're all right."

"So are you, son," James said, and left John getting into the chocolates.

What a night, he thought as he walked back to his room. He was pooped. Maybe he'd relax on his bed and watch the end of *True Lies.*

He'd barely gotten inside and turned on the TV when someone was knocking on the door. It would be Brooke, with or without Dylan in tow, full of fresh plans to entertain her old man. Or worse, wanting to know how his conversation with John had gone. It had gone about the way he'd expected it would. The boy was hurt and humiliated, and the only cure for that was time and another woman.

James opened his door, wishing he'd put out the do-not-disturb sign.

Instead of his daughter he saw Olivia Wallace, wearing a red dress and bearing a plate with a piece of yule log cake. Well, well. Now he was glad he hadn't put out that sign. "What have we here?"

"You never did get dessert," she said, holding the plate out to him.

"It looks great," he said, taking it. "Would you like to come in?"

"Just for a moment," she said. "After dealing with everyone's problems you're probably ready for some time to yourself."

"I am ready for a break," he admitted. "But I've spent a lot of time by myself lately. I'd appreciate some company."

She smiled and seated herself in the armchair.

He held up the bottle he'd confiscated from John. "There's just enough here for a Christmas toast. Would you like to join me?"

"That would be lovely," she said.

James snagged two plastic glasses from the bathroom and poured. There wasn't much left, only a couple of sips each. Young John was going to have a headache come morning. He handed Olivia a glass. "What shall we toast to?"

"How about to Santa?" she suggested.

"Anything but that," he said.

Her gaze landed on the red fabric overflowing the wastebasket. "Oh, I see."

"It's time for someone else to take over," James said.

"I hope you change your mind about that," she said softly. "You were a wonderful Santa."

He merely shrugged.

"Well, then, let's toast to something positive, to the new year and new beginnings.

New beginnings. Was he ready for a new beginning? *What do you think, Faith?*

Out of the blue came another knock on the door. He opened it, and there were both his kids. "Are you ready to do something?" Brooke asked.

Actually, he was.

Chapter Sixteen

All I Want for Christmas Is You

"There are a bunch of games in the lobby," Brooke said. "I thought maybe we could play some Trivial Pursuit."

"You kids go on," James said. "Your old man's going to kick back and have some downtime."

Brooke stood in the doorway, stunned. "But… it's Christmas Eve," she protested.

"And it's only eight," Dylan pointed out. "You can't be tired already, Dad."

"And Santa always stays up late on Christmas Eve," Brooke added, trying to cajole him into co-operating.

"I know," James said, "but right now Santa needs some time off for good behavior."

His daughter peered into the room and, at the sight of Olivia, her eyebrows pulled together into an angry V. "Daddy," she said sternly.

He stepped out into the hall, shutting the door behind him and said, "Brooke," just as sternly.

"You shouldn't be hanging out with that woman," she hissed. "Mom's only been gone a year! It's not right."

"Jeez, Brooke," Dylan said miserably.

"Do you think I'm not aware of that? Do you think there hasn't been a single day this whole wretched year when I haven't woken and asked myself, 'Why get up?' When I haven't wished I was dead, too? I've had a constant ache in my gut, and every time a stranger passed me on the street wearing a smile I've wanted to punch him. I haven't had a good year and I don't need to be reminded of it."

His daughter's eyes flooded with tears. "Oh, Daddy."

James immediately regretted his harsh words. He softened his voice. "I will always love your mother, always be grateful for the life we had together. But, Brooke, tonight I would like to lose the ache, hope that the new year holds some happiness. I'd like to talk with someone my age who's been where I've been. Can you understand that? Can you let me have that?"

The tears had spilled out now and were running down her cheeks. She bit her lip and nodded.

James pulled her to him and hugged her, kissed the top of her head. Then he said, "Now, why don't you go do something fun with your brother?"

She swallowed a sob and nodded again. Then she pulled away slowly, as if reluctant to leave.

"Go on, have fun," James urged. "Your mother would want you to."

From the expression on her face James doubted she was going to have any fun. He suspected there'd be more crying and for a moment he felt sorry for his son. But only for a moment. After the year he'd had, trying to keep himself going, trying to comfort his kids, Santa needed a break.

"Come on, sis," Dylan urged, and gave Brooke's arm a gentle tug.

She let him move her off down the hall, and James slipped back inside his room.

"Is everything all right?" Olivia asked.

"I think it will be," he said. "It's hard to move on."

"Especially for a daughter."

"And a dad. But damn, Olivia, I'm lonesome."

"It's hard going it alone," she said. "And I don't believe anyone should have to if they can find…" Her sentence trailed off.

She didn't need to finish it. "You know," he said, "I think I'm about done trying to go it alone. How about you?"

Her face lit up like the Christmas tree out on the front porch. "Yes, James, I am, too."

"Hello? Did you even hear the question?"

Brooke made a halfhearted attempt to bring her attention back to the game spread out between her and her brother on the upstairs lobby table.

Dylan frowned and threw down the question

card. "Okay, fine. Go mope or make a voodoo doll of Mrs. Wallace and stick pins in it. Come back when you're ready to act like an adult."

"Oh, that's cute," she snapped.

"Yeah, about as cute as the way you've been acting."

"There's nothing wrong with the way I've been acting," she protested.

"Yeah, there is and you know it. Dad's got a lot of years left in him. You want him to spend them all being miserable and alone?"

"Of course not. I just don't want him to rush into anything when he's still so vulnerable."

"Yeah, and Mrs. Wallace would be a huge mistake. That woman's a real bitch," Dylan taunted.

"You don't need to be a smart-mouth," she said, hurt.

He crossed his arms and frowned at her. "Do you want Dad to be happy or not?"

"Of course I want him to be happy!"

"Then, for God's sake, *let* him be happy. And be glad your plan worked. You brought him up here to get his mind off Mom."

"But not to forget her."

Dylan shook his head. "Do you really think he's ever going to do that? Weren't you listening to anything he said back there?"

Maybe she hadn't been.

"If you want to do something—Ping-Pong or whatever—I'll be downstairs," Dylan said, leaving her to clean up the Trivial Pursuit cards. Obviously, neither of her men wanted anything to do with her right now.

She put away the game, feeling unappreciated. All she'd wanted was for them to have a happy Christmas together, to make some new memories. Well, they were making memories, all right, but not the kind that would bring a smile to *her* face.

She wandered down to the main lobby and got a hot chocolate but it didn't help. She should just go to her room and…mope? Was that what she wanted to do? Not really, but her options had shrunk considerably.

She was still trying to decide what to do with her miserable self when Eric Wallace came in from outside, carrying a string of defunct Christmas lights. He was wearing a parka and knit cap, and his face was flushed from the cold. He had a pleasant face, a friendly face, like his mother.

"I thought you'd be with Santa," he greeted her.

"I did, too," she said. "But Santa's busy at the moment. With your mother."

His expression turned wary. "Oh."

She could feel tears stinging her eyes. Oh, no. The dam was about to burst. Sure enough, here they came. "I just don't want him to forget her," she blurted, and then covered her pathetic, bad-daughter face with her hands and howled.

A few seconds later she felt a strong arm around her shoulders. "Hey, I get it," he said. "I really do."

"I know your mother's not a bad person," she sobbed. "It's just so soon. And, oh, I'm such a bitch."

"Come on," he said, leading her down the hall. "I've got exactly what you need."

"A leash?"

He chuckled. "You'll see."

Next thing she knew, they were in the family's private quarters and he was pulling out a bottle of peppermint schnapps from an ornately carved buffet. "Old family recipe," he said.

"My mother and father used to love that stuff," she said. Now her mother wasn't here and, oh, how she missed her. She'd tried her best to plan a wonderful Christmas for her father and brother and herself. Obviously they were coping just fine. The only person who wasn't coping was her. Out came the tears again.

Eric walked over to where she stood and handed her a liqueur glass. "I think maybe we need to make a toast."

"To what?" she whimpered.

"How about to your mom?"

She drew in a shaky breath and nodded. "To my mom."

He smiled and saluted her with his glass, then tossed back his schnapps. Next he motioned to one of the wingback chairs on either side of an electric fireplace. "Tell me about your mom."

And so she did, highlighting her mother's gifts for sewing ballet costumes, making cookies, directing the Sunday school program. "Everyone loved her."

"I can see why," Eric said, and freshened their glasses.

"She loved to bake. Every Christmas we'd go on a regular baking binge, making rolled cookies, gumdrop cookies, spritz cookies. You name it, we made it. We took plates to all the neighbors. And we went to a nearby nursing home and shared them with the residents."

"A lot of good memories," Eric said. He stretched his legs out in front of him. "You ever wonder if she's looking down on you, watching what you're doing?"

Brooke shrugged. "I'd like to think she is but I suppose she's got better things to do."

He was quiet a moment, regarding her. "Do you think so? Really?"

She took a sip of her schnapps. "Yes, I do."

"So maybe she doesn't care if you try to find some happiness without her."

"That seems so cold," Brooke said with a frown.

"Or maybe she *is* watching, feeling bad that you can't let go of her enough to live the life you were meant to live."

Brooke stared into her glass and sighed. "She loved life so much. She was always so happy and she made everyone else happy, too."

"Just like her daughter," Eric said gently.

She shook her head. "It hasn't been me making Daddy happy up here."

"But it was you who brought him. Got him to play Santa, meet new people."

"Like your mother," she said reluctantly.

"Like my mother," he agreed. "Most of us live a long time. There's room in our lives for all kinds of people."

Of course he was right. Deep down, she knew it. She frowned at her glass.

"Who knows what'll happen between our parents, but right now they're enjoying themselves, and I don't think that's a bad thing. Do you?"

She sighed. "No, I suppose not. And the way my father's been this past year, I guess it's not a bad idea for him to have someone new in his life."

"How about you? Is there room in your life for someone new?"

She looked up to see Eric studying her. The spark in his eyes warmed her in places the schnapps would never reach. "Maybe there is," she said.

He smiled. "Would you like to take a walk in the snow? It's pretty out there right now with the Christmas lights on, and you still haven't seen the creek."

"You know, that sounds like a good idea," she said.

Ten minutes later they were walking in a glittering wonderland of snow. "It really is beautiful," she said. "You and your mom have created a wonderful place here."

"You should see it in the summer. What do you do on your summer vacations?"

"Different things," she replied. "Hiking, swimming, traveling."

"That's a lot to fit into a two- or three-week vacation," he said. "Or do you get more?"

"I have all summer off."

"All summer, huh? You must be a teacher."

"How'd you guess?" she joked.

"I'm psychic. I'll prove it by telling you something else about yourself. You like kids."

"Oh, that was psychic." She stole a glance at him. "Do you like kids?"

"Yeah, I do." He stretched out his hand to take hers. "And you know what? We have schools up here."

"Do tell."

"And loads of stuff to do, not just in the summer but all year-round."

"I think I may have to come back and check it out."

"Got a chocolate festival in February," he said, and smiled down at her.

"I love chocolate."

"I know a cool lodge where you and your dad and brother can stay. I bet they'll give you a deal on rooms." With a little tug, he pulled her close, boosting her heart rate. "It's pretty nice up here at New Year's, too. We have complimentary champagne."

"Mmm, that sounds tempting. What else does this place have?"

"Special attention for our guests," he said softly as he slipped his arms around her.

"I like special attention," she murmured, so he gave it to her.

It was a perfect kiss, full of hope and promise. And there, in Eric Wallace's embrace, Brooke realized the ache in her heart was more bearable.

Maybe what her father was being offered, what she was being offered, wasn't so much a chance to move on, away from her mother's memory, but to expand their hearts and lives and to honor that memory. Maybe they weren't being disloyal. Maybe they were being human.

It felt so good to talk, about the long months of caring for his wife, watching her waste away, about the loneliness he'd felt even when he was around people who cared, about how he'd lost his Christmas spirit. And it felt good to listen, too, to hear how Olivia had battled the same loneliness, how she'd struggled to run her business alone, how she'd survived.

"It wasn't easy," she said, "but by God's grace we came out of it. And I believe it made me stronger. I certainly learned I was capable of more than I thought I was. Of course, I'd give anything to have George back, but I like to think he'd be relieved and proud to see that I carried on."

What would Faith think if she could see him? Would she look at that red suit sitting in the wastebasket and be disappointed in him?

Olivia must have seen him frowning at it. She got up, pulled it out and smoothed it against her. "We all go through times when we want to give up, and sometimes we do things we regret later. I'm betting that whoever threw this out might miss it next Christmas."

He walked to where she stood and let her put it in his arms. "You've got a point," he said, and laid the suit out on the bed. "I guess maybe I'll save it. In case whoever threw it out finds he has a need for it."

She smiled at him. "I think that's an excellent idea. And you know, here's another one. Do you like hot chocolate?"

If ever there was a sign, this was it. "Sure do," James said.

"I have some. I could make us hot chocolate with peppermint schnapps."

James wiped a tear from the corner of his eye. "Sounds good to me. Lead on."

And so she did.

"Well," she said, nodding at the bottle and the two glasses sitting on the buffet in the family's private quarters. "It looks like someone else had the same idea. My son, I assume."

"'Tis the season," said James.

"Yes, it is," she agreed with a smile. "And I must say, I'd like to see him find someone and settle down. I'm ready for grandchildren."

"Me, too," James said. "Although it looks like you've inherited a granddaughter this year."

"And what a sweet one she is. I do believe Missy and her children are going to end up being a big part of my life."

"Mine, too, I hope," James said, envisioning

the three of them sitting at his kitchen table eating pizza. It was going to be a good new year.

Olivia got busy in her kitchen making hot chocolate. Nothing from a packet—this was gourmet-style with half-and-half, Dutch chocolate and powdered sugar. Once she'd added the schnapps and topped it all with whipped cream and shaved chocolate, it was a treat worthy of the Food Network.

"Oh, man," James said. "This is great."

"I'm glad you like it."

"My wife and I always used to enjoy hot chocolate with peppermint schnapps in it," he said.

"Oh." Olivia's smile shrank. "I'm sorry."

"No. Don't be. This was exactly what I needed. In fact, it's almost like I've gotten a Christmas present from Faith." Permission to start a new chapter.

Olivia beamed. "I'm so happy."

"You've given me quite a gift, Olivia."

"And that's what Christmas is about, giving true gifts, the kind that touch our hearts."

"What would touch your heart?" he asked, taking a step closer.

She dropped her gaze to the mug in her hand. "I know it sounds silly, but I miss kissing under the mistletoe."

Here was something Santa could provide. Happily. James had noticed the beribboned sprig of mistletoe hanging in the archway between her dining room and the living room. When he'd set down his mug and hers on the coffee table, he took her hand and led her to the mistletoe.

She pressed a hand to her chest. "Oh, James, my heart is fluttering like mad."

His was, too, but he smiled down at her, held her face between his hands and whispered, "Merry Christmas, Olivia." And then he kissed her.

She sighed dreamily and leaned in to him, wrapping her arms around his neck, and he drew her closer and deepened the kiss.

He was only vaguely aware of the sound of a key in a lock and a door opening. Then a voice intruded. "Ho, ho, ho. I'm home."

Chapter Seventeen

I Saw Mommy Kissing Santa Claus

That killed the moment. Olivia sprang away from James, her face as red as a Christmas stocking. James's own face burned as if he'd been toasting it in front of a roaring fire, and he suspected his cheeks were as red as Olivia's.

Even though the newcomer was a stranger, it didn't take much effort to figure out that he was Olivia's second son, Brandon. They'd talked about their families and she'd mentioned getting a call from her younger son, who'd said he'd be arriving late that night. The kid was early, and although James knew how much a parent looked forward to seeing a child he couldn't help feeling a little disappointed that this particular child had made such good time getting to Icicle Falls.

The son didn't appear too thrilled to see him, either. He frowned, saying, "I didn't know you had company, Mom." He dumped his backpack and came over to kiss her cheek. And give James the kind of who-the-hell-are-you look he'd often bestowed on some of the cretins who'd chased his daughter back in high school.

Olivia's face got even redder. "Brandon, this is James Claussen. He and his family are staying here at the lodge."

His mother had raised the boy right. He shook hands with James, saying, "Nice to meet you," although James suspected he felt the opposite.

"Nice to meet you, too," James said. "I hear from your mom that you're an impressive skier."

Brandon nodded.

"My son likes to ski, too," James said. "Did ski patrol for years."

Brandon nodded but didn't say anything. Obviously not in the mood to talk, at least not with the man he'd just caught kissing his mother.

"Well, I'm sure you'd like some time to spend with your son," James said to Olivia. "Thanks for the hot chocolate."

"And thanks for…making the evening so memorable," she said, and her cheeks turned red again.

"My pleasure," James said, and his face flamed afresh. Good Lord, he felt like some randy teenager getting the boot from an overprotective dad. "I'll see you in the morning. Good meeting you, Brandon," he said once more.

Brandon managed a polite smile.

James got out of there, hoping the next time he encountered Olivia's second son, he wouldn't be at such a disadvantage. He shook his head as he went up the stairs to his room. Kids, they sure complicated a man's life—even as grown-ups.

"It's so good to have you home," Olivia said, giving her baby a hug. "My goodness, you certainly got here fast. I didn't expect you before midnight."

"I can see that," Brandon said with a frown.

"Would you like some hot chocolate? And I've saved you a piece of yule log cake."

"Yeah, that'd be great." She hurried into the kitchen to heat up the chocolate. "I thought maybe you'd have your new girlfriend with you," she said in an attempt to keep them as far as possible from the topic of James.

Brandon followed her into the kitchen, opening the fridge and hauling out the cake. "I don't know if that's going to work. Anyway, I thought it'd be good to have just family."

Oh, dear. Here it comes. Brace for it.

"So who's that man you were kissing?"

Olivia's face felt so hot she was sure she could cook on it. "He's a new friend."

"Yeah, you were looking pretty friendly," Brandon said, and he didn't sound all that happy about it. "When did you meet this guy, Mom?"

"Recently."

"How recently?"

"In the past couple of days."

"Shit, Mom. You just met him and you're already…" Brandon didn't finish the sentence. Now his face was almost as red as hers probably was. He got busy cutting himself a piece of cake. "I mean, not to tell you what to do, but you barely know that man."

"I understand," she said stiffly. "But what I know, I like."

"So what *do* you know about this guy?" Brandon persisted.

Since when did her younger son have the right to give her the third degree? She frowned at his back. "Really, Brandon, this is not appropriate."

He turned around. "Hey, Mom, I just don't want to see you get hurt."

"I won't," she assured him. "James is a very nice man."

Brandon took a bite of cake and then pointed his fork at her. "How do you know he doesn't have a wife somewhere?"

"Because he's a widower. He came up here with his children."

"A widower, huh?"

"Yes, and as I said, he's a very nice man." She poured the heated cocoa into a mug, then added a splash of schnapps. "He played Santa at our Christmas Eve dinner." Brandon was frowning again. It was time to change the subject. "Now, how long can you stay?"

"I'm here for the week. Or until your holiday guests are gone."

She had a feeling she knew which guests he was talking about. Well, Brandon would warm up to

James once he got to know him. It was impossible not to like such a kind man.

They'd just settled at the little dining table, Brandon with another slice of cake and Olivia with more hot chocolate, when Eric came in, his face ruddy from the outdoors and a bemused smile on his lips.

"About time you got here," Brandon greeted him.

"Well, look what got dumped on the doorstep." Eric strode into the room and gave his brother a slap on the back. "If you ate all the leftover cake, I'm gonna kill you."

"There's still a piece left," Brandon told him. "So, where were you?"

"Just out wandering around," Eric said.

Out wandering around? What did that mean? Was it her imagination or was her son being secretive?

The three of them visited for another twenty minutes, catching up on everyone's news, and then Brandon said to his brother, "So, you ready for some Ping-Pong?"

"You think you can take me?" Eric retorted.

"I know I can."

"Keep the chocolate hot, Ma," Brandon said to her. "I'll be back soon."

And with that they were off. Hardly surprising. Brandon always had energy to spare. He could only sit for so long before he was anxious to be up and doing something. She watched as her two handsome young men left for some brother time. They were good boys, both of them. She found herself wishing, yet again, that they'd fall in love, settle down and produce some grandchildren.

The prospect of grandchildren brought to mind Missy Monroe and her two little darlings. Olivia smiled, thinking of the fun she was going to have making cookies with Lalla. A woman didn't have to wait for grandchildren, really, not when there were so many children in need of a grandma. And a grandpa, she mentally added, thinking of James. Of course, it was early days yet. Still, a girl could dream. And with that pleasant thought, she went to stuff the boys' Christmas stockings with goodies.

"Who's this James Claussen dude?" Brandon asked Eric as they made their way to the lower-level game room.

"One of the guests."

"I walked in on him kissing Mom."

"No shit," Eric said with a smile.

"She just met this guy, didn't she?"

Eric shrugged. "Love at first sight."

"For Mom or the lodge?"

Eric looked at his brother in surprise. Brandon had always been the more trusting of the two of them. As Mom used to say, he'd never met a stranger. Easygoing and fun-loving, Brandon was always ready to add more people to his friends list.

"What do you know about this guy?" Brandon continued. "I mean, he's here for a couple of days and he and Mom are already..." He scowled.

"He's okay," Eric said. So was his daughter, but Eric decided this wasn't the time to mention that.

"So what do you know about him?" Brandon asked again.

"He's retired, works part-time as a shopping-mall Santa. Or something like that."

"Well, there's a high-paying job."

"The guy's probably got a pension plus Social Security. Probably even a house free and clear. I don't think you have to worry about Mom."

"Well, somebody needs to," Brandon muttered as they walked into the game room.

Eric went to one end of the Ping-Pong table and picked up a paddle. "What's that supposed to mean?"

"I don't know," his brother snapped. "It means whatever."

Eric hit a forehand, starting the ball in motion. "It means you think I'm not taking care of Mom?"

Brandon shot the ball back at him. "I didn't say that."

"You didn't have to. I got the message." The ball zinged back and forth another couple of times. "In case you didn't notice, I've been the one holding down the fort while you ski-bum your way around the country."

"Hey, you're the one who's got a hard-on for this place."

The ball came back to Eric's backhand and he missed it. He picked it up and glared at his irresponsible younger brother. "*I'm* the one who cares about Mom staying in business." He shot the ball back at Brandon.

"What? And I don't?"

"You're never here. Except during the holidays or whenever you want to impress your latest bimbo. Lucky for Mom you're not an only child."

Now it wasn't a Ping-Pong ball that came sailing at Eric. It was a paddle. He dodged it. And hurled his back in retaliation, clipping his brother in the ear.

Brandon swore and grabbed his ear. "What the hell are you doing?"

"Me? Who started this?"

"I wasn't aiming for your head, you prick." Still clutching his ear, Brandon whirled around and marched for the door.

"I wasn't aiming for yours, either." He'd never had a very accurate throwing arm. "Not that there's any brains in there."

Brandon turned and gave him the old one-fingered salute, then kept going.

Fine, he thought. Let the little pissant go off and pout. The truth hurt.

It didn't take long for Eric to remember that the little pissant was his brother and he loved him, even when he was acting like the baby he was. Anyway, Eric hadn't exactly been a model of maturity himself. And on Christmas Eve. Sheesh.

He hurried after Brandon, catching him just before he slipped back inside the family living quarters. "Hey, I'm sorry," he said.

Brandon stopped, staring at the door marked Private. "You're right. I'm not the one who's around, and it's wrong. I was actually thinking of moving back."

"Good. We could use the help around here."

Brandon shook his head. "No, you couldn't. You've got it all under control. You always have." He opened the door and went inside. The lights had been turned off except for the living room lamp, which meant Mom had gone to bed.

Eric followed him. "What are you saying?" he said, keeping his voice down.

"I'm saying you don't really need me here. You never have."

There was a lot of truth in what his brother said. Eric had stepped in and taken over his dad's responsibilities. And the older he'd gotten, the more he'd taken on. Brandon had never complained, so Eric had figured he wasn't interested.

Now the lodge ran like a well-oiled machine. But it ran that way because Eric was always there. He never took time off. And now, after a walk in the snow with a certain brown-haired woman, he was thinking he didn't want to be quite so chained to the place. He wanted the Icicle Creek Lodge to be a family-run establishment in the truest sense of the word.

"We need you more than you realize," he said. He still couldn't picture Brandon coming back and pitching in, but if he was willing to, it would be great.

Another face sprang to mind. He could easily picture James Claussen happily puttering around the lodge, fixing broken toilets, helping string Christmas lights. That would be the only way he and Mom would ever get together because Mom would never leave this place. It was like her third child. If they got serious, would Claussen be willing to move up here? And what about his daughter?

Brandon flopped onto the couch and rubbed his ear. "I don't know. Maybe it's stupid to come back. They say you can't go home again."

"That's bull and you know it." Eric grabbed a bag of frozen peas and tossed it to his brother, and Brandon pressed it to his ear. "Mom would love it if you came back. There's enough for both of us to do. There's enough for *three* people to do."

"Like that guy Mom was kissing?"

"Maybe. They've been eyeballing each other like horny teenagers ever since he and his family got here."

Brandon groaned. "I don't like it."

"Like it or not, it's Mom's life. If she wants a boyfriend, I say let her have one." Man, had he changed his tune. Nothing like a few years of seeing his mom looking wistfully at the happy couples who stayed at the lodge to make a guy think differently.

"What if he becomes more than a boyfriend?"

"Then she won't be alone anymore. That's not a bad thing, Bran."

Brandon frowned. "Nobody can take Dad's place."

"You're right. But maybe Mom's planning to

find a new place for this guy. You gonna tell her she can't? That all she gets to do is sit around here growing old, waiting for us to get married and settle down?"

The frown didn't budge.

"She's lonely. At least, she has been," Eric amended. "I think it's about time she got to have some fun."

"I guess," Brandon said dubiously. "But this old guy better turn out to be on the level."

"He is," Eric assured him. "His kids are nice, too."

"Oh, yeah?" Brandon's expression grew speculative. "Has he got a daughter?"

"He does." Eric pointed a warning finger at his brother. "But she's taken."

Brandon's eyes grew wide. "You and Mom both? Jeez, I move away for a little while and look what happens."

Nothing. For months and months. Nothing. Until Christmas. Eric couldn't help smiling. Way back when Mom had asked if there was anything he wanted for Christmas, he'd told her no, not a thing. And it was true. He'd pretty much given up on finding that elusive woman. But lo and behold, Santa had come to the Icicle Creek Lodge and dumped her right in Eric's lap. It was too early to know how their story would turn out, but he hoped the kiss they'd shared would be the first of many.

He smiled. Those sappy holiday songs weren't

wrong, after all. Christmas was the most wonderful time of the year.

He only hoped he wouldn't wake up on Christmas morning to find out he'd imagined this evening. Or worse, to find Brooke drooling over his little brother.

Chapter Eighteen

Give Love on Christmas Day

John awakened early in the morning with a splitting headache. He started to get up, but the bed began to spin so he decided maybe he should lie back down for a while.

Lying down gave him plenty of time to remember the previous night's romantic fiasco. What a dope he'd been. A man with any brains at all would've seen how one-sided his love affair with Holland had been. Back in the summer when they'd had their rough patch he should have realized it wasn't going to work out between them. Instead, he'd stubbornly fought on, determined to make her his. And why? Just because she was hot? Just because she liked action flicks? There were probably hundreds of women out there who liked action flicks.

Of course, there weren't hundreds of women out there as good-looking as Holland. But that begged the question—what was she doing with *him*? He made an okay salary but he wasn't exactly rich. And he was no Ryan Reynolds. So, why had she gone out with him? Why had she become his girlfriend?

Insight hit him like a giant lump of coal. Making do. Holland had been going out with him only until someone better came along. He'd had an inkling of it last night, and she'd hinted at it when they had their rough patch back in August. "I think we should see other people," she'd said. "I'm ready to branch out." Branching out. Was that what you called it when you dumped your boyfriend?

He'd been good enough for her when they first met. She'd been new to the city, hadn't known many people and had been more than happy to check out the restaurant scene with him. And check it out they had, every place from Wild Ginger to Ivar's, one of Seattle's landmark restaurants. She'd been happy to let him take her dancing, spring for Mariners tickets and movie tickets, and they'd had fun doing it all. Then they'd settled on their favorite restaurants and favorite clubs, gotten into the habit of going dancing on Saturday nights. Fool that he was, he'd thought they were bonding, becoming a couple.

Now he knew he'd been nothing more than a starter boyfriend, someone to help her find her feet in a new place. She'd found her feet, all right, just in time to stomp on his heart. She'd fallen for one of the pond-scum specials where she worked, so she no longer needed John. Plain and simple.

And this trip had been yet another thing she'd

let him spring for. How many more times had she planned to use him before dumping him?

His mother was right. He was dumb when it came to women. Well, no more. No more Mr. Nice Guy. As soon as the bed stopped spinning, he was going to take some aspirin and then drive home. He could still make it back in time for Christmas at his folks', and that sure beat spending Christmas with all the strangers who'd seen his rejection the night before.

Even after staying up late, Missy's kids had begun bouncing on the bed at 5:00 a.m., announcing that it was Christmas morning. Just in case she'd forgotten. She'd given them their stockings and told them to climb back into bed. That had lasted about five minutes before their new dog had started whining to go out. Okay, so much for sleep. Ten minutes later, they were taking a walk in the snow.

Or rather a run in the snow, with Buddy and the kids bounding ahead, Missy following at a slightly slower pace. Wow, she was out of shape. That was what happened when you stood around cutting hair all day. Imagine living up here in the mountains, going for walks in the snow, hiking in the summer. Was there a hair salon in this town?

Even if there was, she couldn't afford to live here. Icicle Falls probably didn't have any affordable rentals. Still, a girl could dream.

And dream she did, planning how she'd decorate her place, seeing herself visiting with Olivia on a regular basis. Lalla spending time with her, too, enjoying her adopted grandmother.

Fortunately, they'd also have a grandparent figure back in the city, Missy reminded herself. Mr. Claussen was such a bighearted man. How she'd lucked out meeting all these great people she had no idea. Maybe it was a Christmas miracle.

Once Buddy's needs were met, she turned them all back to the lodge by way of the trunk of her car, where she collected a starter bag of dog food Dylan had loaded up for Buddy. That should keep the dog happy for about two minutes.

"Now, be quiet, you guys," she instructed as they went up the front porch steps. "People are still sleeping."

"On Christmas morning?" Carlos asked in amazement.

"Older people don't wake up as early. We're going to go back to our room and be quiet as mice. Right?"

"Right," Lalla said, nodding vigorously, then ran inside after her brother and the dog.

At least they weren't whooping and hollering. Once back in the room, she decided to let them open their presents. Lalla had gotten a Disney princess gown, which Missy had scored for 75 percent off at a party store after Halloween. She put it on instantly and modeled it for her mother and brother, spinning around to watch the skirt twirl. It was a cheap costume so there wasn't a lot of skirt to twirl, but Lalla was happy.

Missy had gotten Carlos a couple of miniature

metal cars to play with and a small, super bouncy ball, which he immediately had to try out. After the thing had ricocheted all over the room, making the dog go berserk, she suggested he save that to play with when they got home. That suggestion was rewarded with a pout, which she ignored.

Instead, she said, "Now, look under your bed. I think Santa left you both something."

"Santa already gave us something last night," Lalla said, adjusting her tiara.

"It's from Mom," Carlos said, diving under the bed.

Lalla followed suit, and a moment later the kids came out with their treasures, Lalla hugging the black baby doll to her chest and Carlos dangling the stuffed dog. "Look, Buddy," he said to the dog. "Here's a friend for you."

Buddy barked and thumped his tail on the floor.

"I love Santa," Lalla said happily.

"Me, too," Carlos said.

Teary-eyed, Missy smiled at her babies. This was definitely the best Christmas ever.

She put in a Christmas cartoon DVD she'd found at a summer garage sale and left them snuggled in bed with Buddy while she indulged in a bath, using the bath bomb Santa had given her the night before. This day was going to be special, she just knew it. How could it not with Lalla getting her grandma for the day and Carlos playing with his dog?

And maybe John Truman would sit with them at breakfast.

Okay, don't be greedy, she told herself. It was enough that her children were happy. Her chances of getting someone like John Truman were about as high as a snowman's chance of doing Vegas. Still, it was Christmas.

After her bath she dressed in the jeans and black sweater she'd packed. Cashmere, no less. She'd bought it at a garage sale in one of Seattle's nicer neighborhoods and had been saving it for a special occasion. Today qualified. She took extra time with her hair and makeup, and when she was done she had to smile at her reflection. "Not bad," she murmured. "Not bad at all."

She dressed Carlos in jeans—she was going to have to get him some new ones, since he was already growing out of these—and the red hand-me-down sweatshirt she'd been keeping aside for the holidays. Lalla would wear her princess gown; that was a given. She couldn't help looking at her children with pride when they finally left Buddy enjoying a chew toy and went down to breakfast. They were beautiful children. And good. Maybe they didn't have the finest clothes or go to the best school, but she was going to find a way to change that. Starting today. After all, it was Christmas, and anything could happen at Christmas. Maybe even love.

Once more she had to tell herself not to be stupid. John Truman might have been set free by his girlfriend, but that still didn't put him in Missy's league. Guys like John looked for well-educated women who never went near a thrift store unless it

was to make a donation. Still, he'd enjoyed hanging
out with her and her kids, and when she was with
him she'd felt the attraction. But maybe it had been
one-sided. He'd just been kind to her, and wishful
thinking had turned it into more. Still, the thought
came again. *It's Christmas. Anything could happen
at Christmas.*

The Claussens were already seated at a table and
beckoned her over. They didn't have to ask Lalla
twice. Before you could say *ho, ho, ho* she was at
Brooke's side, showing off her princess gown.

"It's very pretty," Brooke said. "It's a good thing
Santa knows you're a princess."

Lalla nodded. "And Santa gave me a grandma for
Christmas, too. We're gonna make cookies today."

"I hope you'll save me one," Brooke said.

Lalla considered this seriously for a few seconds,
then said, "I think I can do that," making the adults
smile.

Several of the other guests were already at their
tables, too. The Spikes were exchanging presents,
and Missy experienced a moment of jealousy as she
watched Mrs. Spike open a small red satin gift box
to reveal a pair of gray pearl earrings and a matching
necklace, and lean across the table to kiss her husband. Would that ever be her? Not that she needed
a pearl necklace. But, oh, how she wanted to be sitting across the table from a man she loved, giving
him a Christmas kiss. Of course, John Truman's
smiling face came to mind.

She looked around the room. There were Vera

and Jane. There were the Williamses. There was the happy pregnant couple. But she saw no sign of John. Had he left? "I wonder where John is." Oh, crud. Had she just said that out loud?

"You know, I haven't seen him," Mr. Claussen said. He shook his head. "I hope he doesn't leave."

"I would," Dylan muttered. "That was seriously humiliating."

"Sometimes these things happen for a reason," Mr. Claussen said thoughtfully. "Did I ever tell you kids I was in love with someone else before I met your mother?"

Brooke's mouth dropped. "No. I don't believe it."

"We were young, immature. She dumped me. Of course I was heartbroken. But then, a couple of years later, I met your mother. And that was when I realized what I'd had before was…" He glanced around the room, apparently for inspiration, then nodded over to where Mr. Spike was fastening the pearl necklace around his wife's neck. "It was like having a pebble from the beach. Your mom, she was the pearl." Now he slid a look in Missy's direction. "Sometimes it takes men a while to find their pearl. Sometimes they even have to be helped."

Eric Wallace came over to the table, bearing plates with some sort of egg casserole. Missy noticed the smile he and Brooke exchanged. Whoa. Something had happened between those two.

"Someone should go check on John," Mr. Claussen said casually as he took a bite of his casserole. "See if he's coming down to breakfast."

"We should leave the guy alone," said Dylan.

Missy thought Dylan was probably right.

Now Mr. Claussen was looking directly at Missy. "What do you think?"

"I'm sure he doesn't want to see anyone," she said, staring down at her plate. She was no pearl.

"Maybe not," Mr. Claussen agreed. "But then again, I'd feel better if a pretty girl came to my door and asked how I was doing."

Missy looked up to see him giving her an encouraging smile.

"We'll keep an eye on the kids," Brooke offered.

Could *everyone* at the table tell that she had the hots for John? She felt her cheeks warming.

"This is an awfully good breakfast," Mr. Claussen said. "Why don't you go see if he's hungry?"

Okay. She could sit here and do nothing or she could go after what she wanted. Which was it going to be? She pushed away from the table. "I'll be right back."

The aspirin, combined with several glasses of water—well, okay, and driving the porcelain bus—had restored John enough to be able to finally shower and dress. Now his overnight bag was packed and he was ready to go home. That was going to be humiliating, going home with no fiancée. Maybe he'd skip Christmas at his parents', just go back to his own place and watch movies all day. Feel sorry for himself. Yeah, that worked.

The knock on his door gave him a start. Then it

gave him hope. It was Holland. She'd come back to say she was sorry. She'd been wrong. They did belong together.

No, that wasn't happening. And even if it did, he wouldn't take her back. No, sir, not after the way she'd humiliated him.

Hmm. And if he wouldn't take her back, how much did he really love her?

There was the knocking again, timid, as if the person on the other side wasn't sure he or she should be there. Curious, John opened the door to find Missy Monroe. She wore jeans and a black sweater and had little Christmas-tree earrings dangling from her ears.

Holland would never wear Christmas-tree earrings. Holland also wouldn't look as soft and…what was the word he was searching for? *Sweet*, that was it. And sweet wasn't so bad. Nope, sweet wasn't bad at all.

Missy cleared her throat. "I hope you weren't, um, busy."

Busy feeling sorry for himself. He decided not to share that info. "No."

"We just wondered if you were coming down to breakfast."

"I don't think so."

He saw that she'd noticed the suitcase sitting in the middle of the room. "Oh. You're leaving."

"Not much point in staying."

She stood there quietly for a moment. "Yeah, I

guess not," she finally said. "Except the breakfast this morning is really good. And you did pay for it."

He frowned. "I'll pass."

"Yeah, I guess I can see why," she said. Now she looked down at her feet.

So did he. She was wearing little red shoes. Very cute.

"I'm sorry about the dog," he said. Was it only last night that he'd been planning to help Missy with her problem?

"Oh, that's all taken care of. Mr. Claussen fixed everything with my landlady and we get to keep him."

John nodded. Well, somebody had managed to be a hero. He found himself regretting the fact that it hadn't been him. Instead, he'd been wasting his time being a loser.

She cleared her throat again. "I was hoping you'd stay. I know that's selfish of me, considering what you've just been through."

"You were?"

She still kept studying her feet. "I probably shouldn't say this, but your girlfriend was stupid." Now she raised her face and looked at him earnestly. "You're a great guy, John Truman, and there are lots of women out there who'd love to be your girlfriend." Her cheeks grew pink as she continued. "Anyway, I wish you'd come down and have breakfast. And, well, you probably want to go visit your family, but I wish you'd stay here today and play in the snow with me and my kids and then play board games in the lobby by the fireplace. And…get your money's worth." The pink in her cheeks deepened but she held her head high. She stuck her hands in the back pockets of her jeans, and the look she gave him dared him to man-up and face the world.

A cute woman with blue hair begging him to stay made it seem rude to leave. And cowardly. And, under the circumstances, he wasn't anxious to see his family and eat humble pie for Christmas dinner. He nodded. "I guess I could handle some breakfast."

She smiled as if he'd just promised to buy her diamond earrings. "Good," she said with an answering nod.

He stepped out of the room and shut the door on the painful memory of the previous night. As he and Missy went down the stairs, he decided that maybe Missy had a point. Maybe he should get his money's worth and stay until tomorrow.

Chapter Nineteen

Holly Jolly Christmas

James watched John Truman enter the dining room a little like a soldier expecting an ambush. There was only one way to get him past that. "Over here," James called. "We saved you a seat."

John smiled as sober a smile as James had ever seen and joined them at the table. "Thanks," he said.

"Merry Christmas," Brooke greeted him. "The breakfast this morning is to die for. This egg casserole is really yummy. And so is the puff pastry."

He'd barely sat down when Eric Wallace came out of the kitchen with a plate of food for him. He forked up a bite and sampled it. "This *is* good."

"So, what's everyone going to do today?" Brooke asked.

"I think we need to go inner tubing on Snow Hill," Missy said.

"Can Buddy come?" asked Carlos.

"I don't see why not," she told him. She looked

shyly at John. "If you decide to stay, would you like to come with us?"

"Come with us, John," Carlos begged.

John nodded. "I could stay long enough to do some inner tubing."

"Sounds like a great idea," Brooke said, smiling at Eric, who was now back with extra pastries for them all.

Oh, yes, James thought, there was something brewing between his daughter and Olivia's son. And he suspected he wasn't the only one who'd noticed...

"Mind if I join you?" Eric asked.

"The more, the merrier, right?" Brooke said.

"Definitely," John agreed.

"Not me," Dylan said. "I'm going to see if I can find some good downhill skiing."

"My brother can help you with that," Eric told him. He turned and waved over his fellow server, the same young man who'd walked in on James and Olivia the night before. "This is my brother, Brandon," he said to the table at large.

"Nice to see you again, Brandon," James said, although he wasn't entirely sure he meant it.

Brandon nodded and smiled, politely if not warmly.

The smile warmed considerably when his gaze locked on Brooke, and James wasn't too keen on that. The kid was good-looking, probably a ladies' man. He was checking out Brooke as if she were some hot car he'd like to drive.

"And this is my daughter, Brooke," James said,

his voice seasoned with a healthy dose of so-don't-try-anything.

That took the speculation right out of the kid's smile.

They finished the introductions, and Dylan asked about skiing. Brandon's face lit up at that and the two young men began to compare places they'd skied. *Like calls to like,* James reflected, seeing how well they were hitting it off. Surely that was a good development. Maybe Dylan would put in a word for his old man.

"I have to finish helping with breakfast but after that I can show you some sweet runs," Brandon said to Dylan.

"Super," Dylan said, eyes gleaming.

"Daddy, do you want to come inner tubing with us?" Brooke asked.

James caught sight of Olivia, who had come out of the kitchen and was making the rounds among the tables. "You kids go ahead. I think I'll just stay here." Olivia would be busy later in the afternoon, preparing their holiday feast, but James suspected she'd make time for him before that.

Seeing her sons at their table, she joined them. "I guess you've all met my son Brandon," she said to everyone. "He's here for the holidays." She looked at both her sons and smiled. "Christmas is always complete once both my boys are home."

James understood totally. Having your family together was the best Christmas present any parent could ask for.

"I have a princess gown," Lalla announced, tired of being upstaged by grown-ups.

"And you look beautiful," Olivia said, bending over to give her a hug.

"When can we make cookies?" Lalla asked.

"Let's see," Olivia said. "What does your mommy have scheduled for the day?"

"We're going inner tubing," Carlos told her.

"Ah. Well, then, how about baking cookies after you're done?" Olivia suggested. To Missy she said, "That'll give me time to clean up from breakfast and do some of my dinner prep."

"Are you sure this isn't too much trouble?" Missy asked.

"Not at all. I love to bake. And every little girl should have a grandma to bake cookies with. Isn't that right, Lalla?"

Lalla nodded emphatically, making her tiara wobble and the other diners smile.

So the day was all planned. But not quite the way James had envisioned. He'd hoped to at least share a cup of coffee with Olivia later that morning while everyone was out in the snow. However, the woman did have a B and B to run. She didn't have time for coffee breaks with the guests.

She moved on to greet the other guests and the brothers started clearing plates. James supposed he could find plenty to do to entertain himself. But darn, he really wanted to entertain himself with Olivia.

People were beginning to disperse now. The two

older women passed their table and Jane stopped for a moment, laying a hand on John's shoulder. "That girl didn't deserve you."

John's face flushed.

There was no time for embarrassment, though, not when there were children around. "Come on, John," Carlos said eagerly. "Let's go."

"You can come see my doll." Lalla took him by the hand, leading him from the table, Missy falling in step with them.

Yes, it looked like young John Truman was going to land on his feet.

James was about to follow everyone out when he heard Olivia call his name. He turned to see her hurrying up to him.

"You're probably getting ready to go to Snow Hill with the kids," she said.

"Actually, no. I thought I'd hang around here."

"Oh. Well, in that case, would you like to relax with a cup of coffee? I have a little time before I need to get to work."

"Great idea," James said.

"We can sit over in the corner and admire the view." She pointed to the far end of the dining room.

They grabbed cups of coffee and settled at one of the small corner tables.

"I sure enjoyed breakfast," James told her, making her beam.

"I do love to cook."

"And it shows. In the food," he threw in quickly lest she think he was casting aspersions on her figure. "What you've been serving us is as good as anything we'd get in a five-star Seattle restaurant."

"Oh." She waved away his compliment.

"No, I'm serious."

"Well, thank you. Of course, I couldn't manage everything without help. Thank God for Eric. He's been a rock all these years."

"And what about your younger son?" James asked.

"Oh, he's been supportive, too. Although he doesn't love the place as much as Eric and I do. I think he's still trying to find himself," she confessed. She sighed. "Sometimes I worry about him. I'd love to see him meet a nice girl and eventually get married. Of course, I'd love that for Eric, too."

James wondered if she'd had a chance to see Eric and Brooke together, if she'd seen the way they'd been looking at each other. "I think he might have taken a liking to my daughter," he said cautiously. "What would you think of that, Olivia?"

"I think that would make me very happy." She took a sip of her coffee. "You know, we've had so many guests come through our doors over the years, but we've never had a Christmas like this. It's been so special."

"I feel the same way," James said. He reached across the table and covered her hand with his.

She smiled at him, tears in her eyes. "I'm so glad you and your family came to stay with us."

"Me, too," he said. It was early days yet, but he had a good feeling, the same feeling he'd had when he'd first met Faith, that this was the beginning of something that could change his life. As he smiled at her over his coffee cup, he could almost hear Faith whispering, "Merry Christmas, James."

Word got out about the Snow Hill expedition and soon it seemed that half the guests had attached themselves to the party. And it was a party. Brooke found herself laughing as she fell off her inner tube and did a face-plant in the snow. Eric was right behind her with Lalla in his lap and they collided with her and fell off, too, Lalla laughing uproariously.

"Are you okay?" Eric asked, helping Brooke up.

"Never better," she said. It felt good to laugh again. And in that laughter she could feel her mother's presence.

The next to come down the hill were John and Missy with Carlos a few feet behind, the dog racing alongside him, barking. Brooke and Eric dodged out of the way and John skidded on past, shouting, "I'm king of the world."

This was hardly surprising considering the way Missy had been looking at him all morning.

And now here came Vera and Jane, Vera atop her inner tube like a snow lady in a red parka, her plump legs encased in black leggings and boots that could've been around since the first North American Christmas. Jane was wearing ski pants and a parka and had a stocking cap on her head. Her long legs stuck out in front of her and she had her arms raised as if she were on a roller coaster. "Whee!"

she whooped. Right behind them were the Williams girls, big smiles on their faces.

"Come on, Eric," Lalla said, "let's go again." She grabbed Eric's hand and started towing him back up the hill.

"I guess we're going again," he called over his shoulder, grinning at Brooke.

"I guess so," she said, following the two of them. Score more points for Eric Wallace. He was so good with kids; he'd make a wonderful father someday.

She would never have guessed it when she'd first met him, but he seemed to be everything she'd been looking for—he was kindhearted, responsible, fun-loving, good with children. Mama would have loved him.

A momentary sadness slipped into Brooke's heart. If only her mother had lived. She would have so enjoyed this outing.

Brooke remembered one of their many conversations. It had been Valentine's Day, and Brooke had stopped by the house with a floral arrangement. The subject had turned to love, not something Brooke had wanted to discuss since her latest online Mr. Perfect had not panned out.

"Don't worry," her mother had said. "The right man will come along just when he's supposed to."

"I don't think I'm ever going to find the right man," Brooke had grumbled.

"Of course you will," her mother had insisted.

Her mother had been correct, as usual. Eric Wallace *was* the right man; Brooke sensed it way down, soul deep. And he had come along at exactly the right time. This Christmas could have been depressing and hard to get through, haunted by memories. Oh, the memories were still there, but now, balanced by hope and the first stirrings of love, they weren't so painful. She would always miss her mother, but she would go on and live the kind of full life Mama had dreamed of for her.

"You'll move on and live your life, and that's as it should be," Mama had said. "And that's how I want it to be. I want you to do me proud by living every moment to the fullest."

She was doing that today. She was going to be fine. They all were. This Christmas was a new beginning, one her mother would have approved of.

She and Eric and Lalla were at the top of the hill now. He settled Lalla and himself on his inner tube, then smiled up at Brooke. "Race you."

"You're on," she said. She jumped onto her own tube and pushed off and they went down the hill, laughing all the way.

"I'm hungry," Carlos said.

"Me, too," Lalla echoed.

"I guess we'd better run to the grocery store and pick up something from the deli before they close for the day," John said, and they all piled into his pristine car, filling it with the smell of fresh air and wet dog.

"I should have taken my car," Missy fretted, feeling a little guilty. "Now you're stuck driving us to the store."

"Nah," he said. "I would've had to get something to eat, anyway."

"I think Olivia was going to put out some snacks."

"I'm too hungry for just snacks. How about you guys?" John asked the kids.

"I'm so hungry I could eat this much," Carlos said, stretching his arms wide.

"Well, there you go," John said, grinning at Missy.

He started the car and they drove to the store singing "Jingle Bells" at the top of their lungs.

The Safeway parking lot was packed with shoppers buying last-minute items for their holiday meals and visitors to town getting items before the store's early closing at two. She hadn't seen very many restaurants in town that were open. Even the hamburger joint had been closed.

"In a small town like this, family's important," John surmised.

"Another reason to like the place," Missy said as they trudged across the snowy parking lot. "I'd love to live here."

"Would you really?"

"Of course. Why not?"

He shrugged. "According to Holland, it would get boring."

Her, Missy thought in disgust. "Well, I don't think it would. There's too many nice people up here to do things with. If I lived here, I'd be at that skating rink every Saturday."

"Me, too," put in Carlos.

"And in the summer I'd take the kids on picnics in the woods."

"I like picnics," Lalla said. "Do you like picnics?" she asked John, slipping her hand in his.

"I sure do," he said.

Once at the deli counter John insisted on paying for lunch and they purchased fried chicken and coleslaw. "You need your veggies," Missy insisted.

Carlos made a face. "Veggies. Ick!"

But Missy noticed that when they found a table in the café area, he followed John's lead and ate some of the salad.

"I hope Buddy's okay," Carlos said as he finished the last of his chicken.

"We left the window open for him. He'll be fine," John assured him. "He's probably taking a nap. You guys wore him out. You wore *me* out," he added, making Lalla giggle.

But he seemed to have found his second wind once they got back to the lodge. Olivia took Lalla off to bake cookies, and Carlos took Buddy out to the front yard. "I saw some games in the upper lobby," John said to Missy. "Would you like to play one?"

"Sure," she said. Anything to keep John with her a little longer.

The Spikes were seated at a table playing Scrabble, and they greeted Missy and John, then went back to concentrating on their words, leaving the new arrivals to look through the stack of board games.

"Hey, here's Sorry!" John said. "I haven't played that in years."

"I haven't played it at all," Missy said.

He looked at her in surprise. "You've never played Sorry!"

She shook her head.

"Man, what planet were you raised on?" he teased.

Planet Dysfunction. "I didn't exactly have the best childhood," she said, and felt the warmth of shame on her cheeks.

"Oh."

The awkward tone of his voice drove the shame deeper. She couldn't look at him.

"You know, there's no crime in that," he said. "Lots of people have screwed-up parents."

She sighed. "I always wanted a normal childhood," she said as they seated themselves at a small game table. "Every year I'd ask Santa to change my mom into Mrs. Brady." Why was she sharing *this*? Two tears escaped her eyes and slipped down her cheeks, but she quickly wiped them away.

John reached across the table and laid a comforting hand on her arm. "Hey, it's not about how you start in life. It's about how you finish."

She nodded. "I'm going to finish right. I have to, for the kids. I don't want them to have the kind of life I had growing up. My mom was..." She shouldn't share this. "She had a problem with alcohol." There it was, out in the open, in all its humiliation and shame.

"A lot of people do," he said, his voice free of accusation.

"I guess that's why I never touch the stuff. I want to be a good mom."

"You already are, Missy. Anybody can see that."

New tears threatened, and all she could manage was a grateful nod.

"Come on, let's play Sorry!" he said. "Let's not be thinking sad stuff on Christmas."

She nodded again. "Absolutely! This day has been perfect, and I don't want anything to ruin it."

John explained the game and they began to play. She crowed every time she got a game piece out of Start and pouted every time he drew a Sorry! card and put her back in. And she couldn't help squealing when she got three out of four of her game pieces safely into Home.

She pointed a warning finger at him. "I'm going to take you down."

"Oh, no. I'm not dead yet."

And so they played on, moving their pieces around the board. "You know," he said, after he'd drawn his next card, "I'm glad I didn't go home."

"Me, too," she said, smiling at him. And something flashed between them, something that made her heart catch.

Now he looked at her seriously. "Missy, is there anybody in your life?"

"Like a guy?"

"Like a guy."

She shook her head.

"I know I just broke up with someone so it's tacky to ask this, but would you go out with me sometime?"

Would she! "Yes. I definitely would."

He grinned. "It's hard to believe that a few hours ago I thought my life was over."

"It probably felt like it."

He let out a sigh. "I really thought she was the one, you know. But I'm not sure why. I mean, we had stuff we liked to do together. And, of course, she was beautiful."

A lot more beautiful than Missy could ever hope to be. She tried not to make a face.

"But that wouldn't have been enough in the long run. I can see that now. A couple of times today when we were doing stuff, I asked myself, 'Would Holland have liked this?'"

"Well, would she?"

"I don't know. To be honest, I can't imagine her going inner tubing. Or driving around in a car with a big wet dog. Hey, I *know* I can't see her doing that."

"But kids and dogs—is that what you want in life?" Missy asked. She held her breath, waiting for his response.

"Yeah, actually, it is," he said, and once again, the look they exchanged sent a jolt to her heart.

Except that she and John came from two different worlds. "I'm not classy like her."

"No. You're classier. You've got heart."

She blinked in surprise. "That's the nicest thing anyone's ever said to me."

"It's true," he said. Now he shook his head. "Man, Holland did me a big favor by turning me down."

Missy knew Holland had done her one. *Thanks for setting him free and giving someone who really appreciates him a chance.* She smiled and drew a card. It was just the number she needed to get her last game piece to Home and win. "I'm a winner!" she crowed.

"You sure are," he said with a grin.

And just when she thought it couldn't get any better, John remembered he had some Sweet Dreams chocolates left in his room.

"Let's go eat 'em," she said.

Chocolate was always a high for Missy, but sitting beside John on his bed eclipsed even this excellent chocolate. It stirred her up in places that had been neglected way too long. And the way he was looking at her… Oh.

This is how you've gotten in trouble before. "I'd better not rush into anything," she said, as much to herself as to him.

"Oh. No. Of course not," he said, acting embarrassed, as if she'd somehow read his mind.

That wasn't hard to do, since the same thing was on hers. "We should get back downstairs. Lalla probably has cookies made now and will want us to try them."

He nodded and followed her out of the room. But in the upstairs hallway, when she saw the mistletoe, she stopped. "I really don't want to rush into anything, but isn't there something about this stuff?

Like when you're standing under it, you're supposed to kiss someone?"

He grinned. "It's a holiday tradition."

"Tradition is important, don't you think?"

"Oh, yeah." He put his arms around her and all her nerve endings began singing "We Wish You a Merry Christmas." He smiled at her, and her heart did a somersault. "You know, you're really special, Missy Monroe."

"Am I?"

"Yeah, you are," he said softly. And then he pulled her close and touched his lips to hers, and she could feel herself lighting up like a string of Christmas lights.

"Wow," she breathed when they drew apart. "That was some kiss."

"It sure was," he agreed. He took her hand and they started down the stairs together. "You know, I'm beginning to think I was meant to come up here, not because of Holland but because of you."

She smiled at him. "I think that's why I'm supposed to be here, too."

"Funny, isn't it, how things turn out?"

More like *amazing* in Missy's opinion. She just hoped this wouldn't turn out to be some Christmas dream. Because if it was, she didn't want to wake up.

Chapter Twenty

We Wish You a Merry Christmas...

The gumdrop cookies were finished, and there'd been much sampling along the way—of gumdrops, cookie dough and, of course, the final product. Now Olivia supervised as Lalla arranged them on a pretty china plate.

"Your mommy's going to be so proud of you," Olivia said.

Lalla nodded. "I'm a good helper."

"Yes, you are. And you're going to become a very good baker, too." The child beamed at her praise and it tugged at Olivia's heartstrings. It would be hard to see this little family return to the city. Goodness, but she was ready to be a grandparent, ready to bring more people into her life. She thought of James Claussen and happiness filled her. This Christmas had been full of unexpected delights and James topped the list.

Lalla put the last cookie on the plate. "There. All done."

"All right. Shall we go look for your mommy?"

"Yes!" Lalla whooped. Her princess gown was dusted with flour and she had cookie dough stuck to her chin. And with that delighted smile, she belonged on a magazine cover. Lalla Monroe was a beautiful child, both inside and out.

They left Olivia's private quarters, Muffin the cat slipping out behind them, and emerged to discover Vera and Jane in the lobby, sipping tea in front of the fireplace. Lalla ran toward them with her plate. "We made cookies!"

The cookies almost arrived in one piece but Lalla managed to trip over her gown and she fell just before she reached the women, dropping the plate on the carpet and spilling cookies everywhere. She stared a moment in disbelief, then burst into tears.

"Now, now, there's no need to cry," Jane said, and knelt to help put the cookies back on the plate. "They're hardly even broken." She popped a piece of one in her mouth. "Delicious. Did you make these yourself?"

The tears were already drying and Lalla nodded solemnly. By now her mother had come down from the second-landing lobby with John Truman. "Mommy, the cookies are done," she announced.

"And a very nice job she did on them, too," Jane said.

Olivia decided she liked Jane. A lot.

"I assume your carpet is so clean we can eat off it," Jane teased Olivia.

Heaven only knew how many feet had walked on the carpet that day and where they'd been. "Well, we try."

"A few germs never hurt anyone, right, Vera?" Jane offered the plate to her friend. Vera hesitated. "Oh, for heaven's sake, don't be such a wimp," Jane muttered, and snagged another cookie for herself.

Vera took a cookie and gave it a tentative nibble. "Very good," she said to Lalla.

"Thank you," the child said politely.

Jane handed the plate to Missy, and she and John both took a cookie.

"Hey, these are good," John said, and took another.

"Thank you so much," Missy said to Olivia. "You've made my daughter's Christmas."

"I think it was the other way around," Olivia said.

"Did you thank Grandma Olivia for baking cookies with you?"' Missy prompted.

Lalla not only thanked Olivia, she hugged her. "I love you, Grandma Olivia. I don't ever want to leave you."

Missy knew how her daughter felt. She didn't want to leave, either. This lodge, this town, it was all enchanted. The idea of returning to her old life, dealing with the likes of Mrs. Steele and Larry the lech, was downright depressing. *Well, what are you going to do about it?* Good question.

"Now, I'd better go back to the kitchen and get

to work," Olivia said. She gave Lalla a pat on the head and turned to leave.

"Mrs. Wallace," Missy began.

Olivia turned back with a questioning smile.

"I was just wondering…"

She didn't get a chance to share her thoughts because Carlos had come in with Buddy. And Buddy, on seeing Muffin perched atop the reception desk, remembered they had a score to settle.

Carlos had the dog on his leash but Buddy bolted and Carlos lost his grip. Leash dragging behind him, the dog raced up to the desk, put his front paws on it and gave a hearty bark. The cat arched her back and hissed. That didn't deter Buddy in the least. He barked some more and scrabbled to get closer. That was when Muffin decided to scram.

"Oh, dear!" Olivia cried as Muffin bolted and the dog took off in pursuit.

"I'll get him!" John lunged for the dog as he ran after the cat.

But John missed his grab for the leash and went down, crashing into the coffee table and sending cookies flying in every direction.

"My cookies," wailed Lalla as he scrambled back up.

Meanwhile, Muffin made a flying leap and scaled the Christmas tree, making it wobble. And into it charged the dog, followed by John, who was determined to pull him away, followed by Carlos, who was determined to help. Accompanied by cries from

Vera, Jane and Olivia, the tree did a holiday hula, its ornaments swinging wildly. Then it took a bow and, with a swish of branches and a crunch of ornaments, kept right on going down, narrowly missing Carlos and burying both John and the dog. Aloha.

Muffin, who had leaped from the tree, landed safely and ran off into the nether regions of the lodge while Buddy thrashed about, trying to free himself to give chase again. He had his head and half his chest out when a hand surfaced from under the boughs and grabbed his collar. "Oh, no, you don't," John said.

Missy was ready to cry. Or throw up. Or both. "I'm so sorry," she said to Olivia. "I'll cover the damages." Those ornaments hadn't looked as though they'd come from the dollar store. She'd probably have to make monthly payments.

"Don't you worry about that. I've got tons more out in our storage shed," Olivia said as they helped John extricate himself and the dog.

"That mutt definitely needs to go to obedience school," Jane said as John climbed out from the branches, still clutching Buddy's collar.

Missy gave her son the keycard. "Take Buddy up to the room. Now."

When John handed Carlos the leash, the boy said, "Come on, Buddy," and led the dog away. The excitement over, Buddy walked beside his young owner, as docile and well behaved as if he was no relation to the beast who'd just wreaked such havoc.

"All right," Jane said, rubbing her hands together, "a tree-trimming party." She turned to Olivia. "Did you say you had more ornaments?"

Olivia nodded. "I'll go fetch them."

"And a broom," Vera added. "We'll probably need to sweep."

They'd probably need to sweep a lot. Missy groaned.

"Everything will be as good as new before you know it," Olivia said. "John, maybe you can get the tree back up for us?"

"Sure thing," he said, and set to work while Olivia went to get the ornaments.

Ten minutes later, they were all retrimming the tree, Carlos and Lalla helping.

"Look, Mommy, a bird," Lalla said, holding up a delicate red blown-glass bird ornament with an elaborate feathered tail.

"Be careful with that," Missy cautioned. The last thing they needed was to break anything else.

"These ornaments are lovely," Vera said to Olivia.

"I've had them for years," Olivia told her.

Family heirlooms. "The others, did you have them for years, too?" Missy asked weakly.

"Yes, but I was tired of them," Olivia said. She patted Missy's arm. "Don't give this another thought."

"There," Jane said, hanging the last ornament. "It's even prettier than before. Which is really saying something."

"I love an all-red tree," Vera said with a sigh. "I wish I'd put up a tree this year."

"You just did," Jane informed her.

Olivia turned to Missy. "I think you were about to ask me something before we all got sidetracked. Do you remember what it was?"

Missy remembered, but after the chaos her family had caused she felt embarrassed to ask. Still, here was Olivia, looking at her expectantly, wearing a kind smile. "I was just wondering if there are any hair salons here in town."

"Well, as a matter of fact, there's Sleeping Lady Salon. And I know Sarah White, who owns the place. Let me call her tomorrow morning before you leave."

Pinch me. I've got to be dreaming. "Would you?" Missy asked eagerly.

"Of course. I don't know if she's hiring, but if she is you'd fit in very well."

"I'm good," Missy said.

"Are you?" Now Jane was looking at her speculatively. "What could you do with my hair?"

"I don't have my scissors," Missy replied, not sure she was up for a public demonstration of her skills.

"I have scissors," Olivia said. "I used to cut my husband's hair all the time. And the boys' when they were little."

Great. Old, dull scissors.

"Oh, I don't know," Missy said dubiously.

"Then we can give you references," Vera said, jumping on the bandwagon.

"I could use a trim," John said.

Next thing Missy knew, she had a crowd of people in her room, all waiting their turn at the improvised beauty chair in the bathroom. Carlos and Buddy were back and watching TV with Lalla and the room smelled of overheated little boy and wet dog. But no one seemed to mind. Olivia had passed around fresh cookies before going to work in the kitchen, and John had brought the last of the chocolates he'd purchased for the unappreciative Holland. It was a regular holiday party.

"I love it!" Jane declared when Missy had finished updating her hair—a simple cut, a short bob that took ten years off and played up her eyes, which were actually very pretty. "You've got a gift," she told Missy. She smiled at her reflection. "I feel positively sexy."

"Oh, brother," Vera muttered.

But once Missy had finished with Vera, she, too, was preening in front of the mirror.

Both women insisted on having Missy take their pictures. "You can show them to the owner of the salon up here," Jane said. "But first." She turned to Vera. "Let's go freshen our makeup and change into our finery for tonight. If I get a good picture, I might want to put it up on eHarmony," she explained to Missy.

"Good idea," Missy said.

"Really, eHarmony?" John said after they'd hurried off. "Who'd have thought it?"

"I think it's sweet," Missy said. "Everyone needs love, no matter what their age."

He smiled at her. "You know, you're right."

"Sometimes I am," she said. "Okay, dunk your head under the faucet and get your hair wet."

"My mom would be impressed with you," he said from under the faucet.

That made her smile. Except...she came with baggage, two kids by two different dads. Maybe his mom wouldn't be so impressed. Plus she had a tat. "I don't know. I'm probably not the perfect..." *Girlfriend.* She couldn't even bring herself to say the word. Here was where she started waking up from her lovely Christmas dream. "I've made mistakes."

"Everybody makes mistakes," he said, reaching for a towel.

Easy for him to say. He was Mr. Good Guy.

"Not everybody winds up with kids." She looked out to where Carlos and Lalla were sprawled on the bed watching TV, the dog wedged between them. "I wouldn't trade them for anything, though."

"They're great kids." John smiled. "And they've got a great mom."

"I have a tat," she blurted. "I bet your mom would hate that."

"Are you kidding?" He rolled up his sleeve to reveal the tattoo of an eagle on his forearm. "Got it when I was playing basketball in high school. I didn't make varsity."

"So you got a tat? *Because* you didn't make varsity?"

"Yeah. My dad took me."

"Really? Wow!" John had no idea how lucky he was.

"Yeah. He helped me pick out the eagle. I still remember him telling me that just because I didn't make varsity, it didn't mean I wasn't going places." He gave a snort. "I think I'm still trying to get lift-off."

"Me, too."

John smiled at her. "Sometimes you just need somebody along to help you catch the wind."

She smiled back. "You're an amazing guy, John Truman."

"Oh, I don't know about that."

"I do," she said, and gestured for him to sit down.

"Hey, I'm thinking just a little off the ears," he said, and reached up a hand to show her. In the process, he managed a boob graze. His whole face turned red. "Oh, shit, I'm sorry. I didn't mean…"

What a difference from Larry the lech. "I know you didn't," she said. *Santa, if you give me this great guy I'll never ask for anything for Christmas ever again.*

But John was probably wrong. His mother wouldn't like her. His mother would know he could do better.

Wait a minute, she scolded herself. *That was the old Missy. The new Missy is like the eagle on John's arm. She's going places.*

Brooke had to admit that Olivia Wallace had outdone herself. Dinner was everything a Christmas dinner should be, with ham and garlic mashed potatoes, flaky biscuits, a tossed salad and figgy pudding for dessert. An excellent selection of Washington state wine for the adults. Followed by hot cider, tea and coffee. The drinks flowed, and so did conversation among the guests.

"We're going to make this a holiday tradition," Mrs. Spike confided to Brooke as they stopped by her family's table to chat. "We've had such a wonderful time. It's been like a second honeymoon."

"I think we'll be back, too," Brooke said. And long before the next Christmas.

In just two short days, the Wallaces had come to feel like family and this lodge like a second home. Eric had persuaded Olivia to take a break and join them in the dining room for a late-afternoon coffee, and Brandon and Dylan had returned from skiing and joined them, too. Of course, it hadn't taken long for her father to find them. Olivia was like a magnet for him.

She'd noticed that Brandon didn't seem so thrilled to see her father and his mother sitting side by side, looking at each other like besotted teenagers. But he'd get over it, just as she had. If not, she'd have a little talk with him.

That evening the Claussens were invited to the Wallaces' private quarters for hot chocolate laced with peppermint schnapps and cookies. "I'm so glad you could all come," Olivia greeted them. She smiled at each of them, her smile lingering for an extra moment on Brooke. Or so it seemed...

Brooke knew she needed to extend the olive branch, and simply saying, "Thank you for having us," wasn't going to be enough.

So as the men settled in the living room she followed Olivia to her little kitchen. "May I help with something?"

Surprise (more like shock, actually) and pleasure raced across Olivia's face. "I was about to put out the cookies. If you wouldn't mind setting them on the platter?"

"I'd be happy to," Brooke said, coming as close to meaning it as a woman in transition possibly could.

Olivia pointed to the plastic containers and the Fitz and Floyd cookie plate on the counter. "While you do that, I'll finish up with the hot chocolate."

Brooke nodded and got to work. And wondered what she could find to talk about with this woman who'd dropped into her life.

She didn't have to wonder for long. As she set out cookies, she couldn't help asking, "Do these spritz cookies have crushed peppermint in them?"

"I thought it made for a festive twist on an old favorite," Olivia said.

"It does."

"If you like, I'll give you the recipe," Olivia offered.

"Thanks," Brooke murmured. Olivia was being gracious to her and she didn't really deserve it. But she'd take it.

As more cookies came out of their containers, conversation became more relaxed. Olivia told her that the ginger cookies were from a recipe she'd gotten from her mother. Ginger cookies were one of Brooke's favorites. The chocolate drop cookies with the peppermint icing were another of Olivia's creations, as were the cookies iced with nutmeg glaze.

Brooke sampled one and declared it her new favorite Christmas cookie. "My mother would have loved you."

She'd meant that to remain unspoken, but maybe it was a good thing that it had come out. Olivia turned, teary-eyed, and smiled at Brooke. "I think I would've liked your mother, too," she said. "Especially if she was anything like her daughter. I'm sure she was very proud of you."

"I hope so," Brooke said.

She wasn't sure how proud her mother would have been of her behavior during the past forty-eight hours, but she knew her mother would be pleased with her right now.

The men devoured the cookies, then Olivia suggested a game of holiday charades. Watching her father act out Santa's reindeer was highly entertaining for everyone, particularly as he acted out Dancer and Prancer. At one point he pranced right into the coffee table and managed to lose his balance and topple to the floor.

"Dead reindeer!" cried Dylan.

"Oh, *that's* Christmassy," Brooke said with a frown.

"Very Tim Burton," Eric said.

"What were you?" Olivia asked.

"Prancer," her father groaned from the floor.

Next up was Brandon, who deliberately fell down after feigning fright.

"Another dead reindeer?" Dylan guessed.

Brooke snapped her fingers. "'Grandma Got Run Over by a Reindeer,'" she said, winning the game for her team.

"That," Olivia said primly, "is a disgusting song," and everyone laughed.

After charades, Dylan suggested an impromptu Ping-Pong tournament.

"You kids go on," Daddy said. "I think I'm going to stay behind and nurse my knee."

"And flirt with my mom," Brandon muttered as they left.

"I think that's fine with her," Brooke told him. "And really, if she's going to flirt with a man, she couldn't pick a nicer one than my dad."

Brandon shrugged. "Yeah, I guess. He's okay. They just don't need to be in a hurry."

"At their age?" put in Eric. "You gotta be kidding."

"Live and let live, that's what I say," said Dylan the philosopher. "Anyway, it might be okay if they got together. We could have some fun holidays."

Brandon acknowledged that with a nod and another shrug.

Eric sent Brooke a look that about singed her panties. "I'm all for fun," he said.

And after a couple of games with the brothers, he lured her away to a deserted corner of the lodge and showed her exactly what kind of fun he was thinking of. *Merry Christmas. Ho, ho...oooh.*

Olivia had put on a CD of Christmas music and right now an instrumental version of "Angels We Have Heard on High" played in the background. She freshened James's hot chocolate and then sat down with a sigh.

"You're tired," he said. "I should go and let you get some rest."

"Oh, no. Don't. The first week in January is always slow and there'll be plenty of time for rest after you're all gone. And I must say," she added, "I'm going to hate to see you leave."

"I don't plan on staying away for long. I've grown rather fond of this place. And the woman who runs it," he said with a grin. "I'm wondering about New Year's Eve. Are you all booked up?"

"We can always make room at the lodge for Santa."

"Good, because he's planning on coming back."

They both smiled at each other and sipped their chocolate. And there, in her living room, with the music playing and her little tree aglow, he realized he'd been given a very special gift. Santa had gotten back his Christmas spirit.

Chapter Twenty-One

And a Happy New Year!

Missy awoke the day after Christmas wishing she could turn back the clock and start the whole holiday adventure again. But the party was over, and it was time to go back to her real life. Ick. She snuggled under the down comforter, hoping for a few more minutes.

That was all she got, because pretty soon Buddy was whining to go out. And then the kids were awake. Well, nothing wrong with getting in some more time in this winter wonderland.

She savored the early-morning walk in the snow, took in the sky tinged pink and violet, the mighty mountains rising around the town. And back in the lodge at breakfast, her taste buds savored Olivia's fancy breakfast crepes and every bit of conversation with the Claussens, who, along with John, were her breakfast companions.

In another hour or two, she'd be going back to

her life in the city, back to her dumpy neighborhood and Style Savings. *But you've got new friends,* she reminded herself. And a dog. And two happy children. Yes, life could be worse. Still, it was hard not to picture herself moving up here, working in some cute salon, John coming up to visit on a regular basis. Sigh.

There'd been no more mention of Sleeping Lady Salon from Olivia, and Missy didn't feel right bugging her. The woman was busy running this place. She had other things to do besides play fairy godmother to a struggling hairstylist.

Well, Missy concluded, she could find the salon on her way out of town (leave the tree-destroying dog in the car), see if they'd let her send in a résumé. Why not? She had nothing to lose.

She thought of John's eagle tattoo. Maybe she'd get one of those, too. If she ever had the money.

As they stood up to leave, John said, "I was wondering, would you and the kids like to come over to my place next weekend? I've got a Wii."

Carlos had been busy taunting his sister, pulling on her braids, but he displayed his gift for supersonic hearing by jumping into the conversation. "Wii?"

"Wii bowling," John said.

"Oh, yeah." Carlos was all over it.

So was Missy. So she lived in a dumpy neighborhood and had a crappy job. She and her kids had a date with John Truman. She left the dining room with John's phone number and address—and a big smile on her face.

She'd just finished packing when there was a knock on her door. It was Olivia.

"I just talked to Sarah at Sleeping Lady Salon. She'd be happy to have you stop by and see her this morning. If you like, you can leave the kids here with me."

"Really?" This was simply too good to be true.

"She's talking about expanding this spring. She'll need another stylist."

Missy threw her arms around Olivia. "Thank you!"

"Don't thank me, honey. I have ulterior motives. I'd like to see you and your children move up here. I want grandchildren."

Except… "I don't think I can afford to live here."

"I bet you can. I know a young man who has a cottage up on Juniper Ridge. I hear he's looking for a renter."

Could her life, after all those bumpy years, come together this easily? She sure hoped so.

The Claussens were the next to stop at her door. "Thought we'd put your address in our GPS," said Mr. Claussen. "That way we can drop off your dog food and talk with your landlady." Translation: and pay a hefty pet deposit.

Then it was hugs all around and a promise from Brooke to come to Style Savings and get her hair done. How Missy's life had changed since coming to this place. She'd arrived as a single mom with nothing but the hope of giving her kids a nice Christmas and she was leaving with new friends who already felt like family. And…the beginning of a possible romance. Could it get any better?

It appeared that it could. At Sleeping Lady Salon she showed Sarah White the pictures she'd taken on her old digital camera of her impromptu makeovers, and Sarah was properly impressed.

"You're a natural," Sarah said. "I like that."

And Missy liked what she saw of the salon. It was elegant and expensive-looking with big picture windows that revealed a stunning view of the mountains, and a receptionist who made lattes for the customers. With the exception of Sarah, who seemed to be around Olivia's age, the stylists were young and well dressed. It was the kind of place where Missy had always dreamed of working.

"Could you start in March?" Sarah asked.

"You bet!" Missy grabbed the woman's hand and shook it. "Thank you so much! I won't let you down."

"Olivia recommended you, so I know you won't," Sarah said. "But I don't put up with any nonsense. No calling in sick because you stayed out late dancing at the Red Barn or drinking at Zelda's, young lady."

"I've got kids. That won't be happening."

"Good," Sarah said. "See that it doesn't." Then, just when Missy was beginning to wonder what sort of dragon lady she'd be working for, Sarah added with a wink, "And when you get up here I want a makeover like the ones you showed me."

"No problem."

Half an hour later Missy returned to the lodge to find Olivia and John in the lobby, playing Sorry! with the kids. She walked in just as Carlos was pumping the air and exclaiming, "I won!"

"No fair," Lalla said, pouting.

Sometimes life wasn't fair, Missy thought, unable to keep the grin off her face. Sometimes it gave a girl way more good things than she deserved.

Olivia looked up and saw her. "You got the job," she guessed.

"I did. I start this spring. Guys, how would you like to move up here to Icicle Falls, where we can see Grandma Olivia all the time?"

Lalla's loss at Sorry! was instantly forgotten. "Yes!" she cried, bouncing up and down in her seat.

"Can Buddy come?" Carlos wanted to know.

"Of course," Missy told him.

"Yes!" Now both children were bouncing up and down.

"We'd better get going before they break the furniture," Missy decided. "Come on, guys, time to check out."

John got up, too. "I thought I'd follow you back. You might need help with your chains."

Olivia smiled approvingly. "Ah, John Truman, I see a wonderful new year ahead of you."

"Thanks," he said, and shook her hand.

"Hey," he said to Missy as they headed for the door, "I bet that hamburger place is open. You guys want to get a burger before we leave?"

* * *

Olivia watched as Missy and John and the kids went out the door. If ever there was a perfect ending to a story, those two were it. She smiled, thinking about her own story. It hadn't turned out so badly, either.

James had managed to sneak in a moment for just the two of them and had given her a goodbye kiss that felt more like hello. And he and his family now had reservations for New Year's Eve.

She looked around the lodge, at the sleigh in the lobby, filled with presents, the mistletoe, the poinsettias and the greenery she'd draped on the stairs.

Merry Christmas to all, she thought, remembering the famous Christmas poem about Santa. She could hardly wait to see what the new year brought.

Santa Claus Is Coming to Town...Again

It was Christmas Eve a year later and the Icicle Creek Lodge was ablaze with twinkle lights thanks to the united efforts of the Claussen and Wallace men. Inside the lodge good smells drifted out from the dining room, floating down the hallway to tantalize the guests with the promise of a wonderful dinner to come. Poinsettias perched everywhere, and the big tree in the lobby stood magnificent, a study in silver this year, hung with vintage ornaments and tinsel and old-fashioned colored lights. People strolled in from a day of skiing to help themselves to hot chocolate or hot cider.

Jane and Vera sat in cozy armchairs in the lobby, enjoying the fire in the fireplace. "I hear Santa's making an appearance again this year," Vera said.

"He already made an appearance to Olivia," Jane said, happy to have insider information.

"No!" Vera declared.

"Oh, yes. I saw the ring. It's lovely. And they're getting married right here on New Year's Eve."

"Well, I hope we're invited," Vera said.

"We'd better be. I want a piece of that wedding cake. Gingerbread Haus is making it."

"Of course you're invited," said a voice at Jane's elbow. Startled, she turned to see Brooke Claussen, pink-cheeked from an afternoon on the slopes with her fiancé, Eric. They'd be getting married on Valentine's Day. "I need to make it easy for Eric to remember our anniversary," she'd joked.

"So, any special presentations by Santa tonight?" Jane asked Brooke slyly.

"You'll see…"

Jane could hardly wait.

Later that evening, the dining room was full of guests oohing and aahing over the flowers on the tables, the candles, the holiday china and crystal. In addition to the Claussens and Jane and Vera, the Williamses and the Spikes had returned, and there were several new families seated at the tables, ready to enjoy Olivia's cooking.

One couple, who had come in just for the Christmas Eve dinner, sat at a quiet corner table over by the window. Missy Monroe was now living in a sweet little cottage on Juniper Ridge. John Truman, who was coming up for regular visits, sat across from her. Lately he'd been talking with his boss about working from home. And he'd been talking to Missy about finding a house with three bedrooms in Icicle Falls.

Carlos and Lalla sat between them, Lalla swaying in her seat, serenading them with a slightly off-key rendition of "The Little Drummer Boy," while Carlos wolfed down a roll.

Missy smiled across the table at John, who seemed to be having a hard time sitting still.

"What's wrong?" she asked.

"Huh? Oh. Nothing," he said, trying to make his voice sound carefree.

She shrugged and helped herself to a dinner roll. Eric Wallace brought wine to their table, told the woman she looked lovely and then wished them bon appétit.

"So, do you like my dress?" she asked John, obviously hoping for a compliment.

He nodded.

"I got it at Gilded Lily's. On sale." She smoothed the velvety fabric. "It's the nicest dress I've ever had."

"You look beautiful," he said.

"I look beautiful, too," said Lalla, adjusting her tiara. It was certainly an accurate statement.

"Yes, you do," agreed her mother. "But it's bad manners to say so. You have to wait and let someone tell you."

The child frowned. "But what if nobody does?"

"Someone will, don't worry," the young man said.

And so dinner continued, diners enjoying both the food and the holiday atmosphere.

And then dessert was served, an old-fashioned figgy pudding that brought rave reviews from the guests. And as everyone was raving, John saw James Claussen slip away from his table.

Ten minutes later, Santa appeared, bearing a big red velveteen sack of gifts and calling, "Ho, ho, ho. Merry Christmas!" And John began to fidget with his dinner napkin.

"What have we here for Jane?" Santa said, stopping by Jane and Vera's table and pulling out a small box of gift soaps. "Have you been naughty this year?" he teased.

"Of course," she said, taking the present.

"That's what I was afraid of." He laughed and continued to make his rounds.

Exclamations of delight rose around the room as women opened presents to find bath salts or soaps and children received puzzles and coloring books. Then Santa's sack was almost empty and there was only one table left to visit.

"I don't need a grandma now," Lalla informed James as he approached the table. "I have Grandma Olivia. And Carlos has a dog."

"I think Santa has one more big present for you guys this year," James said. "But first…" He held out a wrapped coloring book to her. For Carlos he dug deep in his bag and found a small car. Then he tipped the bag and shook it. Nothing came out, and the expectant smile on Missy's face faded.

"Well, now, that's odd. I seem to have run out of presents. Oh, wait." James reached inside his suit and pulled out a small black velvet box wrapped with a gold ribbon, and Missy put a hand to her mouth and gasped. "This is for you," he said softly, and laid it on the table in front of Missy.

Hands shaking, she picked it up and opened it. Then burst into tears.

"So, Missy, will you marry me?" John asked eagerly.

"Yes!" she cried, and bounded up from her seat to run and hug him as the dining room erupted in applause.

"We get a dad for Christmas?" Carlos said in awe.

"And another grandma," John said, before kissing Missy.

"Two grandmas," Lalla said breathlessly.

"What a difference from last year," James said later as he and Olivia sat in her private quarters enjoying hot chocolate laced with peppermint schnapps.

"I'm so glad it all worked out for those two," she said, snuggling against him.

"I'm so glad it worked out for *all* of us," James said. "Are you ready for our big day?"

"I'm more than ready," she said. "It's going to be so wonderful to have you and Brooke up here year-round."

"I'm glad she was able to get that teaching job."

"Who knows, maybe this time next year we'll be expecting a grandchild."

For a moment James's smile was wistful, but not for long. Faith would have been happy to see how his story turned out, he reminded himself. And it couldn't have turned out better. He took one final sip of his hot chocolate, then set it aside and dimmed the lamp next to the couch. With a sweet, willing woman beside him and a future bright with promise, it would be silly to waste this rare moment of solitude.

"Have I told you recently that I love you, Olivia Wallace?" he asked softly.

"I seem to remember you mentioning it," she said, giving him a dimpled smile. "But feel free to repeat yourself."

"I do love you," he said, and took her in his arms. And then Santa went off duty for the night, and it was just James Claussen and the woman he loved, ringing in Christmas together.

* * * * *

Acknowledgments

I have several people to thank for helping me make this book happen. First, a huge thanks to the brain trust: Susan Wiggs, Elsa Watson, Anjalee Banerjee, Lois Dyer and Kate Breslin. You're all proof that girlfriends are the best present a woman could ever get. Thank you, also, to my incredible agent, Paige Wheeler, who is always there for me, and to Paula Eykelhof, my beloved editor, who is simply brilliant. I'd also like to thank Mike at the Aberdeen, Washington, animal shelter for not only giving me a tour of the facility but also giving me a crash course in the business of caring for animals. I wish all of you a merry Christmas and a stocking full of joy.

Recipes from Olivia

Christmas is the season for goodies, and when it comes to creating wonderful treats, no one can beat Olivia Wallace. She wanted to share her favorites with you.

Gumdrop Cookies

(Makes about 3 dozen)

Ingredients:

1 cup butter, softened
1½ cups granulated sugar
1 egg
1 tsp vanilla extract
1¼ cups chopped gumdrops
½ cup shredded coconut
2¾ cups flour
1 tsp baking soda
½ tsp baking powder

Directions:

Preheat oven to 350°F. In a large bowl, cream together the butter and sugar until smooth. Beat in egg and vanilla. Add gumdrops and coconut. Combine remaining dry ingredients in a sifter and sift into creamed mixture. Mix well, then form into small balls and place on ungreased cookie sheets. Bake 8 to 10 minutes or until golden brown. (It takes 12 to 15 minutes in Olivia's oven.) Let stand on cookie sheet 2 minutes before removing to cool on wire rack.

Old-Fashioned Bon-Bon Chocolate Cookies

(Makes 3 dozen, unless kitchen helpers
sample the dough…)

Ingredients for cookies:

¾ cup butter
1 cup sugar
1 egg, well-beaten
½ tsp vanilla extract
2 tbsp milk
2 squares semisweet chocolate, melted
2½ cups flour
¼ tsp salt

Ingredients for peppermint frosting:

¼ cup softened butter
2 cups powdered sugar
1–1½ tbsp milk
Peppermint extract (start with just a drop, as it's
strong!)
Red food coloring

Directions for cookies:

Cream together butter, sugar, egg, vanilla, milk and
slightly cooled melted chocolate. Sift in remaining dry ingredients and mix well. Refrigerate for

2 hours before working with the dough. Then roll into balls and place on ungreased cookie sheet. Bake 10 to 12 minutes in a 350°F oven or until a toothpick inserted comes out clean. Cool on a wire rack.

Directions for frosting:

Cream butter into powdered sugar, then add milk, extract and red food coloring and mix well. When cookies are cool, top with a small dollop of peppermint icing.

Breakfast Casserole

(Serves 12 to 15, depending on what size
you cut the servings)

Ingredients:

10 eggs
½ cup flour
1 tsp salt
1 pint cottage cheese
1 lb Monterey Jack or Pepper Jack cheese, grated
½ cup melted butter
1 cup chopped onion
1¼ cups chopped mushrooms

Directions:

Preheat oven to 350°F. Break eggs into a large bowl
and whisk with a fork until mixed. Add the next five
ingredients. Sauté onion and mushrooms and add
to the egg-and-cheese mixture. Pour into a buttered
9 x 13 casserole dish and bake for 35 minutes. Left-
overs can be frozen (if you have any!)

Merry Christmas from Olivia

This Christmas,
visit four of your favorite towns
in a Christmas collection from
four of your favorite authors!

"These are three of my favorite authors! I hope you'll join me in visiting the towns of Cedar Cove, Whiskey Creek, Icicle Falls and Cold Creek as everyone gets together for Christmas!"
—Debbie Macomber, #1 *New York Times* bestselling author

Available now, wherever books are sold!

Be sure to connect with us at:

Harlequin.com/Newsletters

Facebook.com/HarlequinBooks

Twitter.com/HarlequinBooks

MTFC1723

New York Times Bestselling Author

BRENDA NOVAK

Discover a brand-new *Whiskey Creek* romance all about heart, hope and happily-ever-after...just in time for Christmas.

Eve Harmon has always enjoyed Christmas, but this year it reminds her of everything she *doesn't* have. Most of her friends are married now, and that's what Eve wants, too. Love. A family of her own. But the B and B she manages, and even Whiskey Creek, suddenly seem…confining.

There's simply no one in the area she could even imagine as a husband—until a handsome stranger comes to town. Eve's definitely attracted to him, and he seems to have the same reaction to her. But his mysterious past could ruin Eve's happily-ever-after—just when it finally seems within reach. And just when she's counting on the best Christmas of her life!

Available now, wherever books are sold!

Be sure to connect with us at:

Harlequin.com/Newsletters

Facebook.com/HarlequinBooks

Twitter.com/HarlequinBooks

#1 *New York Times* bestselling author

SHERRYL WOODS

takes you back to Chesapeake Shores for another heartwarming holiday season.

As the only child of a single mom, Jenny Collins wanted nothing more than to be part of a large, rambunctious family like the O'Briens. Ironically, though, when her mother married into that family, Jenny found herself feeling more like an outsider than ever.

Now, after years in Nashville as an established songwriter, Jenny's drawn back to Chesapeake Shores to collaborate on a Christmas production…and to make peace with the past. As if that's not challenging enough, Caleb Green, the singer who broke her heart, has followed her to town, and he's determined to win her back.

With the help of a little O'Brien holiday magic, will Jenny and Caleb find a way to make sweet music forever?

Available now, wherever books are sold!

#1 *New York Times* bestselling author

STEPHANIE LAURENS

ushers in a new generation of Cynsters in an enchanting tale of mistletoe, magic and love.

Six Cynster families gather together at snowbound Casphairn Manor to celebrate the season in true Cynster fashion—and where Cynsters gather, love is never far behind.

The festive occasion brings together Daniel Crosbie, tutor to Lucifer Cynster's sons, and Claire Meadows, widow and governess to Gabriel Cynster's daughter. Soon the embers of an unexpected passion smolder between them.

Claire believes a second marriage is not in her stars. But Daniel is determined. Assisted by a bevy of Cynsters—innate matchmakers every one—Daniel strives to persuade Claire that trusting him with her hand and her heart is her path to happiness. Then disaster strikes, and by winter's light, she learns that love— true love—is worth any risk, any price.

Available now, wherever books are sold!

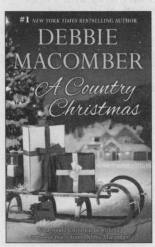

REQUEST YOUR FREE BOOKS!

2 FREE NOVELS
FROM THE ROMANCE COLLECTION
PLUS 2 FREE GIFTS!

YES! Please send me 2 FREE novels from the Romance Collection and my 2 FREE gifts (gifts are worth about $10). After receiving them, if I don't wish to receive any more books, I can return the shipping statement marked "cancel." If I don't cancel, I will receive 4 brand-new novels every month and be billed just $6.24 per book in the U.S. or $6.74 per book in Canada. That's a savings of at least 22% off the cover price. It's quite a bargain! Shipping and handling is just 50¢ per book in the U.S. and 75¢ per book in Canada.* I understand that accepting the 2 free books and gifts places me under no obligation to buy anything. I can always return a shipment and cancel at any time. Even if I never buy another book, the two free books and gifts are mine to keep forever.

194/394 MDN F4XY

Name	(PLEASE PRINT)	
Address		Apt. #
City	State/Prov.	Zip/Postal Code

Signature (if under 18, a parent or guardian must sign)

Mail to the Harlequin® Reader Service:
IN U.S.A.: P.O. Box 1867, Buffalo, NY 14240-1867
IN CANADA: P.O. Box 609, Fort Erie, Ontario L2A 5X3

Want to try two free books from another line?
Call 1-800-873-8635 or visit www.ReaderService.com.

* Terms and prices subject to change without notice. Prices do not include applicable taxes. Sales tax applicable in N.Y. Canadian residents will be charged applicable taxes. Offer not valid in Quebec. This offer is limited to one order per household. Not valid for current subscribers to the Romance Collection or the Romance/Suspense Collection. All orders subject to credit approval. Credit or debit balances in a customer's account(s) may be offset by any other outstanding balance owed by or to the customer. Please allow 4 to 6 weeks for delivery. Offer available while quantities last.

Your Privacy—The Harlequin® Reader Service is committed to protecting your privacy. Our Privacy Policy is available online at www.ReaderService.com or upon request from the Harlequin Reader Service.

We make a portion of our mailing list available to reputable third parties that offer products we believe may interest you. If you prefer that we not exchange your name with third parties, or if you wish to clarify or modify your communication preferences, please visit us at www.ReaderService.com/consumerchoice or write to us at Harlequin Reader Service Preference Service, P.O. Box 9062, Buffalo, NY 14269. Include your complete name and address.

ROM13R

SHEILA ROBERTS

31618 THE TEA SHOP ON	___$7.99 U.S.	___$8.99 CAN.
LAVENDER LANE		
31470 MERRY EX-MAS	___$7.99 U.S.	___$8.99 CAN.
31454 THE COTTAGE ON	___$7.99 U.S.	___$8.99 CAN.
JUNIPER RIDGE		
31432 WHAT SHE WANTS	___$7.99 U.S.	___$9.99 CAN.

(limited quantities available)

TOTAL AMOUNT	$	_____
POSTAGE & HANDLING	$	_____
($1.00 for 1 book, 50¢ for each additional)		
APPLICABLE TAXES*	$	_____
TOTAL PAYABLE	$	_____

(check or money order—please do not send cash)

To order, complete this form and send it, along with a check or money order for the total amount, payable to Harlequin MIRA, to: **In the U.S.:** 3010 Walden Avenue, P.O. Box 9077, Buffalo, NY 14269-9077; **In Canada:** P.O. Box 636, Fort Erie, Ontario, L2A 5X3.

Name: _____

Address: _____ City: _____

State/Prov.: _____ Zip/Postal Code: _____

Account Number (if applicable): _____

075 CSAS

*New York residents remit applicable sales taxes.
*Canadian residents remit applicable GST and provincial taxes.

HARLEQUIN® MIRA®
™ www.Harlequin.com

MSR1114BL